UNNATURAL
MOTHERS

UNNATURAL MOTHERS

a novel by
Renate Dorrestein

translated from the Dutch by
Wanda Boeke

Women In Translation

Copyright © 1992 by Renate Dorrestein

English translation copyright © 1993 by Wanda Boeke

Originally published in Dutch as *Ontaarde Moeders* by Uitgeverij Contact, Amsterdam, The Netherlands.

All rights reserved. No part of this book may be reproduced in any form without prior permission from Women in Translation, 3131 Western Avenue, Suite 410, Seattle, WA 98121, except for the quotation of brief passages in reviews.

Publication of this book was made possible in part with financial support from the National Endowment for the Arts and the Foundation for the Production and Translation of Dutch Literature.

Cover illustration and text design by Kris Morgan.

Library of Congress Cataloging-in-Publication Data

Dorrestein, Renate.
[Ontaarde moeders. English]
Unnatural mothers : a novel / by Renate Dorrestein ; translated from the Dutch by Wanda Boeke
p. cm.
ISBN 1-879679-06-X
I. Boeke, Wanda. II. Title.
PT5881.14.06705813 1994
839.3' 1364--dc20
94-16877
CIP

Printed in the United States of America
First edition, October 1994

10 9 8 7 6 5 4 3 2 1

II

Of All Women, Of All Times

Last night in the hotel lounge I saw a man who looked like Zwier, and was shocked to find that my heart still skipped a beat at the unexpected sight. He was sitting on a Chesterfield sofa under a potted palm, leafing through a magazine.

I myself was just leaving the cocktail bar, where a German businessman had asked me what a woman like me was doing in this part of the world all by herself. I was on my way to the desk to pick up my key so I could lock myself in my room for the rest of the evening, which is the wisest thing a woman alone in this part of the world can do when German business types show up on the scene. This one appeared to me to be the kind who'd packed his own blood plasma in his suitcase in the event something should happen to him in the Nairobi Hilton. He offered me a Scotch and soda before he launched his question. I hadn't been sitting at the bar for more than two seconds even, anticipating the prospect of a drink, as why else would one go to the civilized world, so there was no choice but to tolerate the man's sitting down next to me. He was actually serious: he really wanted to know what had prompted my pretty legs to trot all the way to Africa. So I said that I'd just spent two months on Mount Kenya where the astounding flora of the Rift Valley reaches its peak: the slopes are overgrown with vegetation that, as a result of the climactic conditions, has assumed monstrous proportions. I'd gotten there just in time for the colossal flowering pillars of the giant lobelia that only blooms once every seven years, its mulleins easily reaching a height of six meters.

As I was telling the German about this I saw before me once again the huge camphor trees, too big and too heavy for their own root systems, so they fall over sooner or later to rot away in obscurity, and at that moment I was more certain than ever that I prefer the helpless plants of the field to people with signet rings on their little fingers. I don't fit in with the German white collar crowd, and I also probably don't belong in Hiltons. Perhaps I should never have come here. I mean, I'm not the kind to perch on a bar stool wearing a short black dress, mascara and lipstick—even if I do play the part quite convincingly. Besides which it's a practical dress. It's been with me for years.

Convention demanded that I in turn ask the German what he was doing here, but I didn't bother because Germans are all invariably, as far as I know, employed in the pharmaceutical industry anyway. Despite their never having seen a malaria mosquito up close, they produce and sell terrific antimalarial pills along with the best of them. Oh well, live and let live, that's my motto.

We had another drink. Meanwhile, the conversation didn't flag a bit, interested as the man was in my giant lobelias. The attention he exhibited concerning the subject made me fear the worst: he was the kind who was going to eat up my words as if he could never have his fill, which in his case would definitely take some time. Presumably he wasn't out for the pleasures of my body at all—on closer inspection he seemed more the type who needed a warm hand to hold out there in the great unknown: Daddy's in Africa, Daddy's a little scared, there's a witches' brew of a city out there outside the Hilton waiting to get him, a city that's like a concussion, with as many slums, mutilated beggars and stinking markets as white apartment buildings and wide boulevards. What he'd like most is to latch on to me with those fleshy tentacles of his, particularly now it turns out I'm such a tough cookie, just back from the tropical wilds. Vati wants a babysitter. But for him to remain assured of my company, new topics of conversation had better be found quick. Before I know it he'll switch from lobelias over to me. How come a woman like myself got caught up with botany: that might well be his next move. Well, that's a long story.

Of course it doesn't matter what I say. As long as he hears the sound of my voice. I can start with my own conception as far as he's concerned. My father, I might just as well tell him, begot me by my mother shortly after the Dutch national collection movement 'Open your wallets, close your dikes' started. It was the age of mopeds, the housing shortage, the Drees Cabinet and the migration to Canada; and Article 451 of the Criminal Code forbade the public sale of condoms. Unfortunately my mother wasn't as fertile as women in the postwar era were expected to be: after her first daughter she had to wait eighteen years for me. Not like her. My mother's a person who likes to take her fate into her own hands. Her own fate along with that of others. For me, too, she had plans. I had to do better than my sister. Not that that was so difficult: at eighteen, right after I was born, she got married, and that was that.

My birth, Herr Sticklebauer, took some doing, although, as the story goes, from the moment my father's spermatozoa finally found their way to my mother's ovicell, I remained alarmingly under what was considered the desirable weight. The incubator was, so to speak, standing by. I must have been the kind of anemic, pathetic embryo you sometimes see in those pictures used by opponents of abortion to try to command a respect for life, one of those bony fetuses with desperate hands on which all ten little fingers are visible when the creature still isn't any bigger than a pea. Do you know what I'm talking about?

Anyway, you'd think that an undersized kid like me could quickly and easily be brought into the world, but the opposite proved to be true. Just a hair and my mother would have bled to death during delivery. She often recounted, gloating to some degree, that I'd almost killed her. Losing quarts of blood and being torn beyond repair were the feats by which mothers in the fifties could rake in a good deal of respect. Grueling deliveries were a pet topic of conversation, over a filter cigarette. Motherhood, therefore, seemed to me a miserable and bloody business. Count me out.

But what does an utter stranger in a hotel bar in Nairobi have to do with all that? My life is mine, and others should stick to theirs. So when I could see that another scotch was about to be ordered, over which everything but the kitchen sink in my life would have to be laid out on the table, I quickly left the bar and walked to the desk to ask for the key to my room, whereby I saw a man sitting in the lounge who reminded me of Zwier.

For an instant I thought it really was him. Which of course could easily have been possible, since he's probably in Africa as often as I am. After all, I can't forbid him to be there.

During the brief moment I thought I was standing there face to face with him again after all these years, my breath caught in my throat. He was still equally attractive, with his dark curly hair and that tall, lean body that's athletic without being annoyingly muscular. As always, he was tan and slightly unshaven, and he was sitting there completely engrossed in his own thoughts, that brooding look I know so well on his face. Not a man needing a warm hand, no. A man of surprisingly high voltage. Somebody that makes you think: I better save you from yourself. I'm the only one who can understand you and, if necessary, forgive you. What a challenge a man like Zwier is. Who's going to discover the diamond in the rough and polish it? Who else but me?

In the next instant, when I realized that it was a stranger who, like myself, was staying at the Nairobi Hilton, I was, to my dismay, disappointed. But what did I want? To step up nonchalantly in my short black dress? He wouldn't even have recognized me with mascara and lipstick on. I would have had to introduce myself. Hey, Zwier, do you know who I am? You're married to me, remember?

On second thought I should be grateful that it was only a double. Heaven only knows what would have gone through Zwier's head if I suddenly popped up in his life again. No, it was much better this way.

I've always thought that it was better this way. For everybody.

What, I'm not leading a rich and satisfying life? Good grief, if there's anybody who can call herself the architect of her own destiny, it's me. I've always escaped under my own power from situations that pinioned or bridled me. I've been blessed with the energy of six and the courage of ten. It couldn't be expressed in any other way. Nobody's going to keep me down. Now that I'm thirty-seven, I can ascertain that I'm simply not to be kept down. Sometimes that requires a sacrifice, but in the long run even this won't change anything in the quality of my life. If I want to study giant lobelias, I'll go to Mount Kenya. And when the project's done and I've got a couple of days free, I'll park myself in a good hotel where they pour tea from silver teapots. Tea that can't compare with the *chai* that boys sell on the street, but that isn't the point. I mean, I can come and go as I please. I'm not responsible to anybody. Not to anybody. And that's worth a lot to me. More than I can ever put into words. And for the rest my life happens to be my life, and it's nobody's frigging business.

    The man who looked like Zwier, at least from a distance and then really only from the side, jumped up when a woman and two children stepped out of the elevator. All three were wearing safari outfits. Europeans are almost always equally ridiculous the moment they set foot on this continent. The first thing they ask is whether there are black mambas in the air-conditioned Nairobi Hilton lounge. Their little daughters were twins even, I noticed, as they walked by. What a terrible thing to be a twin. But a couple of self-satisfied parents like the Zwier-look-alike and his blond goddess certainly never entertained that thought. Always a mouthful about what's good for children, and meanwhile. That kind of thing just makes my blood boil, although I should know better. Or you might suddenly get an obstruction somewhere, an embolism or something like that, and then you can't climb Mount Kenya on your life, belongings strapped to your back and all. And really, that's the only thing that matters. One time I got on my motorcycle simply because I wanted to go hundreds of miles up the road to where you can walk through a mangrove swamp, somehow clearing a path over the prop roots. Under those green trees with their glossy leaves the atmosphere is somber, the air warm and humid, and the water in the streams running through the mud flats is dark, and everywhere there's—but I'm digressing.

When the happy family in their goofy suits had left the Hilton, no doubt on their way to a phony joint like Under The Palm Tree, I picked up the magazine the man who'd reminded me of Zwier had been flipping through. A *Time* from a few weeks back. The cover story was about the inventor of the birth control pill, a Dr. Gregory Pincus, written on the occasion of the twenty-fifth anniversary of his death.

Not that I can now recall who'd been the most upset when it turned out I'd forgotten to take the pill, Zwier or me.

But anyway, it's all for the best this way.

Mamma, mamma, the Africans shout when they see a European woman. A white woman, you're supposed to say these days, and why not? If they don't know you speak Swahili, they use 'mamma' by way of 'ma'am'. The logic of this is striking, for what woman escapes motherhood? A point for Africa. Mamma, mamma.

In all honesty, I'd love to have my name whispered in my ear again. 'Bonnie?' Zwier would sometimes mumble. And I'd ask, "Yes? What?" But he only said Bonnie to say Bonnie. He enjoyed that, it excited him, or maybe he'd just forgotten what he wanted to say, how should I know.

Once up in my room I called room service. An indifferent but courteous waiter brought a bottle of Scotch up to me. I almost fell victim to the temptation of putting it on the German businessman's tab. You know, just for fun. But then I pictured him stumbling upstairs, reaching out with his sweaty hands. As for me, I never sweat.

The bottle within arm's reach, I turned to the *Time* magazine. In theory, there was no reason why I shouldn't acquaint myself with the history of the birth control pill. Knowledge is, after all, power. Oh, sometimes I can really make myself sick. That's what you get when you live alone. You start thinking in complete words and phrases, as if you're always talking to somebody. Knowledge is power! Right. I got down to reading.

Paleoanthropologists in the distant future, according to the article, will one day look back at our moment in time and establish that Dr. Pincus' discovery of the ovulation suppressant was one of the most revolutionary developments in human history, comparable perhaps only to the moments when humans stood up on their hind legs, tamed fire, discovered the wheel and learned to break matter up into atoms. In 1955, after women had been subjected for three and a half million years to their fertility, Dr. Pincus discovered that this could be controlled by means of progesterone. Dr. Pincus liberated women from their unswerving biological destiny. From the moment the pill was put on the market in the first half of the sixties, women were able to decide for themselves whether and how often they wanted to bear children.

It would figure that I just happened to be born at precisely this turning point in human history. Isn't it ironic? According to *Time* I belonged to the first generation of girls that grew up with the reassuring prospect of practically airtight birth control devices. Boy, wasn't I lucky.

As it happens, I remember my first pill very vividly. I'd had to lie, cheat or steal to get it, one of the three, because the pill wasn't included in health insurance policies back then, nor were abortion or those pregnancy tests where you have to urinate into a beaker and then do something with a little stick, those tests you can't buy if you happen to find yourself in the Hadar Valley, for instance. That's a thing some Sticklebauer should do something about. Gap in the market.

I assume I grabbed some cash from my mother's household money to buy my first pill. Three strips in a little box, manufactured by the Organon Company in Oss. Those Krauts are fine, but them Dutchies are better in this respect: Holland, as I understood from *Time* magazine, was one of the first Western European countries where the pill was manufactured. Be this as it may, when I punched one out of the aluminum strip, my mother knew nothing about it, obviously. She'd have preferred to bury sexually mature girls up to their necks in boiling hot lava, or sew their crotches shut. So I couldn't discuss my primary concern with her, namely, that that all-important pill was so small. You couldn't tell anything about its shattering hormonal charge just by looking. If only it did the job. I swallowed it, a gamble as it were, and also at my own risk, because barely ten years later we'd be given a scare by reports that the pill was carcinogenic. But now I'm getting ahead of the story. When I punched my first strip, the skies were still unclouded, and I was sixteen, or seventeen. In order for people to form a picture for themselves of the social backdrop: when I'd reached that most remarkable age (never sixteen or seventeen again!), we found ourselves in the era of the first Dutch women's lib movement with the 'crazy' Dolle Minas, the Tomato Demonstration at the City Theater in Amsterdam, the clearing of Amsterdam's Dam Square of protesters by the Dutch marines, and of the Nobel Prize for economics going to Professor Jan Tinbergen.

The father of the pill, Gregory Pincus, according to *Time* magazine, never received a Nobel Prize.

Dr. Pincus decided to study the suppression of ovulation thanks to a woman. Details like this aren't lost on me. I'm not the kind of person who always fearfully hastens to declare: "No, no, I'm not really a feminist." Her name was Singer or something, wait, I'll get the article; here: Margaret Sanger, feminist and pioneer in the field of birth control in the United States. Already around the time of the Second World War, Sanger attempted to promote the entry of the diaphragm into that country, until she realized that the continual failing of her mission evidently coincided with the fact that in order to use the diaphragm, an *immoral act* was required. She was the one who asked the celebrated biochemist Pincus if he couldn't develop a contraceptive that was in no way related to the genitalia: meaning, an oral contraceptive. It seems neither of the two ever wondered whether anything could be done about the mobility of spermatozoa. Presumably they both argued along the lines of the following adage: the one who bears the baby can keep it. And so it was ovulation that had to be suppressed.

But then mine had always been irregular. And in the tropics you often can't keep track at all of your hormonal affairs. And OK, so I turned out to be pretty disorganized, but putting little x's in a diary just doesn't happen to be the thing for me, and I'm really not the only one. So all in all it seems to me that it was a little optimistic on the part of the *Time* journalist to claim that since Dr. Pincus only children that were wanted have been born.

Besides, what do you gain by being wanted? I was myself one of those children who was passionately longed for, and I can't say that it made my life any simpler. A wanted child becomes her parents' *be all and end all in life*. The average person can handle a lot more love than she deserves and the average child is conceived to occasion this. Go ahead, kid, pull that one off. I might have a lot of things on my conscience, but at least I was never guilty of that kind of sublimated systematic selfishness.

Aside from that, it's all for the best this way. Whatever others may think. I've always known that it was really all for the best this way.

So I, a woman alone in Africa, alone in the world, drank another glass of Scotch to the twenty-fifth anniversary of Dr. Pincus' death, may his wisdom be praised, even though as far as I'm concerned the congratulations were gratuitous. Anyways, as Zwier would say. Whenever Zwier changed the subject, he always said "Anyways..." But there was a bit more going on with Zwier than that. If his stopgaps had been the only problem, I would simply, like every other wife vexing herself gray, still be with him. But I left. And Zwier isn't a man to take being abandoned lightly.

Anyways, in the wake of the efforts undertaken by Pincus and Sanger, many more contraceptives were developed in the second half of the twentieth century, according to *Time* magazine. Are you listening, Zwier? You dog. You always thought I didn't have a head for numbers or statistics. Ha! Listen up, boy: aside from about a hundred million pill users, there are now another sixty million women wandering around our good planet Mother Earth with an IUD, and another sixty million women that have been sterilized, and in addition some five million are using a contraceptive implant (Norplant brand levonorgestrel) or an injectable contraceptive (depot-medroxyprogesterone acetate from Depo-Provera). Those last categories we find particularly in the Third World, the spatial equivalent of what we consider prehistoric in the temporal.

That prehistoric humans differed much from us is something Zwier didn't believe; that was one of his hobby horses. He just blindly assumed that one era of history doesn't really differ from another. His field of study covers roughly three and a half million years, and you're not going to take a magnifying glass to a hundred odd centuries or so. On the contrary, you only see that practically all human experiences are the same for all people, of all times.

In brief, the prehistoric human also loved, she hated, she clubbed her enemies to death, she worked and she passed the genetic material of her ancient ancestors on to her descendants. The only thing that distinguishes me from her is the fact that I understand the miracle of fertilization. Except, who, after years of having enjoyed a carefree love life as offered by the Organon Company, still thinks about the miracle of fertilization at all? Point for me.

I drank another Scotch to that, sitting in front of my window on the third floor of the Nairobi Hilton, with a view of the churning, steaming city. For some reason or other I always feel at home in African cities. At home in Africa.

Zwier would be able to explain that: wasn't our foremother originally from this part of the world? On this continent, millions of years ago, the first human-like creature stood up on her hind legs. Indeed, no trifling matter. Paleoanthropologists have called her Lucy, because when they were sorting out their incredible find (the bones of the first hominid!) they happened to be listening to a Beatles tape: "Lucy In The Sky With Diamonds."

Lucy!

Amusing, isn't it, that present-day science posits that humanity has a woman to thank for its existence, not a man, not one of those assholes like Zwier, cursèd be his spermatozoa! That man's seed was a little too lively, if you ask me.

Anyways, so there I was, sitting in front of my window with its view of Nairobi when I could have been relaxing in a hot bath. But I couldn't shake my thoughts from the past, although I've always believed that you have a memory solely for your own pleasure and use: people shouldn't let themselves be bullied by it. A person has to move on, nature wants to move on, as you can see with plants—if you pinch them off, they seem to manage to develop another strange offshoot somewhere: everything that burgeons and blooms is impelled onwards.

It was so disconcerting to me that as a result of Dr. Pincus and Zwier's double I was busy looking back and rehashing old affairs, that I almost polished off the entire bottle of scotch. For this I was promptly punished during the night by an exhausting dream: I dreamed that I had five or six children by various men, and that I just kept wiping noses and teaching fumbling fingers to tie laces. Touching scenes. Heart-warming. And that Daddy came home from work and that I'd pour him a glass of genever. Meaning five or six, and all of the men in a row on the sofa.

So homey.

At breakfast I was in a pretty sorry state. I was just drinking yet another glass of orange juice when the situation took a turn for the worse: my German friend came into the breakfast room. He appeared to be extremely pleased to see me sitting at a table all by myself and, without further ado, he pulled up a chair. Had I made plans for the evening? If not, he'd love to take me to one of those nice clubs one heard so much about, like Under The Palm Tree. He looked both adventurous as well as scared to death at the prospect when he made his suggestion. Oh, Herr Sticklebauer! And what were we supposed to talk about all evening? Not me again? Sure, who else. The alternative was even less attractive to me. Well, let me see, where did we leave off? Oh yes: my earliest youth. We're still on relatively safe terrain, in any case. All right then.

I was an unhappy child—I was angry and rebellious.

There was, you should know, sir, something of A Secret in our family and there's nothing that can make a kid as contrary as having to spend its days in the vicinity of a good secret without being made privy to it. Nobody told me why my sister had fallen into such profound disfavor that even her name was hardly allowed to be mentioned. And rest assured that my mother could keep her mouth shut. Her silence was deafening, and at three I'd already figured out that her lips were sealed for all eternity once she had decided not to talk about something. To get to know about even the most ordinary things I had to move heaven and earth. Unthinkable that something as interesting as the miracle of fertilization would ever spontaneously pop up in conversation! Where I came from was side-stepped, until one day on the front page of the newspaper, behind which my father was hiding, I read and spelled out the word RAPE. When I asked what it meant, we were just about to sit down to dinner. My mother gave my father a particularly urgent look, at which he immediately left the room, and she and I had a talk about the facts of life.

As a prelude, my mother first tersely unveiled voluntary sexual intercourse. It sounded pretty far-fetched to my ears. The idea that my mother would put up with something like that from my father didn't want to sink in, as she hardly tolerated his occasionally laying his hand on her arm. About the phenomenon of rape she was even more terse. That only happened to sluts. She set her lips in a tight line when she said that. Can you picture it, sir?

The German was buttering a croissant and gazing at me, his eyes filled with hope. No, I said quickly, I've got very different plans for this evening, unfortunately.

You see, I still intend to amuse myself here before I have to step aboard the airplane in a couple of days. Even if only because in The Netherlands I'll have to play the role of the obedient daughter again: on the rare occasions that I'm in the country, I simply can't get around visiting my mother. She drives me crazy. Every conversation with her sooner or later comes down to the same thing: she has never quit showering me with reproaches.

But I'm just not going to pay for a single mistake my whole life. Spare me your righteous indignation, Mother! All over the world, every single day, children are neglected, abused and left to fend for themselves. Dedicate yourself to them! Go work for UNICEF!

Oh, good heavens, now the Zwier family had to come rushing into the breakfast room. Daddy Zwier, Mommy Zwier and the lovely little Zwier twins. Today they were again all decked out in tasteful camouflage colors. They were an unbearable sight. They sat down and looked around hungrily.

I promptly ordered another cup of coffee from one of the countless white-liveried waiters to prove to myself that I wasn't going to be driven out by the Zwiers, which was stupid of me because Herr Sticklebauer took this as proof that I wanted to share his company for a while longer, thereupon starting in on another dinner invitation some other evening, then. We had, meanwhile, as Europeans in diaspora, automatically become so intimate that he let it slip out that his first name was Hubert.

Hubert?

Wasn't that the patron saint of the hunt?

Meanwhile, Mommy Zwier, two tables away, was examining the menu as if she were preparing for a final exam. What would constitute the healthiest breakfast for her family totally preoccupied her. This was one of those women for whom motherhood was a sacred calling, you could see that right off. This was a woman, if you were to shove a microphone in her face, to declare with sugary eyes that motherhood simply happens to be a woman's office. After all, doesn't a woman have a hole between her legs? Not by accident! It is the intention of creation that babies should tumble out of there. Otherwise she'd have been made without a hole—her biology speaks for itself!

Hasn't anything changed in all these centuries? Nowadays you're allowed to have a cute little job on the side, if you like, but bearing and raising children you're bound, bearing and raising you're bound, if for no other reason than that women have been doing this since the dawn of humanity. You're supposed to bulge to bursting with motherly urges, merely on the basis of that hole between your legs. The absurdity! Well, if we're going to start that way, I can think of a couple of other things to boot. It might, for instance, rightfully be claimed that women, by virtue of their physique, are born, are created, are preordained to be raped, and that on the basis of their biological potential there's nothing they want more.

That's something for sluts, said my mother disparagingly when I'd seen the word RAPE in the paper; my mother who thinks I've broken the laws of nature. It seems to me, however, that rape is an experience that's even harder to avoid than motherhood. Don't man and woman find each other in the most amazing fashion this way? The manner in which her natural office dovetails with his natural calling!

What did I know, in the era of the bikini, the color television and sales tax, when I started living together with a boyfriend in a cold attic. One day he started slapping me around. I was twenty. I collected coupons and points; I had a whole kitchen drawer full of them, not from some domestic urge but from poverty. For a total of eight thousand points you could get one free teaspoon. I was in no way aware that my position wasn't unique. I thought I was the first woman in history to get beaten. It didn't occur to me to hit back. Not until I got my nose broken was the limit reached. I summarily ordered my heavy-handed lover to leave the place, which of course wasn't something to be arranged of an afternoon. To save my skin I sought temporary refuge with a girl who was a fellow student to wait for the moment that my apartment would be vacated. I returned there just once to reach an agreement about its contents. On that occasion he tore off my clothes.

When I was lying on my floor a moment later under somebody who moaned that I was his and would stay his, when, in short, I was informed for the first time that my body wasn't my own, when it was imparted to me that I was property belonging to somebody who, as he said, had the right to do with me as he saw fit, my mother of course wasn't around to stand by me.

In no time I was all pulp on the outside and raw on the inside. If I didn't squeeze my eyes shut I could see that my rapist was wearing a sweater I'd washed for him for years. At some point I'd even mended the collar with a wool whose color at each washing matched less and less. As I lay there on my attic floor, every time my eyes caught those tender loving stitches, I had to clamp my jaws shut to keep from screaming out loud. At least I wouldn't end up with a child as a result of this, thanks to Dr. Pincus.

I was hoping, twenty years old, that my nose wouldn't be broken again, that I wouldn't have to feel that sharp snap and hear that nauseating cracking sound. I did take care not to struggle. If I had been able, I would have stopped breathing, in order not to provoke him unnecessarily.

In vain I tried, just as when I got beaten, to act as if it didn't concern me. But what I'd always succeeded in doing while being slapped around, didn't work this time. I couldn't divorce myself from this. I had to experience every everlasting second. I could easily have sung a thousand times over, backwards and forwards, all fifteen verses of the Dutch national anthem, that's how long it lasted. My bulwark in faith Thou art, Oh Lord, my God. I tried to make a deal with Him. All my scholarship money for the poor in

Calcutta if it stopped right now. My bid went higher and higher the longer the ordeal lasted.

Not God, but I myself finally made an end to it, when I took the reins into my own hands: I knew that the man in that sweater almost immediately ejaculated if I squeezed his balls.

You could say that at an early age already I had a nose for bad men, but anyway.

Well, I consider mine to have been just about the least dramatic rape in the history of humanity: unfortunately, every woman will, at least once in her life, be confronted with the surprise that somebody considers her his property. In the newspaper we often read about considerably more gruesome cases. The only thing I wanted to say with all this is: nobody needs to come at me with romantic arguments about my natural office. The day I helped my rapist achieve his climax I stopped believing in all that. And that's why, later on, I was able to do what I had to do.

I left my husband, I left my daughter. So what?

Let's be realistic for heaven's sake: the child also has a father, right? We didn't hear anybody gripe during all those innumerable centuries when it was the other way around, when it was the fathers who took to their heels? The concept of unnatural fathers didn't even exist, until we recently discovered that they even rape their own daughters. But as a mother! As a mother you're considered unnatural a whole lot quicker. After all, as a mother don't you automatically and solely live for your child? The instincts they foist on you! What if you happen to refuse to have them? Because you've figured out that there's something fishy going on, something that has to do with power-play, for instance? I'm certainly not Lucy! And I'm not obliged, like the average wife vexing herself gray, to act like I'm crazy either, am I? No, as far as

I'm concerned, the father, at least if he isn't a rapist, will be the caretaking parent of the future. He has been created for it, as it were. He's got two hands to do up laces, a lap to sit on, and by definition a big brain that many a tot can profit from. In the near future we will be reading cover stories about this, mark my words. I mean, in my day you didn't even *notice* you had a father. Mine was a foreman at a gravel pit. The days he put in were long and he came home tired. The only thing I remember about him is that he always called me princess. Does her majesty want milk or buttermilk? The canal along which he used to bicycle home was deep, and I was only eight when he was dredged up. The day before I'd had an argument with him—I don't even know what about anymore. If he'd displeased us, we didn't talk to him, Mother and I. That's what I'd been taught. My last memory of him is, on the evening before he died, how he fruitlessly attempted to win me back.

When they had retrieved him from the canal, my mother took me along to identify him. Naturally, I was, all of eight years old, her help and mainstay. Her most precious possession. Do you get the picture, Herr Sticklebauer? Hubert?

At the morgue they opened one of those drawers and drew the sheet back a ways. Nobody asked: "Is this really appropriate for a child to see?" But I've already said enough.

My father's face was so swollen up that it was unrecognizable. That's why the sheet had to be completely removed, so that it could be established whether or not there was evidence of the scar from an appendectomy. His body, too, looked like it had been pumped up with gas. He took up a lot more space dead than alive, and between his legs there was a monstrous swelling.

I had never seen my father naked before, and I knew for certain that he didn't want me to look at him now either. But I couldn't get rid of the image of his gigantic organ protruding spongily from the seaweed on his loins. It was the most awful thing I'd ever seen. That was what had engendered me. The miracle of long-awaited fertilization had fulfilled itself in my mother by means of that swelling.

For a long time after that, I used to inspect myself before going to bed for lumps and blisters. A few years later when I started getting vague masses on my chest, my first thought was that my contaminated hereditary material had finally caught up with me and that my final hour had come. Had my father still been alive, I would have called him to task. But he'd skipped out.

It's my personal opinion that, in general, fathers have been skipping out for far too long. While Vati's all smiles, Frau Sticklebauer in Frankfurt is wiping snotty noses. And later she'll be blamed for everything. All the little Sticklebauers' neuroses will be on her account. That in itself is reason enough to refuse the honor: as a mother in our world, which is totally segregated on the basis of sex, you are always and unavoidably the ultimately blameworthy party. Didn't I do a fine job of turning the tables!

Later, when she's old enough, she'll thank me. None of that stifling symbiosis for her—and believe you me, I know what I'm talking about. I was myself left to the mercies of a mother. Weren't we all? So we should all know better.

Or else, she'll have to stop and think about what the laws of reincarnation teach, namely, that we choose our own parents: in the circular path of our existences, each time we return to earth, we seek out consciously and precisely those circumstances that are required to fulfill the demands of the next phase of our karma. A comforting perspective. The teachings of reincarnation neutralize, as it were, the phenomenon of parents. It's just because of your karma, dear, that you have to grow up motherless.

And listen: you'll have to agree with me that there are only very few children who don't have to be pitied because of their parents. You really aren't the only one. Parents are almost always terrible.

They know no limits. They're always doing too much or too little. Most grown-ups are in vehement agreement about this when they look back on their own childhood. Even when they're well along in years, they're still busy settling the score.

Seen in that light, it may even be the case that the failure of parenthood is simply handed down from generation to generation, and that it's somehow just part of life. There are, no doubt, mysterious cosmic reasons for this phenomenon, but it might also just be almightily impossible to be a good parent. Except that, *qualitate qua*, there's no subject about which I admittedly know less.

You understand what I'm telling you?

I've always wished you the best of everything. Really. Zwier's teeth, for example, because between the two of us he always had the best teeth.

Now I think I'll go take an extensive siesta to make sure I'm in top form tonight. That's funny—I'm crying. Oh well, a person's got to cry every once in a while. It doesn't mean anything. I should take a bath, put on some make-up, put on something nice and sneak out, past the bar where Vati Sticklebauer's fearfully hitting the Scotch, hoping some motherly type will come along and take pity on him.

Bummer, Hubert.

A couple of hours of dancing and I'll be my old self again. It isn't at all like me to shut myself up in a hotel room—you only get morose thoughts that way. That isn't my style at all, really. In fact, I'm always bright and cheery, absolutely carefree, I'm not somebody to cause problems. Whatsoever.

I

Like Mother, Like Daughter

At the airport it's busier than ever. The crowd in the departure lounge is so packed, that in just a couple of minutes Mary Emma has already lost her father. One minute he's still walking right beside her, the next his tall form has disappeared in the swirling mass. As far as the eye can see people are crowding each other out in this filthy, sweltering place. Voices rant in English and Swahili, beet-red tourists block the way with mountains of bags and backpacks, African businessmen in impeccable suits hurry from one over-crowded ticket counter to the next. Nobody pays any attention to the girl in her faded t-shirt, squeezing her way through the masses at Jomo Kenyatta International Airport, in search of her father. She is carrying a bag that's too big for an eleven-year-old. Locks of blond hair stick to her face as she works her way through the jungle of sweating bodies. The legs of her jeans are too short, and her skinny bare arms have the unhealthy dull yellow color that white skin takes on after a lengthy stay in the tropics. "Daddy!" she shouts in a shrill voice. A porter, laden with baggage, curses for her to move aside. Gasping for air she sprints off. In passing, she knocks over a suitcase and someone roughly grabs her arm and yells at her, at the precise moment that a flight is being announced. In a panic, she stops a couple in safari outfits. "Was that the plane to Frankfurt?" she cries. "Didn't they just say Frankfurt?" The man and the woman walk on, shaking her off routinely as they have been shaking raggedy children off their entire vacation.

In her desperation, Mary Emma drops her bag. When she bends down to pick it up again, she suddenly notices that the buckle of one of her sandals is broken and that her toes are black. She had imagined her departure from Africa to be very different—first, a weekend in Nairobi to buy new clothes and to take a bath in an expensive hotel. That's what he'd promised. But in the end, here she is, filthy, wearing beaten-up shoes, having to go to Europe where it's wintertime, on top of it all, and she doesn't even have a sweater. She grabs a passing stewardess by the arm. "Check-in for Frankfurt?" she inquires shakily.

The woman leans towards her, already half-obliging because she isn't being asked for hand-outs, and for a moment Mary Emma is reassured by the smiling mouth turned her way. Then she sees that it isn't a real mouth, it has only been painted on the face, with friendly, curving corners. The eyes, too, have been drawn on with thick black rims, and the eyelids have been colored in blue. Her father's digging, sweeping and sifting students always look very different. They're sun-tanned, have white wrinkles around their eyes and trickles of sweat in their muscular necks. They wear their dull hair in messy topknots and ponytails. They wear men's boots through the sand and the mud, they roll their own cigarettes and drink straight out of the bottle. They lie around under jeeps with wrenches and four of them can lift up a side of beef to skewer it on a spit. They'll call out: "C'mon Em, go find something to do, I'm not your nursemaid." They only like potsherds and soil records. They have had to move heaven and earth to be able to spend at least one season digging with her father.

"Frankfurt!" Mary Emma pleads.

"Over there," says the stewardess, with a disapproving glance at her shoddy clothes. At the same moment Mary Emma sees her father standing in line in front of a ticket counter. His denim shirt is drenched with sweat. With an automatic movement of his hand he combs his dark hair out of his face without looking up from the paperback in which he is engrossed, while pushing his baggage up some with a foot. He'd even get on a plane to Baghdad if she wasn't around to take care of him.

Mary Emma dashes over to him. She wraps her arms around his waist and pushes her face into his side. "I'm back again," she mumbles into the folds of his shirt. While she inhales his familiar scent, he murmurs some kind of response and briefly tickles the back of her neck. Then he turns the page and is once again engrossed in reading.

Leaning up against him, the girl feels the anxiety that her father too will dissolve, evaporate, disappear, slowly but surely withdraw. Mary Emma Zwier, orphan.

With a sigh of contentment she sits down on the floor and takes off her sandals. She pulls her sneakers out of her bag. Carefully she ties the laces. "Look, Dad," she says.

"Shipshape, soldier," says Zwier without looking up. He's got at least twenty names for her: she's his soldier, his one and only millstone, his all-time chocolate bunny-rabbit, his dearest ball and chain, his brave warrior, the favorite nail in his coffin.

But truly shipshape the sneakers are not, even though they're better than the sandals. Dejected, Mary Emma sees how dirty they are, and at the same time her eye catches the girls standing right in front of them in line with their parents. They are the same age as she is. Pink legs protrude from their snow-white shorts. Their fresh striped blouses have been crisply ironed. Their glossy hair fans out neatly combed over their shoulders.

"Daddy," says Mary Emma, getting up. "All those people are still ahead of us. It's going to take hours. Can I still go to the bathroom, quick?"

He looks at her over the edge of his book. His eyes peer absently from behind his glasses. He nods.

As fast as she can, Mary Emma runs to the ladies room. There, in the mirror, she can see that she's in even worse shape than she feared. Her t-shirt isn't just faded, it's stained and wrinkled too, and her face is streaked as if she'd been crying in her sleep last night lying on the back seat of the Land Rover. Although she does know better. She honestly won't let on to her father that she would rather stay in Africa, especially now that he's so ecstatic about his new assignment. For an archeologist, it isn't easy to find work in Holland.

The water from the tap is lukewarm. But at least there's enough, whereas on one of Zwier's digs you're mostly allowed to have a bath only when you absolutely can't stand the smell of yourself in your own sleeping bag for a minute longer. Mary Emma washes her hands thoroughly first, with the greasy soap in the dish, and then splashes handfuls of water on her face. When she looks in the mirror she can see reddish brown trickles running down her forehead: the ineradicable dust of Turkana. After hesitating briefly, she flops her head over the sink and turns the tap on again. Groping for the soap, she rapidly rubs it all over her scalp. But she is startled to find that rinsing her hair isn't so easy with the lukewarm water. Maybe it'll help if she dabs up some of the soap with a couple of paper towels. She wrings out her hair as best she can and gives her head a good working-over with a few grayish sheets of paper. Instead of soaking up the soap, they fall apart in shreds that get sucked on to her hair. When she looks up, dismayed, she can see in the reflection of the tiled room a black woman watching from a distance, a child with decorative little braids in her hair holding her hand. Look at yourself, thinks Mary Emma. She turns the tap on full blast and sticks her head under to rinse away the flakes of paper. In a little while when her hair's all dry, maybe you won't see the suds anymore. Her eyes sting. But she's a brave soldier, she never cries, and certainly not at Jomo Kenyatta International Airport under the gaze of strangers, and absolutely not on special days like today, now she's on her way to a new life.

———

Over four thousand miles away, Gert Balm is, as usual, selling floor wax and Alka-Seltzer in his drugstore. Some time ago there used to be a gravel pit in this remote corner of The Netherlands; but now there is the Binnenmars Café, the Stormvogel Carrier Pigeon Association and an historic monastery well.

With the holidays around the corner, Gert Balm is busier than usual: people need candles, Christmas tree ornaments and napkins decorated with holly boughs. While he is offering advice on cosmetics and tallying them up on the cash register, wrapping up shampoo and aspirin, he doesn't succeed as he normally does in downplaying his smile. Today his clients can get a good view of the teeth that line his jaws like rows of crooked tombstones. He nods and confirms: tonight his guests are coming. Hopefully the girl speaks some Dutch, his English isn't very good, and he doesn't know the first thing about any African languages. He opens a drawer and points: samples she can play store with. A play store, he says cheerfully, is a lot more fun of course than a real one. But, if his little niece would like to stand behind the register, he'll tell her she can go right ahead, that he will.

By the end of the morning, Gert Balm is dead tired.

―――

At twenty-seven thousand feet up, a light lunch of chicken, broad beans and rice is being served on board Lufthansa flight 581. Zwier has some white wine with his lunch. He hasn't had any alcohol in a long time and feels the drink go to his head almost immediately. He promptly requests another little bottle from the stewardess, which she brings with a smile. Her fingers brush his as she hands it to him, and she lets her other hand lightly and briefly rest on his shoulder. "Danke schön," he says, keeping his irritation in check. It is puzzling to him what women always mean to see in him at first glance. Even his female students are unable, despite their constant sarcasm, to conceal their interest: "Could you, for a change, possibly take note of what I'm saying, Professor, sir?"

When the stewardess lingers beside his seat, Zwier demonstratively turns to his daughter. "Taste good, bunny-rabbit?"

She nods, her mouth full.

"If you keep it up, you can have my dessert when you're done." To his relief, out of the corner of his eye, he can see the woman slink off down the aisle. He screws the top off the little bottle of wine and pours himself another glass, which he downs in a couple of swallows.

"Is this butter or cheese spread?" asks his daughter, studying a cube wrapped in aluminum foil.

"Cheese spread," Zwier says absently, "to put on those little crackers." He stares off over her head out the window where there is nothing to be seen but the immeasurable blue sky. An awful despondency takes hold of him. He finishes off the rest of his wine.

"It's fucking *butter!*" his daughter exclaims.

"No four-letter words, we're on our way to the civilized world."

"But you said it was cheese spread!"

"Then I made a mistake," he says in a tired voice. If it hadn't been for her, he'd still be in Africa.

"But I really wanted cheese spread."

"All of Holland," snaps Zwier, "is covered with cheese spread. Soon you'll be able to have as much as you want."

"OK, but I mean now."

With a great effort he manages to say, "Don't whine, Emma." She's flying from one continent to another and still manages to find something to complain about. When he was her age, his most exciting excursion had been to go together with his father to look at the trains as they raced by on the embankment of the dike. That one's going all the way to Rosendaal, his father would say, impressed, or, the slow train from Amsterdam's late again. Meanwhile, they would eat treacle sandwiches they had brought in a paper bag. "Just finish your plate," he says curtly. I've given you the whole world. Isn't it ever enough?

With a sullen look on her face, his daughter spreads the object of her disdain on a miniature cracker. Then, suddenly perking up, she asks, "Will it be cold?"

"Bitterly cold," he replies.

"But what are we going to do, Daddy? We don't even have any jackets!"

"Stores," reassures Zwier, "are plentiful in Holland, too." But what kind of an impression will it make on those people in Sibculo if he arrives in the middle of winter without having taken along even a cardigan for his daughter. Guiltily he thinks: when we're in Frankfurt, there will be time enough. He'll buy her some warm clothes that she can put on right away so she'll be sitting on the airplane to Amsterdam just like any other ordinary Dutch girl. At the thought of how few hours separate him from The Netherlands, Zwier can feel his spirits sink even lower. In a newspaper one of his students had received from home, he had chanced to read that his homeland at that moment found itself in the era of the *grand foulard*, city-district councils, the new illness myalgic encephalomyelitis or ME, and the fin-de-siècle feeling. Zwier has no idea what city-district councils do or what a *grand foulard* is, let alone what the rest is all about, and he would be most pleased to keep it that way. Let the sea simply swallow up that stupid little country. So when they get there it won't exist anymore—everything will simply have been solved, like in a dream where the house in which you lived all your life is suddenly missing among the familiar house fronts along the street. There won't be any Schiphol Airport anymore, and no more over-crowded highways, no tulip fields, no twosomes living under one roof, no employees' councils, no taxes called for by the Provincial Board for the Maintenance of Dikes and Polderland, no more counters and tellers' windows. Where once the nation of mist, herring and forms in triplicate had been, there would now be nothing but a gaping hole in which all that deadly decency and those millions of regulations to maintain order and respectability still gurgled faintly.

Zwier delights in this envisioned solution for a few moments. However, it is unfortunately beyond any doubt that in several hours he will irrevocably see the lights of Schiphol Airport loom up below him in the dark.

Somewhere in that darkness, three weeks ago on a somber December evening, all the fuses had blown when the Sibculo Merchants Association turned on their Christmas lights for the first time. Night had descended with a bang over the entire village. In every house, children had screamed in terror. They had dropped their toys, stumbled in the dark to knock against the edges of tables, smashing their teeth through their lips.

However, because God knew that He couldn't be everywhere at once, He had luckily made mothers—and where there's a mother, there's a tea-cozy and a tea-light: it wasn't long before a little flame flickered behind each window, in the dim light of which the fright could be kissed away. Safely on a lap, most of the toddlers began to think it was a great adventure. The occasional one still whimpered a little, but gradually a marvelous silence took hold of Sibculo. No sloshing of washing machines, no rattling of model trains, no zooming of vacuum cleaners, no bleeping of computers, no grinding of blenders, no roaring of power drills, no bleating of televisions, no humming of refrigerators. Grouped together in their homes, the villagers almost felt like prehistoric cave dwellers. They tried to imagine how their remote ancestors had passed the long winter nights. With meaningful looks, the adults gazed at one another over the flames of the candles and then, in unison, allowed their eyes to drop and rest on their children. In the end it wasn't such an impossible question as to how one killed time when people were still crawling around in the gloom of prehistory. Then the lights flicked on again and Sibculo returned to the twentieth century.

This happened, as was already mentioned, three weeks before, which on the clock of eternity is less than a second, but in the Christmas rush, everybody had forgotten the incident. Only Minnie de Kraaij, who, ever since her husband's death, sees cosmic clues everywhere, harbors the secret suspicion that on that evening there was evidence of an obvious omen. For weeks already she has been keeping a wary eye on the blinking lights of the sign from the elegant capital at the top of the street down to and including the exclamation point on the front of Balm's Drugstore.

Merry Christmas And A Happy New Year!

In the living quarters behind the drugstore, there is no sign of Christmas lights. All day long, the indeterminate gray light of the shortest days of the year has held sway. And yet, Meijken Balm has been unable to bring herself to turn on one of the lamps in the dark corners of her over-furnished living room. The mere thought of the battle to get herself up and out of her chair caused her body to protest. It has a will of its own which is usually stronger than hers.

How did Meijken Balm get through this long, dull, dark day? She wouldn't be able to say, herself. In one way or another, the hours usually slip by of their own accord, while she sits motionlessly in her chair. And every afternoon of course Minnie always comes by for an hour or so. This winter she and Minnie are doing healing. Meijken herself would have liked to do some numerology this season, or lay tarot cards, but Minnie has a need, since she's become a widow, to keep going deeper. For her, she is wont to say, the point is finding the answer to a single significant question: what is a person's role in the universe? In silence

Meijken doesn't believe people play any role of import in the universe, in any case no more significant a role than that of, let's say, any old virus: at least everybody still needs throat lozenges, or an antibiotic. In Meijken's eyes, the virus has only one serious rival for the title of champion of the cosmos, and that is the calorie.

Following Minnie's visit she has treated herself to the split pea soup that Gert prepared for the evening meal. He believes in eating foods that are in season. After making the soup, he went off with a big piece of cardboard (ZWIER FAM.) to Schiphol. Since the moment the door shut behind him, Meijken has been listening to the ticking of the pendulum clock and to the other gentle sounds her house produces. As is so often the case, she feels a bit listless, tired of sustaining her body. Sometimes she doesn't know herself whether she's awake or sleeping, whether she's in a dream world or the real one. Is it, for instance, really true that she married Gert Balm, pharmacist in Sibculo, thirty-seven years ago? She seems to remember that she didn't want to have him. But at the time, of course, she had no choice, that was the whole point. Eighteen she was when she crossed the threshold of this house as a bride. After that she never again set foot outside the door. In the thirty-seven years that she hasn't seen the out-of-doors, she could have learned Chinese, or studied law. But Meijken Balm doesn't like having to use her brain. Ultimately she would like not to be in any state at all to think. She prefers to wallow in the merciful numbness of her slumber into which, time and time again, she sinks like a hippopotamus into a pool of mud.

Does Meijken Balm, after decades spent in between four protective walls, know anything about pools of mud? Sure she does.

Disquieted, she sees that the moment at which her guests will arrive is fast approaching. The past few weeks she has nurtured a vague hope that at the last minute something would come up. It was only when her husband spelled out ZWIER FAM. with a magic marker on a piece of cardboard that she realized there was nothing left to hope for: as the minutes pass, her guests are irrevocably coming closer and nothing will stand in the way of their presence in her house and in her life.

Mary Emma's head is still abuzz from the landing, so that she saunters along behind Zwier in her new red jacket and green cardigan from Frankfurt without paying much attention. Not until the end of the concourse, when they've passed the gates for flights to Baltimore, Harare, Rome and Algiers, does she observe in alarm, "This isn't where customs is, Dad."

"Should've said that right away," mutters Zwier.

"We walked the wrong way," concludes Mary Emma. She has to pee, but swallows her question on seeing how awkwardly her father turns around. That's due, no doubt, to all that wine. "Come on, Dad." She takes his hand.

But he comes to a standstill and with a wild look in his eyes starts patting his pockets. "Do you have the passports?"

"Daddy, come on," she laments, "I gave them to you, you were going to hang on to them, you said so yourself." She starts hopping from one foot to the other as her father, cursing under his breath, bends over the backpacks and overnight bags that they never check in anymore since the time they lost all their baggage in Tanzania. "Look in the side pockets, first," she implores, "don't go and take everything out!"

He isn't listening. "Hold this for a sec," he says, his voice unsteady as he stoops, holding a bundle of clothes out to her that exude the smell of Africa.

"That stuff'll never fit in again. We'll never get the bag closed if you take everything out."

"Just help me out, Em."

"But it isn't my fault you're always losing things."

"And no moping." He now opens her bag as well and digs around in it. With an expression of horror he produces a stuffed whale covered with bald spots. "D'you really have to lug this thing around?"

"That's Jonas," says Mary Emma.

"We were going to travel light!" admonishes her father, swaying to and fro. He looks so incensed and he's breathing so heavily through his nose that Mary Emma says dejectedly, "But Victor Hugo can't be without him."

He straightens up. With his thumb he pushes his glasses back on the bridge of his nose. He states, suddenly articulating very distinctly, "Now don't be difficult, Emma."

"I'm not being difficult! Victor Hugo inherited Jonas from me!"

"I had to leave a lot of things behind, too. This entire undertaking is supposed to be a new beginning, and that means you can't drag everything along with you."

"But I'm carrying him myself," counters Mary Emma with a dry throat.

"That isn't the point."

"I don't want to have a dumb father like you," she blurts out.

"Then go find another one," he barks as he dumps the clothes he's pulling out of her bag on the ground.

"You're messing everything up," Mary Emma whimpers, ignoring, in her befuddlement, the ominous portents. She bends over to pick up a blouse. At that moment, like a shot, her father straightens his back, grabs her by her wrist and jerks her upright. "Go ask that gentleman if he wants to take you. The one in the blue suit over there. He's bound to be a better father. Hurry up. Or do I have to go ask him for you?"

Mary Emma looks at him uncertainly, her arm in the vise-grip of his grasp. Mostly, he doesn't get into these moods when other people are around.

"Go on," says Zwier through clenched teeth. He almost pulls her arm out of its socket.

"No," she screams, "no, Daddy."

He says nothing, no matter how hard she struggles. Grimly he starts dragging her along. "Sorry, Daddy. Sorry, I didn't mean it like that," she sobs, as her knees scrape over the floor. "I want to stay with you."

He halts abruptly, lets her go and turns around. She can tell by his back, as he is walking towards the bags, just how angry he is. He grabs the clothes spread all over the ground and shoves them back into the bags. From a distance, Marry Emma watches him as he steps on to the beltway with as much as he can carry, to let himself be conveyed in the right direction. Shaking, she picks up the backpack that is still lying on the ground. It is even heavier than her own bag. When she buckles the belt, she sees the passports in the open side pocket.

At customs she breathlessly slips into line behind her father and with downcast eyes presses the documents into his hand. "You see, you were the one who had them!" he fumes.

"Sorry, Dad," whispers Mary Emma. She clutches his sleeve to be able to stumble into The Netherlands pressed as closely as possible against him.

For Mary Emma Zwier, The Netherlands consists of one single place, and that is Leiden, where her Grampa used to live. He even taught her how to ride a bicycle, along the railroad tracks, when they were there on sabbatical once. Bicycling's tough in Leiden, with all those little hump-backed bridges. There aren't a lot of people who know the art of bicycling in Leiden. That, Grampa always said, takes a real helmsman. In fact, she preferred to sit on the back of his bike since, for someone who's spent the larger part of her life in the desert, Leiden is a veritable metropolis.

Of Sibculo, Mary Emma has no notion whatsoever. The word village only makes her think of how Dutch villages are always described and portrayed in books and magazines: full of red poppies, farms, country lanes and hay wagons you can go for a ride on. She hasn't been prepared for the collection of ugly, square, dark-brown brick houses surrounded by extensive chick- and calf-fattening sheds. Luckily it's dark already. That will spare her the disappointing panorama of Sibculo tonight. And tomorrow she'll realize it's only a question of waiting for the summer to come before Sibculo reveals its hidden beauty: obviously there's some reason for all those campgrounds in the vicinity. Later on in the year, Sibculo will no doubt be more to her liking.

In the meantime, however, Mary Emma's simply trying to stay awake in the back of her newly met uncle's car, after her long and eventful day. Her father, in the front seat, is snoring loudly, and so she has to listen for two to Uncle Gert's stories. He lisps as he talks—he's got a problem with his teeth, he apologizes, and whenever he eats firm things, if he should, for instance, by accident as it were and without thinking bite into an apple, which in principle can happen to the best of us, into let's say a Granny Smith apple, one of those hard green ones, he runs the risk, and who'd want to take that chance, at least you always assume that most people know better, although in his own time he's met up with some choice examples of the opposite kind, please help remind me so I can tell you about that, but as I was saying...

When the car stops, Zwier opens his eyes. For a moment he is disoriented. A blast of cold air hits him: his fellow passengers have already gotten out. Zwier worms his tall self out of the car as well. He places his feet tenuously on the earth of Sibculo. Something's flashing in the dark, and right above his head he deciphers the radiant phrase:

Merry Christmas And A Happy New Year!

"Same to you," mumbles Zwier, looking around at the street where he has landed. He can see a couple of stores and a Rabo Bank.

"What?" asks Gert Balm eagerly, having opened the trunk to take out the bags.

"Nothing. That we're here already!" says Zwier, rushing over to offer a helping hand. He gives his daughter her bag and takes his own from Gert Balm. "Sorry I dozed off on the drive back. Sometimes you get so wasted from flying." As long as there's no alcohol on his breath.

"That's all right," says Gert Balm. He takes the bag out of Mary Emma's hands, shuts the trunk and motions them inside. When he opens the door, Zwier can smell camomile, peppermint, floor wax: the smell of Holland.

"This," says Gert Balm, with a sweep of his arm indicating the shelves displaying cough syrup, tooth paste and shower gel, "this is where I earn my living." He sucks audibly on a tooth and runs his hand over his balding head. Then he throws his guests a glance filled with anticipation.

Zwier makes a vague sound of approval. He's dying for a cup of coffee. Gently he pushes his daughter, who is eagerly looking at the assortment of salty licorice, ahead.

"No, no, this way," says Gert Balm.

They walk through a narrow passage behind the cash register toward the living quarters. Zwier maneuvers his bags. Watch out for the paint, flashes through his mind.

"Well, here we are," his host announces, opening the living room door. Zwier can make out heavy furniture, and standing on a low set of cupboards which in another flash he knows to be a sideboard, the *dressoir* in Dutch, is a gilded coach with little white porcelain horses spanned in front. He turns his gaze away from it, aware all of a sudden that there's another person in the place.

"Hello," says Meijken Balm from somewhere in the room. At first he can't see her; such is the extent to which her motionless figure in the dim corner is a part of the furniture. But then she makes an attempt to get up out of her chair.

"Don't get up," says Zwier, caught by surprise.

"Have a good trip?" asks Meijken.

"An excellent trip," replies Zwier, walking over with an outstretched hand. He sets his course by a little side table. Only a few short steps now still separate him from his hostess. He hopes he has been able to control his expression. The enormous armchair in which Meijken Balm is sitting must, with time, have completely conformed itself to her body: she lies imbedded in it the way an old stone finds a natural bed in the moss into which it sank at the beginning of time. You occasionally see photographs of archeological digs where stones like this have been found, a young man in khaki shorts beside one pointing out with authority that some of these colossal boulders represent breasts, still others the cylindrical blocks of thighs so characteristic of the mysterious, prehistoric idols from a time when there were still goddesses.

Zwier is not a man for The Goddess. At the sight of the mass of Meijken Balm's fat, he isn't so much awed as filled with revulsion. Speechless, he shakes the surprisingly small hand that is extended toward him. He coughs. "And this," he says, "is Mary Emma." He hopes his daughter won't stare. She can stare in an extremely disagreeable manner. He nudges her furtively.

"How do you do, ma'am," says Mary Emma without taking her eyes off the golden coach.

"Aunt Meijken," Zwier corrects her. Shake hands. Make a good impression. This is our only chance.

"Aunt Meijken," his daughter echoes with a breezy smile at the gigantic woman. She doesn't seem to notice anything unusual about her.

"Please sit down," says Gert Balm with a generous motion of his arm, "and I'll go make some coffee."

"But maybe Mary Emma wants to take a look at her room first," proposes Meijken. Her voice sounds somewhat girlish, and for the first time Zwier has to think of his wife. The same melodious intonation. For the rest, no greater difference could be imagined than between Meijken and Bonnie. "So Emmie," he manages to say, "what do you say?" He lays his hand on her shoulder and gives it a quick squeeze.

"It's late already," Meijken persists. "Maybe she'd like to go to bed right away. She must be exhausted. And besides, the same may very well go for you, after such a long trip."

"Oh, no, really," Zwier starts, to be stopped short by the discomfiting thought that perhaps he couldn't do his hostess a greater favor than by immediately retreating again from the claustrophobic living room behind Balm's Drugstore. Suddenly he is painfully aware that he was the one, single-handedly and bluntly, to invite Mary Emma and himself here.

"Gert," says Meijken. She looks around, bothered. Then she says in a tone of voice that wavers between irritation and indulgence, "He's gone to make some coffee. I guess you'll have to find the stairs yourselves."

"We'll manage," opines Zwier, quickly fumbling for the bags.

"You can't miss it. Naturally we only have one guest room. But that won't be a problem, I'm sure."

"Not at all," Zwier agrees.

"Gert even papered it," says Meijken with unmistakable disapproval.

"All that effort," Zwier makes an attempt.

"He says it's clouds. To me they look like sheep." Meijken shrugs her gigantic shoulders, and adds, "Whatever."

But, as a rule, don't things look completely different after a good night's rest? You can be so quickly mistaken. You're liable to think the worst straightaway, whereas sometimes things turn out to be much better in the end.

———

To Meijken's relief, the following morning right after breakfast, Zwier announces that he wants to go meet his new employer already. And Gert, pale and resolute in his white pharmacist's jacket, has already claimed the child, engrossed in a pile of magazines, and taken her along to the store. It reminds Meijken of how he used to try to extract Bonnie from Mother's claws and coax her into a visit to his Aladdin's Cave.

For some time Meijken moves through the quiet house. She opens doors and closes them again. Then she lets herself flop, perspiring, into her chair, allowing things to take their own course. Ever since she topped five hundred pounds, she only fits into this one special armchair that her husband reinforced underneath with a steel chassis. The seat has been supplied with extra springs, on which many cushions, filled with the finest down, have been placed. Her comfort is his highest priority. The soup-maker. The tea-brewer. The pillow-stuffer.

Bored, Meijken lets her hands rest on both sides of the globe of her stomach and wonders what it must be like to fly from Africa to Europe. She can't picture it. Only once in her whole life did she herself cross the border, the consequences of which she is still experiencing every day. She shuts her eyes, but instead of wide-open, unknown spaces, she sees herself, unexpectedly, long ago, beneath the clear sky, the wind in her hair, against the background of the bank of the Vecht River or the woods around the village. With long strides she walked past aromatic trees, her head thrown back and laughing from pure anticipation, simply because she was alive, because she was eighteen in the age of the motor scooter, the rumba, the stiletto heel, the strapless bra and jazz favorite Pia Beck. While walking she'd tell herself her life story. She waved her slender arms while she imagined her future. She took major decisions. She was certain about everything. Except that she would be buried alive between four walls.

Straining herself to the utmost, she smoothes back a couple of locks that have strayed from her big bun. She hears clinking sounds in the kitchen. It is already much later than she thought; she must have fallen asleep. Any minute Minnie will be coming in with the tea, tea that constricts or is meant in fact to dilate the arteries, whichever, according to what Minnie considers necessary. Once they went to school together, with aprons on and braids in their hair, but why should it be Minnie, of all people, who remained loyal to her all those years? Day in, day out, she shows up around teatime. She is there like the rain is there, or the unshakable rhythm of day and night in which the earth slowly rotates.

Meijken pulls herself together when her friend enters the room with the tea tray. She can see a little bowl with Christmas wreath cookies on it, and prepares to hoist her mighty arm up.

"So," says Minnie, "I thought I'd come a little bit earlier today." Her dark eyes dart back and forth, searching for traces. With her foot, Meijken shifts the pile of ladies' magazines that the girl had been leafing through this morning out of plain view.

Minnie notices nothing, she pours tea that is green and fragrant, sits down on the sofa, comfortably settles her feet on the taboret and says, "Alright, shoot."

"Don't tell me," exclaims Meijken, "you got yourself another pair of shoes."

Distracted, her friend stretches out a foot with a slender instep. Her ankles can still be encircled by one hand. "Think they're nice?"

"How many pairs does that make anyway? You're getting to be like Imelda Marcos," says Meijken.

"Shoes? Sixty-two pairs," replies Minnie contentedly. She caresses the red patent leather for a moment and then straightens her suit jacket with an elegant little flourish. Of late she has been wearing tailored jackets, size 8, as if she were somebody's secretary, and her dyed black hair is cut fashionably short, in a style her late husband would have detested. Gazing down at her new pumps, she mutters, "It better stay dry this afternoon."

Meijken glances out the window. The barren courtyard has a dismal air about it in the gray light. She wiggles her toes in her slippers. "According to the weather report, there's supposed to be snow showers later this afternoon," she remarks with unexpectedly malicious pleasure.

"Then Gert will have to take me home in the car later on," says her friend. "Say, he's pretty enamored of your guests, isn't he?" A slight smile crosses her face. Minnie has a weak spot for Gert Balm. As a single woman you develop a keen sense for the qualities of others. The death of her spouse has enriched Minnie in a certain way: it is just as if she has only now realized just how much unconditional love she is, in fact, capable of.

"Did I tell you already that he's been down in the cellar every evening?" asks Meijken.

"He's suddenly found a hobby then, don't you think?" considers Minnie.

"What hobby, I wonder," says Meijken, "that he's always got to have the key in his pocket."

"Luckily, maybe," Minnie contemplates. "Otherwise you'd probably be tempted. Just like Blue Beard's wife."

"That he kept all those corpses," says Meijken. "I always thought that was strange. Even when I was little."

For a moment her friend appears to be interested. Then it occurs to her that it's Blue Beard's brides that Meijken is talking about. "Somehow he still loved them," she supposes vaguely. "After all, love can hold out very well over the grave, they say." She stretches her fingers, twists her double wedding band and suddenly utters a soft, cackling laugh.

Inadvertently, Meijken observes her own ring, solidly imbedded in ballooning, pale flesh, and sips at her tea.

"But as I was saying before," Minnie continues, "that those two come on over just as you've got the exclamation point on the front of the shop. That has to mean something. Meijken! What's going on in that head of yours? Seems to me you've got a lot to say."

Various excuses dart through Meijken's head. Then she says, surprising herself, "But I don't feel like it."

"Oh," says Minnie. She starts rummaging through her purse as spots start to appear on her neck. She looks hurt, rejected. We'll never, Meijken thinks, get too old for that. At that moment, the telephone rings, and she stiffens.

"The telephone."

"That'll be Mother." The relief she feels at being able to elude Minnie's curiosity is stronger for an instant than her disgust at what is now in store for her. Meekly, Meijken heaves herself up out of her chair by powerfully pushing off on the armrests. Hauling her weight up like that causes a wavy sensation in her head, and she sways. She feels perspiration building up in every fold of her flesh.

In the hallway, the telephone rings imperturbably. After all, Mother knows she's always there. She herself condemned Meijken to an existence between these four walls.

And behind the festive exclamation point on the front of his store, Gert Balm sells mascara and corn pads. He beams. It's true, the new wallpaper in the guest room was a big success. The little one even said: "Little lambs on the wall." Little lambs! In Dutch, without an accent. And then you don't have the heart to say they're clouds. Children have such an imagination, it just goes to show. He shakes his head. No, she isn't here right now. She's gone to see her new school already. He would have liked to go with her, but then, he's got a business to attend to. And that it has to be so brisk out. Hopefully she won't catch cold, coming straight from the tropics as she has: viruses will have a field day with her. But that's how they are with everybody, that's part of nature.

Almost nauseated by her powerlessness, Meijken replaces the receiver, after Mother, with a minimum of words, has simply demanded the guests. The familiar feeling of humiliation has settled in throughout her body, even in the remotest parts. The passage of years changes nothing about the fact that she's still Mother's daughter, as long as Mother is alive.

With a sinking heart, she looks at herself in the mirror beside the telephone. She leans forward and, to torment herself, studies the face that lies hidden under her quivering jowls, her fleshy cheeks, her gray skin that never feels the outdoor air: Mother's high cheekbones, her straight, thin nose, her regal forehead. Handsome and inflexible she rises up out of Meijken's flesh, with the slim figure about which the neighbor ladies had incredulously agreed: "And that after two children." That on her account she had had to sacrifice her fabulous body for months on end, that's what Mother probably blamed Meijken for the most. But it had been her own idea.

―――

And little Mary Emma?

Twenty-eight pairs of eyes stare at her. Brown eyes, blue eyes, gray, black, green, some behind lenses that magnify her and bring her into focus: Mary Emma Zwier, eleven. She is standing in front of the blackboard and stares back with an increasing sense of panic. She sees blond, brown, black hair and reddish, curly, straight, long and short hair against a backdrop of drawings in harsh angry colors, hanging every which way. The heat ducts radiate so much heat that the whole classroom seems to pulsate like a head tormented by throbbing pains. "...and never been to school like the rest of us. That will take some getting used to, won't it?" Mary Emma retains with difficulty. She clears her throat. "Yes," she says mechanically. And then, because she doesn't want to be out of the ordinary, quickly adds, "Not at all."

The concussion laughs. Mouths gape, sounds of ridicule burst forth, mouths full of perverse pleasure: did you see that weird Mary Emma Zwier?

"And such an unusual name," the voice continues. "Merryyemma. You don't often hear that."

"Well, so what?" she says loudly, scaring herself.

A silence has fallen in the overheated classroom with its steamed up windows. The cruel mouths that wanted to eat her raw just a few seconds ago, now cup themselves shut over teeth with and without braces. In the blue, brown, gray, green and black eyes some interest has been kindled. Let's see how Mary Emma Zwier pulls it off.

"Are you," the voice asks after a moment's hesitation, "named after someone? Is anyone in your family called that?"

"No," says Mary Emma, on the edge of a strange fit of laughter: just imagine, her father being called Mary Emma. At once she feels rooted to the ground, her breath catches in her throat: all of a sudden she doesn't know what her mother's name is. She has forgotten her name. For a few seconds she is too upset to speak. Then everything that she does still remember about her knots up inside, wells up and out. "My mother," she blurts out, "went off to Mexico on her motorcycle."

The class hisses, startled or awestruck, and gets ready to start buzzing and crackling like a jungle of telegraph poles, messages will be fired back and forth—agitation, Aztecs, Harley Davidson, and who washes and irons Mary Emma's jeans, then? No wonder Mary Emma Zwier looks like a bundle of rags. The voice says quickly, "And Mary Emma's father, her father is Professor Zwier, the famous archeologist. He has worked all over the world, but now he is here. Why do you think he came here?"

"For the monastery well," the entire class automatically brays in unison, leaping on an easy question.

"The medieval monastery well of Sibculo," confirms the

voice, resuming its dampening work, dribbling Sibculo like medicine into twenty-eight pairs of ears. The eleven-year-old citizens shake their heads briefly, in surprise, but the exotic vision is already gone, they're back in the classroom where it's too hot to convert rebellious feelings into action. Waiting, their arms crossed, they take in the strange little girl.

Mary Emma can see that they're the kind of kids that will shove silly putty up your nose and mouth if they don't like the way you look, and then roll you in stinging nettles. She takes a step closer to the teacher, who is making flattening motions as if she were using an iron while she administers sleeping pills in the form of words in a lulling voice: "Merryyemma's going to have a really nice time with her relatives, until her father gets a house." Collectively the tamed class pictures domestic scenes: an aunt pouring a glass of chocolate milk, a house that has to be decorated or furnished, father reading the paper under a floor lamp and the child that gets called indoors because it's time to eat. The class yawns disinterestedly. Here and there they scratch themselves. Outside it has started snowing slightly, and in a half an hour Christmas vacation begins.

"Well Merryyemma," the teacher wraps it up, "it was really nice of you to come today so we could all get to meet you. And we'll be seeing you again after the new year."

It is only now that Mary Emma notices that she has an imitation mouth too. And disapproving eyes: we know our little pumpkins, that's what we've been trained to do, see if you can take issue with that, missy Zwier, you little troublemaker.

Mary Emma bows her head. She has already blown it, in her new cardigan with two frogs and the words *Frog City* appliquéed on it. That's where the enchanted princes live, her father said when she had picked it out in the duty-free shop. She wants to run away and hide behind his back, hide from the twenty-eight pairs of piercing eyes and the indifferent painted face—but then they'll see that her father doesn't wear any socks and they'll laugh at him because he's barefoot in his shoes: a foot has to be able to breathe, Zwier always says, the foot is the most important means of human transportation. For over three million years, humans have moved around barefoot, from here to there. Humans are nomads; a person owes his feet, or in your case, her feet, a lot.

"Did you want to ask about anything else?" her teacher inquires with barely restrained impatience. She taps the floor with the pointed toe of her shoe.

Mary Emma shakes her head. She tries to straighten her shoulders.

"Well, hurry along then," says the teacher glancing at the scratching class. Thorn in the side, she thinks, pensively staring after the girl who has shut the door behind herself. She has heard all the stories, even though she isn't from around here. Even to this very day all of Sibculo condemns the scandal. With a mother like that—on a motorcycle!—the child will no doubt turn out the same, runs in the family. But such a good-looking girl surely has a good-looking father.

In the hall Mary Emma has trouble pulling up the stiff zipper of her new red jacket. She zips it up over her chin and buries her nose in the upturned collar that contains a hood, behind snap buttons. You can unroll it and then tie it tight around your chin with a little drawstring. Victor Hugo has a jacket that's exactly the same, except it's blue, to hide in. Keeping her gaze fixed on the floor tiles, Mary Emma hurries down the hall, past coat hooks piled with the coats of unknown children that make for unknown smells.

Outside in the empty schoolyard she stands still. Wet snow is falling; before the flakes melt on the ground they look just like white pebbles strewn in the sand. They make Mary Emma think of the trail she and Zwier have left on the globe, like nomads moving from one dig to the next: everywhere there are bright white envelopes with their next address inside, forming a dotted line that must be easy to follow over the face of the earth, from Mexico.

The sound of the school bell startles her out of her daydream. At almost the same instant a bunch of whooping children bursts out the door. She breaks out in a sweat. They'll catch her and then torture her. Her thoughts tumbling over each other, she runs as fast as she can to the bicycle racks where Victor Hugo is waiting for her, hidden under his blue hood. Let's...let's play spaceship, Victor Hugo. We're aliens, we were dropped here from outer space. We came in one of those UFOs and we'll get right back in if we don't like it somewhere and then we'll disappear in the nebulas of the universe. What's that in Dutch, Dad, how do you say UFO? Hey, Zwier! I asked you something. The truth, Zwier. What are we doing here in Sibculo?

"An archeologist of his repute! In that old well of ours!" Minnie remarks. "There's something strange about that, don't you think?"
    Meijken has started slicing the Christmas wreath spice cake that Gert had intended for after dinner with coffee. She sprinkles extra powdered sugar on the slices and slowly licks her fingers while she asks herself how on earth Minnie has managed once again to steer the conversation in this direction. And that's how it'll be from now on, and worse: everybody will grab the opportunity of Zwier and the child to discuss subjects that Meijken wants to keep quiet about. Unaccommodatingly she replies, "He's got at least a year's work here, he says. That'll give him a nice opportunity to settle down in The Netherlands again. The girl's going to have to go to high school soon. Their years of roaming are over." With a guilty conscience she thinks: Gert will have washed Mary Emma's hair, won't he, before sending her off to her new school? How neglected the child looks. Her father as well, in that shabby suit jacket. He's probably cold wearing it.
    "In my opinion, either that well's more interesting than we always thought, or that brother-in-law of yours amounts to less

than what everybody makes of him," Minnie follows up on her train of thought. Her beady little eyes are sparkling.

With heavy arms Meijken sets the cake on the side table that Mother had to give up along with the rest of her furniture when she went to the nursing home. She says, "Or, in the interests of his daughter, he's making do for a while with work that's really below his level."

Minnie lets out a short, hard laugh. "He's really got you, hook line and sinker. He managed that pretty quick."

"Don't be so ridiculous," says Meijken. To her own surprise she actually sees before her all of a sudden how the man who calls himself her brother-in-law lifts a piece of bone with utmost caution out of the dust of ages. He holds his find up to the light. His arms under his rolled-up sleeves have hair on them. Each hair grows in exactly the same direction. For a second, Meijken holds her breath.

Her friend helps herself to a slice of cake. "To me it seems like a pretty unhealthy profession. Always under the ground, among old skeletons. Typical, though. You know my theory, don't you?" Minnie's theories are numerous and often relatively limited in their validity. And since she has become a widow, she has appropriated more leeway than ever. Never again does she have to say: "Excepting the good ones, of course." Nowadays she can restrict herself only to generalities. She relaxes and animatedly sets sail. Since the dawn of mankind, already, says Minnie, the you-know-whos have been more interested in death than in life, that's why that unhealthy concern for other people's graves. Just think about it, from the moment, in some prehistoric time, that they got up on their hind legs and thereby freed their hands, they've used them to beat each other to death: brute strength and loutish violence have, for men, from the very beginning, been the equivalent of life. I'm just saying it like it is, says Minnie: even their most intimate desires they express in a manner reminiscent of a wild boar. And then they think that all that ramming and jamming is supposed to contribute to the salvation of the world, no really, I mean it, you can tell by their attitude, particularly with young men in jeans, they're always walking around with their fingers on their crotches, thumbs hooked in belt loops and their fingers pointing at their alpha and omega—or the way they sit across from you on the bus, legs wide apart, hands around their balls, *around* their balls, Minnie repeats, I'm probably more romantic than is good for me, but that's disgusting to look at, isn't it?

"So what were you doing on a bus?" Meijken asks, having listened to her friend's explanation with only half an ear because Zwier's face has just loomed up in front of her mind's eye, with that caged expression of his, both alert and driven at the same time. He could well be lonely. After everything he's been through. Inadvertently she allows her gaze to fall on the rolling landscape of her body, wrapped in a caftan sewn by Minnie. She always manages to pick colors that don't suit Meijken. Beige is a disaster, unless you're talking about those expensive raincoats you can belt snugly around the waist, those coats in *Casablanca* and such. With a feeling of disillusionment Meijken takes the last piece of cake.

"What was I doing on a bus? I wanted to go to Zwolle," Minnie replies, "to do some Christmas shopping. But am I right, or not?"

"I'm sure you are," Meijken gambles. "But anyway, isn't it about time we started with our healing exercises?"

"Our chakras really aren't going anywhere," Minnie observes. She waves her empty teacup and makes a sour face. "Or are you trying to get rid of me before Master Professor comes home?"

"He's got a name," says Meijken. "His name's Zwier." How long would it be, she's thinking, before worms and maggots have relieved the bones of five hundred pounds of tissue? Buried deep beneath her beige drapery lies a skeleton that archeologists in the distant future will lovingly hold in their hands.

"Zwier," Minnie mocks her. She allows one of her Imelda Marcos-shoes to jiggle up and down on her foot. Then she sets her cup back down on the table with a thump. "I don't understand you," she intones, "welcoming him here."

Disconcerted, Meijken says, "What do you mean?"

"If Bonnie knew you'd brought him here."

"Bonnie," snaps Meijken, "couldn't care less."

Minnie takes a cigarette and lighter out of her purse. With short puffs she starts to smoke; the scent of menthol drifts through the room. "You were always jealous of her," she starts up suddenly. "From the moment she was born. From the moment your mother was pregnant, even."

In the silence that follows her words, the pendulum clock ticks audibly and behind the wall the doorbell of the store rings: a very ordinary Friday afternoon.

"You only took Zwier into your home to be mean to Bonnie," Minnie concludes, exhaling a large cloud of smoke. "Otherwise you would have been on her side. If my sister had dumped her husband, personally, I'd never welcome him with open arms."

"I didn't have any choice," Meijken defends herself. "He just announced he was coming."

"But you don't owe him anything. How long have they been separated now? Nine years?"

"What difference is it to you?" Meijken exclaims. Minnie and her impertinence! Minnie thinks she can do anything she pleases. She no doubt thinks she's indispensable.

"I," says Minnie, stubbing out her cigarette among the cake crumbs on her plate, "happened to be very attached to Bonnie. Even though I never endorsed her just leaving without her child. I can't think that's natural." She purses her lips, shakes her head. Some things are sacred, and Minnie is an upstanding woman. She doesn't allow her personal preferences to influence a moral judgment. You can't turn a blind eye to the despicable patches in someone's character. And the truth must be spoken. "Myself, I raised four," she says. "And I won't deny that it's nothing but sacrifice, sacrifice and more sacrifice, but a child happens to need a mother." She leans over towards Meijken again. Her face unavoidably floats nearer, it's impossible to get around her penetrating eyes. "But aside from all that," she says eagerly, "wasn't she delectable? Remember? Bonnie Bonbon. That's what the boys used to call her. Oh, it's all coming back to me now. Delectable. Even as a baby."

Meijken can't prevent herself from nodding her head. That's precisely what she had thought at the time. She feels her defenses crumbling away, as if she is falling under the influence of hypnosis.

"A real Sunday's child, like all afterthoughts," Minnie says dreamily.

"Yes," Meijken agrees apathetically. Mother, pitied all around, who had to wait eighteen years after Meijken, while everybody around her just kept on bearing children and raising them, bearing and raising.

Only when she gets a side ache does Mary Emma slow down. As soon as she hears the cheering of children's voices behind her she doesn't think twice, but slips into the shoe store on the other side of the street. Panting, she pulls the door shut behind herself.

It is a very ordinary store, with shoe boxes stacked up along the walls and everywhere displays of fashion boots and slippers. Near the cash register two women are chatting. One is wearing a matching cardigan and knit jersey over a skirt, the other a winter coat with strips of fur. Their impeccable hairdos gleam like space helmets, glinting whenever, in the course of the conversation, they nod their heads. Unconsciously, Mary Emma imitates their manner. The women turn around unperturbed: "Jesus, Em, are you pulling my leg?" They don't even take notice of her. Undisturbed, they continue their conversation in low voices. "A downright disaster, a crybaby like that."

"Well, I don't even want to think about it, you know. Mine were never any trouble at all."

"She's a nervous wreck. She can hardly stand it. She says sometimes she'd simply like to run out of the house. She says: kids like that are capable of driving their own mother out of the house. But just a moment, I've got a customer." The woman with the friendly face in the cardigan turns slightly and looks inquiringly at Mary Emma.

Mary Emma sees all kinds of things at once that she will have to try out in front of the mirror some time: a dimple in the cheek, a raised eyebrow, a lock of hair straying down over the forehead. She can feel her eyes are sucking everything in. Get rid of that look in your eyes, her father always tells her, you aren't a puppy, are you? "Do you have socks too?" she asks timidly.

"Go see for yourself, in that rack over there." The woman turns back to continue her conversation. "She's afraid she won't be able to answer for herself if this keeps up."

"Has she had him checked?"

"Three times already. Each time she actually wanted to leave him there at the clinic."

Their voices jingle on while Mary Emma goes over to the socks and haply pulls a pair out of the rack. Light blue: at least they'd go with Zwier's denim shirts. And thanks to the crocheted edging with lace trim his feet will be able to breathe. If only they have them in his size. She takes the socks over to the counter.

"Yes, a fine choice," the woman says. She taps the socks with a pink lacquered nail. Mary Emma looks at her large, soft cheeks and is reminded of whipped cream pastries sprinkled with powdered sugar. This morning in one of Aunt Meijken's magazines she read that facial powder can add that necessary finishing touch to foundation.

"That'll be twelve guilders ninety-five," the woman says, and Mary Emma thinks: at night, try a bluish powder, in artificial light it'll give the face a porcelain glow. Possessing such knowledge gives her a glorious feeling, so it takes less effort than usual to muster the courage to ask something.

"Do you also have them in a larger size?"

"Say!" the other woman exclaims suddenly, "Aren't you Balm's niece? Well, I'll be! I'm your neighbor. I live next door to Gert. So, you came here yesterday with your father. Nice for you both that it's snowing just now, isn't it?"

"Gert was worried about whether you'd speak Dutch or not," says the saleswoman.

"But Daddy and I talk Dutch almost all the time," Mary Emma defends herself.

"You'll be able to enjoy that for the rest of your life, all those languages, all those countries. My, haven't you seen a lot of the world. How on earth did you manage to go to school?"

"Simple," says Mary Emma, surprised. "I had text books and workbooks. They got sent in the mail."

"And that it happens to be snowing," the other woman muses again. "Have you seen snow before?"

Mary Emma shrugs. "Lots of times. At Grampa's in Leiden. I was there five times even."

"Leiden? Boy, you certainly get around. And here we were thinking you'd never been in the country, always traveling around like that."

"Daddy had to go to the university sometimes, you know," Mary Emma says in astonishment. "Once a year almost every year. And we'd stay with Grampa. But now he's got a place in Benidorm."

"In Spain! I'm sure he misses those Dutch winters."

"And the friendliness. What did you think was the friendliest place, where you had the most fun?"

Mary Emma considers. That question, for some reason or

other, has never come up before. Do you like it here, Mary Emma chocolate bunny-rabbit Zwier? If he asks that way, she's almost always sure that her father thinks they're in an excellent place, or that the work's moving along well. She has never heard him talk about places being friendly or fun. And he really does know what's important. "At Grampa's," occurs to her: he was always going on about how fun this or that was, to comb your hair and wash your hands.

The women smile. Their space helmets glitter. Beneath them triumphant little bleeps go off: did you hear that? Did you hear what Mary Emma Zwier said? That child's been all over the world, but there's no place she'd rather be than simply at her Grampa's.

Mary Emma wallows in their approval. She'd like another twenty questions fired at her.

"And what have you enjoyed the most till now in Sibculo?"

"That my mother was born here," says Mary Emma, proud of her knowledge, happy with her response.

The women exchange glances. "Oh," says one. "By the way, what size were you looking for?"

"Ten, that's forty-four," says Mary Emma. She wipes her clammy palms on her jeans and then feels around in her pocket for her change purse. "Forty-four?" the saleswoman echoes.

Mary Emma nods. Are my feet and I, Zwier asks her time and time again, finally the same age this year or are we the same size? What do you think? He gets a kick out of things like that. "He's very tall," she says by way of explanation. She can feel she's beaming. Why are you beaming, soldier? Because you're the tallest daddy there is. They've got a game called sack of coal—he'll throw her across his back, he'll grab her by her legs and swing her around in the air, where shall I toss this coal, out of the way, out of the way, watch out lady, and then she's suddenly straddling his neck and he'll shout: climb up, you can go higher, just hold on to my hair, put your feet on my shoulders, I'll hold on to your ankles, keep going, the ladies and gentlemen of the audience are waiting for you, here are the acrobats. Are you a Zwierio or not?

"Oh, for your father," realizes the woman with the whipped cream face.

"Yes, but in size forty-four," Mary Emma says again. She pulls out her money. All Dutch guilders. We're living here now, bunny-rabbit, my big, grown-up girl, no Emmie, you're getting too heavy, think of your old father, well alright, for the last time. The Zwierios!

The woman opens a drawer under the counter and studies the contents with an exaggerated shaking of her head. "Of course I don't have men's socks in mint," she says in a funny tone of voice.

"Mint?" Mary Emma repeats, perplexed, "I want light blue," she says, shyly touching the socks. Suddenly, she notices that there's dirt still hidden in the cracks of her skin.

"It's *the* fashion color for girls your age. Cute, though, so refreshing. Will dark blue do for your father, or does he wear black?" asks the talking cake. She pulls out a pair.

"But he doesn't like that kind of pattern," Mary Emma blurts out shrilly. "He only likes plain colors." How was she supposed to know that fathers and daughters are supposed to wear different kinds of socks here? Who'd ever come up with something so absurd? And if you break that rule, you'll get a fine, for sure. Oh, mercy, Zwier had said on the plane, we're going to the land of fines again. What do you mean, Emma? You must know by now what a fine is? My God, what are we going to do with you in the civilized world? What is it, a ticket. A paper. You get one if you park in the wrong place.

Not understanding, she had tugged at his sleeve, "So, do you get one for free, Dad?"

"I've got plain colors, too," says the woman soothingly,

laying out a half dozen pairs on the counter, "all plain. Choose whatever you like."

"Just think of how nylon has changed the world," the other woman sighs. "Like computers. Or what they've got now, what are they called?"

"Microwaves?"

"Those, too, but I meant fax machines." They stare at each other in amazement when the shop door slams shut behind Mary Emma Zwier.

And behind the blinking light of the exclamation point on the front of his store, Gert Balm wraps aftershave lotion and eau de toilette in silver gift wrap and punches the keys of the cash register.

Merry Christmas And A Happy New Year!

In the drawer under the counter is where his gift for Meijken is: a leather case lined in red, with nail files of various grades, little scissors, clippers, manicure tools to prod with and others to push the cuticles back. Every time he unzips the lovely manicure set, his anticipation grows. Last year he had made a mistake with those little rhinestone hair-combs that turned out to be no match for Meijken's thick, heavy hair: they kept slipping out of her bun before he'd had the chance to ask her whether he could undo it.

For thirty-seven years Gert Balm has been spying on his wife every night when she takes her hair down and brushes it out with indifference. His heart aches as he watches the way she roughly attacks the tangles. If it were up to him, he would minister to the wild tresses strand by strand, he would carefully separate them without tearing at them and first delicately untangle the knotted ends. He imagines combing a portion of the hair to the side, so that the white hairs underneath become visible, like the underbelly of an otherwise dark animal. It touches him that Meijken's gray hairs try to hide themselves, while their camouflage is now, just before her fifty-fifth birthday, getting thinner and thinner. He can picture how he would lay bare her vulnerable neck and how his fingertips, while brushing, would feel each little lump and bump of his wife's skull and perhaps gain more of an understanding of the thoughts that resided within. But intimacies like this demand planning and organization.

Gert Balm takes one last lingering look at the manicure set before closing the drawer again. With a feeling partly of triumph, partly of tenderness, he thinks: she can't reach her feet.

In the living room behind the store, Minnie again shifts a little closer. "And the child," she drills on, "what's she like?" Let those who will think that their thrusting power propels the world, but Minnie de Kraaij knows better: it is by women's voices discussing various situations with each other that Mother Earth is driven to her indomitable rotation, so that each time day again follows upon the night. Actions don't interest Minnie. She wants words, analyses! Minnie wants to go deeper.

"Is she like Bonnie?" she asks, leaning back again, comfortably stretching her legs.

In distress Meijken fingers the small wart that has recently started growing on her upper lip and thinks of the little girl who calls her aunt. Mary Emma is very attractive to look at, with that almost perfectly triangular shape to her face and that unusual combination of thick, dark eyebrows and caramel-colored hair. Only her teeth detract from the whole, they are too narrow and pointy, like those of a hamster. Down to the smallest detail her features reflect the face that Meijken has tried for so long and so hard to forget.

"Just as good-looking?" Minnie persists.

"Yes," admits Meijken.

"And blond?"

"Yes," Meijken says softly.

"And you and your parents, all three of you so dark. Bonnie always stood out."

"Yes," Meijken says again. But there was a good reason for this: there's blond hair in my family, on my grandmother's side, Mother had said. Sometimes it'll skip a generation or two. You see it happening so often.

"If that child's blond, Bonnie's genes must be stronger than those of that Zwier," Minnie speculates. "Like mother, like daughter. That's always for the best, I think. That a child has its mother's genes. You know my theory. I mean, nowadays, with all our know-how about the miracle of reproduction."

Meijken stares at her. Then, in spite of herself, she asks, "Are you talking about the pill?" Right away, she envisions whole generations of women punching pills out of foil strips. Never to bear, never to raise children again. From choice! Unexpectedly, beneath the lid of her soul it starts to stew and simmer.

"No, no," says Minnie impatiently, "I'm talking about genes, Meijken. Genes, chromosomes in particular. Seems to me we've got plenty of know-how about them these days." She lights up a cigarette and settles down to delve into the subject properly. It has, she says, been common knowledge for ages, after all, that the male Y-chromosome is in fact a deficient female X-chromosome. Not to speak pejoratively about you-know-whos, but the point is: their imperfect hereditary material simply keeps spreading. We'd already have landed on Venus as a more advanced civilization, says Minnie, if we'd only prevented them from stagnating the progress of humanity with their miserable DNA! Speaking in terms of the average, the way I look at it anyway, says Minnie, they are of less consequence than your toe and mine put together and they aren't worthy even to suck on them, or on whoever's toe, much less, in so-doing, reproducing themselves. Now, am I being too romantic again, Minnie wonders, or can't that already be done by means of more responsible techniques, just with synthetically perfected seeds cultured in a dish or in a bottle or something?

Meijken glances at the clock. Seems it's about time for a drink. She heaves herself up and out of her chair and goes over to Mother's sideboard. By rolling her weight slightly to one side she can just reach Mother's crystal glasses on the top shelf.

"Don't you think so?" asks Minnie with an expectant look on her face.

"Sorry, you were saying?" mumbles Meijken, pouring sherry.

Minnie utters a sigh. "Oh, I was just talking to myself," she says crossly, "about the need to take a hard line, put up our mitts. Good heavens! Only now it occurs to me that the uterus *is* shaped like a fist! Doesn't that mean something? Maybe I can send in a letter about that to the editor of one of those feminist magazines they've got these days."

Meijken has no notion as to what her friend is talking about—and the thought that she probably hasn't missed much strikes her as particularly painful. With a heavy heart, she considers the walls surrounding her. She feels utterly discouraged, as if she has been locked up in her own living room for a hundred years already, with Minnie's babbling in the background. Hadn't it once appeared to her that life consisted of more? Desperately she tries to look back through the tunnel of time, but there's no end to it: it must have been sometime in the Pleistocene Age that she was eighteen, wandering freely through woods and fields while she told herself about her life—or maybe it was even earlier, at the time of the Big Bang, when land was being pushed up to the surface of the seething primordial seas. Good grief, thinks Meijken: the ground is moving under her feet: in the earth's core hot magma is cooling down to granite interspersed under pressure with ore-bearing layers. First mica crystallizes, then feldspar and then the remaining magma finally petrifies into quartz. Sun, wind and rain start hammering and tearing at the landscape of corded gneisses, schists and moraines. The ice advances some four times, the meltwater alters the shapes of coastlines and widens rivers, and all the while great chunks of rock are being crushed by the force of the ice and smashed out over the top of the earth's surface. And somewhere along the line, the first hominid appears faraway in the distance. Here we come! With all our unique, individual experiences that will be shared by all people of all times, here we come with everything that we will hand down from mother to daughter, our shortcomings, our fears, our dreams. We have come down from the trees, and somewhere on earth, far from here—but we still don't have any sense of here or there, we only live up to the horizon—somewhere on this slowly rotating planet that scares us with its incomprehensible lengthening and shortening of days, one of us promptly stands up without further ado, just as in present-day Sibculo each roughly fourteen-month-old baby suddenly realizes that it's time to get up on its hind legs and therewith participate in *la condition humaine.*

Meijken, out of breath and whizzing back to the here and now of her living room behind Balm's Drugstore, becomes aware of Minnie's face hovering just above hers. "Meijken! You were completely gone there for a minute."

She nods groggily. The walls are there again, or still.

"Just tell me if you're going to start on your healing exercises! You scared the living daylights out of me. Luckily I could tell by your breathing."

"I think I just spontaneously dove into a deeper layer," Meijken says, startled, accepting the peppermint candy her friend offers her.

"Where were you?"

At the beginning of creation, Meijken wants to say, but in the healing handbook no mention is made of a return to prehistory, when iron was still in the mountains where it should, actually, have stayed. "Why are we doing this, anyway?" she complains.

"Because we're looking for our roots," is Minnie's immediate response. "Every civilized person should do that. We already don't have a clue as to where we're going, so for god's sake, can't we at least know where we came from?"

Stamping her feet from cold, Mary Emma stands in the portico of Huisman & Sons Butcher Shop, across from Sibculo's single point of interest, the old well where monks in the beginning of the fifteenth century used to get their water. All that remains of the monastery, thirty feet away, is a couple of tombstones that have fallen over, beneath which, it has recently been suspected, there is a medieval crypt. The butcher's window interests Mary Emma a lot more: on display, is a sleigh filled with sausages, hams and roasts, pulled by a reindeer made of bacon fat. The longer she peers at the butcher's wares, the more words occur to her in Dutch she thought she had forgotten: soup bone, veal, olives or pigs in a blanket, German farmer's sausage, her Grampa from Leiden's list from a to z. She could easily go inside and place her order just like any other Dutch child. At that thought she can feel a chill run all the way from the top of her head to the base of her spine: as a youngster, her mother surely must have been sent here with a shopping basket and a grocery list! She'll have opened this door countless times and stood in line in front of the counter waiting her turn. Here, in this entryway, as a little girl, her mother must have bent down to pull up her sock or take a pebble out of her shoe. Maybe she even stood for a second on this exact same broken tile. For a moment, Mary Emma can't budge. All around her wet sneakers there is a crisscrossing of footprints, of tracks imprinted in the sticky snow. Her mother has been here.

On the other side of the street, Zwier leans over to inspect one of the monastery's tombstones in the late afternoon gloom. He jots something down in a notebook and then starts pacing back and forth with stiff strides as the snow drifts down. Two men in heavy loden coats follow at his heels. Occasionally, when he stops, they almost bump into him.

From the stoop by the butcher shop Mary Emma watches how her father loosely sketches something in the air with one of his long arms, a lay-out, a plan, an idea. He's going to catch a cold like that, in his suit jacket and no socks on. "Let's go take a look and see if Daddy isn't almost done," she whispers to Victor Hugo. She waits for the right moment: as soon as Zwier, across the way, turns aside to say something to his companions, she trots across the street.

Around the monastery well, a dense little bed of shrubbery has been planted, full of thorns that viciously snag at the legs of her pants as she works her way, puffing and panting, towards the pride of Sibculo. She bends over the natural stone rim and can't keep herself from snorting in disdain: only five centuries old. But whatever is underneath the surface, Zwier always says, can be considerably older. Considerably older. Her father digs his way through time like a mole. Because, as he says, people just like searching for their roots. They think, says Zwier, that the past is full of secrets that must be understood. But, if you ask me, Stone Age folk were no different from you and me: they loved, they hated, and they took their lives as seriously as we do. Except that that can never be illustrated by stratigraphic probes and artifacts.

Mary Emma stares down into the depths of Sibculo's disappointing monastery well. For Victor Hugo's amusement she tosses in pieces of gravel that make sharp noises as they ricochet off the sides.

A short distance away, the gravel crunches. "Hi, Daddy," she calls out, looking up.

Her father comes closer, hands dug deep in his pockets. He scrutinizes her with an absent look. He says, "I'm going to be busy for a while longer."

"Me, too," says Mary Emma. She leans down and grabs a

handful of gravel. Each chip has a pointy white snow-cap on that promptly melts in her hand.

"Can't you go play some more?" Zwier asks. "Then we can go home together in a while." Behind him the loden coats shuffle their feet.

"I already played," says Mary Emma. She tosses the stones over the rim.

"Don't do that," says her father.

"Why not?"

"The idea is that we're going to be digging here, and not that it all gets buried under an extra layer of stones." He is already turning away toward his companions.

"Was I ever a crybaby?" Mary Emma asks without raising her head.

"Sure," Zwier says over his shoulder, "go ahead, and I'll see you later."

"Daddy!"

"Yes? What is it?"

"Professor," one of the loden coats intervenes, laying a hand on Zwier's sleeve. People shouldn't do that, they shouldn't beg for her father's attention or bother him when he's talking, that really ticks him off.

"Did I always cry?" Mary Emma persists, "or was I quiet, too, sometimes?"

Zwier tucks a shirt tail farther in his pants. "Come on, Em. Do you have to start that right now, this very minute? I'm working."

"When, then?"

He hesitates. "Just a moment," he curtly tells the others, before coming over and standing beside her at the edge of the well. He puts his arm around her. "Just one minute more, OK? What games did you play today? Did you have fun?"

"Spaceship. That Victor Hugo and I were aliens."

"Aren't there any other children around, then?"

"Man, they're all at school," says Mary Emma. Caught off-guard, she bites her lip. First at the school, then at that shoe store—soon there won't be any place where she can still show her face. Shrinking, shriveling Sibculo.

"I'll hear all about it tonight," her father says.

She quickly adds, "We were a space rescue team."

He starts to rock to and fro on the soles of his feet. His eyes turn away behind his glasses. I'll count to ten, Emma, I'll count to ten. If she were alone with him, she'd take care, but the presence of the two shadows makes her reckless. Excited about her own discovery, she repeats, "A space rescue team, Daddy."

"That's wonderful. Wonderful."

"We rescued crybabies that had been abandoned by their mothers."

Zwier squats down so suddenly that she jumps back. He grabs her shoulders and thrusts his face close to hers. But his voice is flat, as if he were tired all of a sudden, when he says, "All babies cry."

"But how do you know?"

He gets up abruptly, at the same time swinging her up and plopping her down on the rim of the well.

"I know that from a book."

"What book?" she inquires eagerly.

"A book I bought when you were born."

She clutches his lapels, asks him, "And did it tell you what you were supposed to do when I cried?"

"Walk," says her father, "I walked miles with you." He loosens her fingers, gives them a squeeze. "All babies cry. That's very normal. Come here, give me a kiss."

She starts to giggle and wriggles in his arms, "You're tickling me, hey Zwier, you're tickling me!"

"Be polite," he tells her as he lifts her to the ground.

"Only if you put on a scarf," she retorts, "or else you'll get sick."

"That's enough now. Go play. I'm not through yet."

"You could get pneumonia."

"Enough's enough, Emma."

"And no socks!" Exuberantly she scoops up another handful of snow-stones from the ground.

"And what did I just say?" her father raises his voice. "Don't throw anything in the well!"

"But what am I supposed to do?"

"Stop it, Em!" He quickly lowers his voice, "Just stop it, for heaven's sake." He jerks her up by her sleeve from her slouched position so that the fabric of her new jacket makes a ripping sound. Her arm slides out of the smooth lining, she loses her balance and falls down on her knee on the sharp gravel chips. She gasps for air, but she doesn't want to be a crybaby.

"Do you understand?"

"Yes, Daddy," she says breathlessly. "Sorry, I forgot. I won't touch anything again, really!"

He pulls her to her feet and gives her a shove. "There's a field. Go there and play."

"You won't forget to call me when you go? You won't go without me?"

Zwier makes a snorting sound. He throws his head back and looks at the pale half-moon above shrinking Sibculo.

"Will you call me, Dad?"

But he's already on his way back to the tombstones, behind which the loden coats are still just barely visible against the dark sky.

Only when she is sure that her father won't look around does Mary Emma hobble over to Victor Hugo, huddling in the shelter of the well. "It isn't so bad," she whispers comfortingly, "I only lost a little piece of skin."

She carefully pokes at her knee through the rip in her pants. "You see," she mumbles, "it's only blood. Then it always seems worse than it is. Just like the time I got that hole in my head." She doesn't have a handkerchief with her. But the Inuits don't have handkerchiefs either. They put snow and ice on their wounds instead of bandaging them up; she saw that for herself in a *National Geographic*. That one Inuit's leg with a harpoon sticking out of it. With her eyes shut, Mary Emma presses a handful of snow she scraped together from among the gravel chips on to her knee. The iciness shoots through her like a spearhead. She rocks her upper body back and forth. But she has to hurry up. She has to go look for that field. Otherwise Zwier won't know where to find her later on. She gets up stiffly.

The only thing that can still be distinguished in the near-darkness is a narrow path winding across the little park. Limping, obedient, she follows the well-trodden trail. The path makes a wide loop around the well and then leads to a piece of overgrown terrain that gradually slopes upwards. There's lots of juniper bushes, some of them like pillars, others with wide crowns or with creepers running over the ground, but all of them equally evil-looking. In the dark they look just like people puffing themselves up or then again making themselves very small. As the undergrowth gets denser, Mary Emma walks slower and slower. She is reminded of scary fairy tales and the way in which Zwier's students always told them to her, annoyed, hastily: "And then Hansel and Gretel were sent into the forest by their parents and there they were eaten up by a witch. What do you mean, how come? The witch was just hungry." One time in Ethiopia, where everything had gone wrong, where equipment had been stolen and where paleoanthropologists who were messing around with the graves got underfoot, all the female students had gotten together and handed in a letter of complaint to Zwier. What's this all about, asked Zwier, a feminist tribunal or something? They had stamped on the ground with their boots. Are we here to do fieldwork or babysit, Professor Zwier? If we wanted children, we would have had them ourselves. Nothing personal, Professor, but that macho attitude has gotten really old. This isn't the Holocene Age. We, the young women had shouted angrily, aren't living in Lucy's time anymore, goddammit!

That Lucy!

Lucy, or rather the world famous skeleton that was given that name and that possibly belonged to the very first human ancestor, or possibly the last apish one, had made prehistory, or rather paleoanthropology, so glamorous that no honest archeologist could stick a spade in the ground anymore without droves of fossil hunters horning in. A potsherd, Zwier had said bitterly, is merely a potsherd, but a finger bone is a different story entirely, bunny-rabbit, and that's what's getting on my girls' nerves: the minute we finish neatly measuring everything up and plotting everything out in the blistering heat, there's another nonsensical order from the sponsor that we can't get into the ground because some bright person, who's pro- or anti-Lucy, has told him that there's fame to be found in this or some such area with a jawbone inspected by an expert. Do you think it so strange that the girls are a little irritable? Could you maybe humor them a little more, Emmie, old warrior of mine? I already have my hands full with them without you making them still more obstinate and unmanageable.

Yes, Dad, Mary Emma had said in the darkness of the tent. It had itched like crazy under the gauze patch on her temple: it felt like maggots had crawled through that hole and into her head and that they were laying eggs in every fold of her brain. Maggots got babies all by themselves. They couldn't be put on the pill. Lucy, or rather Australopithecus afarensis, couldn't either. Lucy had born and raised, born and raised children, three and a half million years ago. Otherwise human beings wouldn't be here today. Or maybe they would be, but that depended on your denomination.

"Emma, what is the main characteristic of Australopithecus afarensis?" Zwier sometimes asked her when there was company.

And Mary Emma, proudly, "That was the first one to stand up, that only used its hind legs to walk." "Her legs," Zwier would then always correct her.

As he had pulled her over beside him on his cot, he had said indignantly, "God knows I'm not an antifeminist, but I think I deserve some respect, the way I'm raising my kid single-handedly in the desert. Tell me, Emma, how many fathers do you think would do that? I could easily have sent you to a boarding school. As long as you get that into your head. And don't scratch at your Band-Aid or it'll start bleeding again." Then he'd held her on his lap and said that the situation was a little tense right now, and then people sometimes did crazy things. So she shouldn't be angry with her old father.

Mary Emma had quickly shaken her hair over the accusing patch. She almost tripped over her words as she said, "It doesn't matter, Dad. Really. Really."

Maybe, he'd said after a short silence, they could go to Addis Ababa this weekend and buy something nice. Mary Emma had laid her head on his shoulder. He smelled of sweat and dirt. "My millstone," he'd murmured tenderly, pulling her closer. "Do you have any idea," she'd asked, suddenly sleepy, "why Hansel and Gretel's parents sent their children into the forest?"

"I'd have to look it up," Zwier had said. "I really don't remember. Ask the girls. I still have a lot of writing to do."

Reluctantly, Mary Emma had stolen outside into the African night where nothing stirred. Sometimes you'd step on something in the dark by accident and then you'd be in hot water. Especially since Lucy. She wasn't, in fact, against Lucy. On the contrary, it was a comforting idea that you were part of one big family with all the people on earth. That they could send you from here to there and you'd never have to feel lost. She had groped her way along to the tent where Zwier's students read their feminist magazines, because they, too, wanted to be part of a family that spanned the globe. They were nudging each other, reading a letter sent in to an American magazine out loud:

> *To the editor:*
> *We protest the degrading manner in which on the cover of the previous issue you showed a wolf as symbolizing a man. That is species chauvinism of the first order. The violent acts perpetrated by men cannot be attributed to 'animal instincts,' any more than they can be attributed to the provocative behavior of women. Feminists have known for a long time that women aren't responsible for the outrages to which they have always supposedly tempted men: isn't it time that we stopped blaming animals?*
> *Helene Aylon*
> *Batya Bauman*
> *Feminists for Animal Rights*

That was the kind of thing her father's students had on their minds! Plus having to remember to take along enough pill strips for the trip—no little accident for them, the way Professor Zwier's wife had had not too long ago! Which accident, Mary Emma asked, a little frightened when she heard them whispering. You, they had said shaking their heads, you really weren't planned, you know, they'd have had you aborted for sure if they'd been in a civilized place, go ask your father, you were definitely a mistake.

A surprise, corrected Zwier, pushing his papers aside to take her in his arms, you were the biggest surprise of my life.

Mary Emma pulls her zipper up even higher and forces herself to keep on walking. Of course there aren't any wolves in Sibculo, or else her father wouldn't have sent her into the woods. She climbs the hill past the juniper bushes. When she has reached the top, she suddenly hears children's voices below her. Behind the underbrush, a smaller field is to be seen lower down, with two soccer goals, a basketball hoop and a jungle gym. A tall lamppost diffusely lights an area in which snowflakes are floating down like dust particles in the beam of a slide projector. Three boys are riding their mountain bikes around in circles in the white grass. There is no other possibility than that they're from Sibculo's one and only elementary school. Silly putty and stinging nettles flash through Mary Emma's mind. She ducks down behind a bush. If only Victor Hugo doesn't start bawling. "They're rough," she hisses, "they're jerks, they're mean. Nasty fucking shitheads! Just look at my knee! How do you think that happened? Well?"

Hidden down in the bare undergrowth she nurses her knee. At least a solution has been found as to what she'll say to Aunt Meijken and Uncle Gert when they ask her how her pants got torn. Guiltily she bows her head: obviously they found the wet sheets stuffed under the bed. But that's what you get with a baby like Victor Hugo—and you shouldn't ever lose your patience with little children, it's written in all the books.

She is suddenly shivering from the cold. Why hadn't Zwier waited until summer? Then at least she could have gone to junior high school right away, instead of being delivered into the hands of those stinging nettle-kids and that powder mouth for half a year first. It isn't logical on her father's part to want to settle down in the middle of the school year.

In the underbrush, Mary Emma throws her arms around herself. It could well be a long time before she'll hear him calling her that he's ready.

At the stroke of six, just as Minnie, unasked, is pouring them both a second glass of sherry, footsteps can be heard in the hallway. Gert Balm appears in the entrance to the living room, one shoulder higher than the other and jutting his balding head forward a bit, the way he always does when there's company. "Ladies," he says cautiously.

"So, Gert," says Minnie, "did you do a lot of selling today?"

He sucks on a tooth as he unbuttons the top button of his white jacket before buttoning it back up again. Finally he replies. "It's a busy time of year." It sounds like an apology.

"Come in, why don't you," says Meijken.

"Or shall I start making dinner?" her husband proposes. "It's past six already."

"They sure are late, those guests of yours," Minnie observes, raising her glass before emptying it in a single gulp.

"Maybe they've gone to do a little shopping," Gert Balm speculates. "I don't believe Zwier even took any socks with him."

"Go and get some cocktail nuts," Meijken tells him.

"But what should I do about dinner, Meijken?"

"As long as they didn't get lost," Minnie ponders.

"Lost? In Sibculo?" remarks Meijken. "That's a good one."

"Maybe waiting a little bit longer is the wisest thing," her husband wavers.

"Nuts, Gert."

"Kale and potato stew," he says, finally coming into the room. "I thought it would be nice to make something traditional for their first Dutch meal. Don't you think so?" He bends down by the sideboard and takes out a bag of peanuts.

"Over here," Meijken says before he can go put them in a little dish one by one.

"Tell us, Gert," says Minnie as she pours herself still another drink from the bottle, "what's your impression of the visitors?"

Meijken cuts her off. "Now I remember what I wanted to ask you!" she addresses her husband. He turns his head towards her expectantly. Sometimes she wakes up at night and then it turns out he is leaning over her with the exact same expression in his eyes, and his face, with its prominent, gaunt jaw line, so close she can count his pores. At moments like that she is startled to realize that he doesn't really notice her circumference, that he is looking straight through her gigantic, spongy body, still seeing the girl that she smothered in fat. "What?" he asks.

"A Christmas tree!" says Meijken. "They sell trees on the square, don't they?"

He stands there, bewildered. He rubs his hands. "Do you want a tree?" he asks after a couple of seconds.

"Yes," says Meijken.

"Then I'll go get you one," says her husband. He leans over and gives her a kiss on her forehead. She begrudgingly puts up with it. After all, there are worse men. There are enough, she surmises, who would expect something in return. "Why don't you go right now," she insists before she loses her patience once again. "You've still got to make the beds."

After he has closed the door to the living room behind himself without a sound, Minnie remarks with the confused indignation resulting from three glasses of sherry, "Are you really going to let Gert make their beds? Is there something wrong with this Zwier that you're giving him the velvet glove treatment?"

"Mary Emma had a little accident," Meijken explains. "She needs clean sheets."

"Still a bed-wetter, at eleven?" exclaims Minnie. "That child can't be happy. Obviously she misses her mother."

"She's done without her for so long already!" Meijken blurts out. She checks herself. "All that excitement of the trip must have given her a bad turn." What on earth, she thinks, ashamed, was I doing this morning, going up to their room as soon as they left? Why did I drag myself all the way up there? What did I expect to find in those bags?

"And Gert just slogging away," Minnie sums up thickly. Then she recalls something. "But I *meant* it, what I just said to him: what *does* he sell the whole livelong day? Whenever I need something he never has it."

"Well, then you just go get it somewhere else," says Meijken, who has no idea what her husband sells. She wouldn't even know how his shop is set up anymore. The last time she was there was over ten years ago. Weight-loss products had then just become the rage, and overnight he had put bags of dissolving powders on display that were supposed to suppress the appetite, and cans of liquid putty that were supposed to be meal substitutes, all without a single calorie. After taking one look at the new products, Meijken had turned around and walked out. Her husband had promptly gone to Sloot's Bakeshop to get some chocolate-covered cream puffs. "You'll see," she says darkly, "that he's down in the basement night after night to tinker on some present he's putting together for me."

"Oh come on," says Minnie, bored. She read a theory somewhere last week, she explains, about how houses should be built smaller in The Netherlands. After all, what does a spacious kitchen lead to? To the installation of a king-size refrigerator. And what's to be found in a refrigerator like that? "A bottle of sherry," says Minnie, "I swear, that's what that man wrote, an architect or something."

"So?" offers Meijken, suddenly exhausted.

"And with the sherry, along comes the neighbor lady," Minnie winds up victoriously. "Get it? That was his theory: put two women together and right away things get discussed that the average man would rather leave be." She turns up the collar of her blouse. "We just happen to go deeper." Then, with a look of regret, she gets up. "I can't leave Harold waiting any longer."

Harold is Minnie's cat. Minnie suspects he's a reincarnation of Mahatma Ghandi—he has the same expression—so she can't bring herself to have him castrated. "Oh darn it all," she comments, "now Gert's gone and it's still snowing." She looks regretfully at her pumps, then raises her head and says, "Nothing's happened to them, your guests, I mean, that they're so rude about coming back?"

In the quiet following Minnie's departure, the furniture seems to take up more space than usual. An uncommon feeling of claustrophobia takes hold of Meijken. There we are again. She sighs. But that which is the heaviest to bear must be the weightiest. Those had been Mother's words once, too. The truth, said Mother, is such a *modern* concept. We never knew about that, and nobody went on about it either, as long as we grew up proper and decent.

Meijken plants her feet firmly on the floor and pushes off: a piece of liverwurst is just what she needs. At that moment, the phone in the hall rings. How thoughtful, she thinks, at once forgetting about her hunger, that he should call to say he's going to be late.

"Hello, Zwier?" she inquires into the receiver. Her smile vanishes. She braces herself. "No, Mother," she stammers. "No, Mother, they aren't back yet."

2

The Caring Society

It's almost seven by the time Zwier turns homeward after his first inspection of Sibculo's well. He carries his daughter all the way on his shoulders, holding her ankles protruding thin and breakable from her pant legs. He's beside himself with rage. The scum. Ganging up on a little girl. It makes you want to break their legs. They wouldn't just walk away with banged-up knees if he got his hands on them.

"Don't pull on my feet like that," Mary Emma complains.

Zwier is gripping her ankles tightly. "Hang on a little longer, honey," he says as he presses his head against her. "Would you like me to sing something for you?"

Eagerly, "Yes, Daddy! The dove song!"

"The dove," says Zwier, disarmed. But just as he is about to start singing, he is struck by the pervasive silence of the village. It is unnaturally, eerily quiet. Only people who usually keep their mouths shut live here; who don't ask their creepy sons what they were up to just now. A person can get away with anything in Sibculo, beneath that blanket of silence. Just think, the neighbors might hear! You can be sure that the people in all those houses are cupping glasses to the walls. Is there a hint of scandal to be ferreted out? Oh, no, not here. Without a sound Sibculo breathes, waiting for the unspeakable.

At the thought of what might have happened to Mary Emma, Zwier really flips. He has never stopped to think about the dangers of a dark city park. He can feel himself starting to sweat in his light-weight clothes. He is already falling apart over his responsibility for her. There's no room for new worries.

"Sing the one about the boy and the dove," she insists.

Zwier clears his throat. Then he starts in on the first line of the song his own father always used to sing for him, about a boy who takes the eggs out of a bird's nest. As a boy, he would chime in with the refrain, sketching the fate of the mother dove left behind alone, as loudly as possible: "And the woods resounded so *sadly,* rookoo, rookoo, rookoo." You could draw out the word *sadly* till it gave you goose bumps. So safe the world was back then, with no greater evil than the stealing of eggs.

"And the woods resounded so sadly," sings Zwier, and his daughter's high voice chimes in. Gert and Meijken will reproach him for having left her alone for so long, in the dark, in a strange place. Sibculo isn't the desert! In Sibculo you have to stand guard over your daughter, and anybody who calls themselves a parent knows that. Go ahead, heap some more burning coals on my head, thinks Zwier bitterly.

Mary Emma's voice now rises above his. Her *sadly* sounds so melancholic. You can hear she knows what she's singing about. My father just leaves me to fend for myself.

"Keep singing," she pleads when his voice hitches. Mechanically he starts in on the couplet where the cruel Bart makes his move and takes off with the eggs. At home, even though the lyrics make no mention of it, Bart naturally had a father as well as a mother: after all, Bart lived in the era of nuclear families. He didn't have a father who had to be everything to him and who was therefore always falling short.

"And the woods resounded so sadly," Mary Emma and Zwier lament in deadly quiet Sibculo which might as well, if it were left up to Zwier, disappear with its creepy boys, historic monastery well and all, off the face of the map: reality is still worse than he had suspected months ago on receiving the letter in Africa telling him he might go look for a burial ground under Sibculo's monastic well. At that moment he had just found the depiction of a praying mantis on a rock slab that had surfaced from under a previously skimmed layer; a fleeting thought had just crossed his mind about the makers of such paintings—to be precise, he'd thought: it must have been the social misfits who had embellished their world with blood, feces or vomit, those who were unable to hunt, those who were unable to kill, who were left behind in their own filth when the tribe went off to hunt. And he went on thinking, Zwier went on thinking: while the women were meanwhile bearing children and raising them, bearing and raising, therefore having no time to kill or to embellish caves. My god! thought Zwier, and for him it really was a new thought, so here it is: my god, it wasn't until more or less the end of the twentieth century before the hand that always stirred the cereal could also wield the pen and brush! And for a brief moment he'd had a highly positive feeling about himself as being somebody who valiantly recognized at least that women were people too. All of this had been on his mind when Zwier, who thanks to Bonnie, he admits, did a lot of pondering about what has been so unjustly termed the women's issue ("If there weren't any men, there wouldn't be any women's problem"), was handed the letter by one of his students in which he had been informed of a job in Sibculo.

"And the woods resounded so sadly," he sings, his daughter on his shoulders, stumbling through dark and silent Sibculo. Since this afternoon he knows for certain what he had dreaded then, immediately on reading his letter: a slightly quick-witted third-year grad student would already be bored to tears with that well. But never for a moment had he seriously considered that Mary Emma wouldn't be safe here.

"Rookoo, rookoo, rookoo," Zwier and his daughter sing, and in the distance Sibculo's Merchants Association's good wishes twinkle at them:

Merry Christmas And A Happy New Year!

In the store, Mary Emma is placed on the counter. Embarrassed about the consternation she has caused, she fiddles with the drawstring on her hood, while her uncle agitatedly digs around for cotton wool and gauze dressing. Slowly but resolutely her aunt swells nearer, like a large ship. "That looks nasty," she says. "And that on your first day here! Let's take off those pants, or else we can't get at your knee properly."

Zwier tugs Mary Emma's sneakers off without undoing the laces. "Those socks are just plain soaked," Meijken observes, shaking her head.

"Tomorrow," Zwier declares in a threatening tone, "tomorrow I'll buy some decent apparel. But don't you start telling me that I'm falling short of the mark too."

Aunt Meijken looks disconcerted. "I didn't mean it as a criticism," she manages to say. She turns to Mary Emma with a smile. Her gigantic arms rise up like zeppelins. "Let me help you out of those pants first." She pulls socks and pants down in the same surprisingly quick motion and wads them up. Right away she shakes them out again. "What do you want me to do with these, Zwier? Wash them or throw them away?"

"Daddy!" Mary Emma whispers, upset: she doesn't have another pair of pants.

"I just said we were going to go shopping tomorrow," her father says measuredly to her aunt. But he seems uneasy. He feels Mary Emma's cheek, her forehead. "I'll just go get you a blanket, honey." He pats her on the leg and turns around, almost bumping into Aunt Meijken. "Sorry," both utter in unison. Zwier makes a gesture for her to precede him into the corridor.

Alone with her uncle in the store, Mary Emma is suddenly painfully aware that she has had the same underpants on for weeks. She shifts backwards on the counter, while Uncle Gert takes a pair of tweezers in hand and disinfects them in alcohol. His reassuring smile exposes the whole cromlech colonnade in his mouth. Mary Emma can't help staring at it. As if he has read her thoughts, he taps one of his teeth and says in a conspiratorial tone, "Milk teeth. I never changed them."

She doesn't know what to say.

"Shall we?" he asks. "Will you tell me right away if I'm hurting you? Then I'll stop."

She nods. It occurs to her only now how incredibly clean he is. Even under his thin hair his scalp looks like it gets buffed every day. Yesterday, in the duty-free shop, she wasn't allowed to try anything on, the lady said that right away, with a chilling look at her dirty clothes.

"What a brave girl you are," says her uncle, picking bits of grit out of her knee with his tweezers. He makes clucking, shushing sounds all the while. She hopes nobody is looking in through the store window, watching how he's fussing over a little bit of sand and gravel. Now he's dripping iodine on the scrape and his face contorts. Above his balding head Mary Emma looks with shame at the display of beauty aids. Colorsport has Tummy Tone with seaweed extracts for stomach and waistline, there's Hip & Thigh made from ivy and butcher's-broom for the upper leg, and Tone-Up, a shower gel with fortifying effects; the fragrances one can choose from are: Ocean, Peach, Magnolia and Avocado. "And now all we need is to put a nice dressing on it," says her uncle. His white hands cut off a piece of gauze.

"But then I can't take a bath anymore!" she starts. "And that's what I wanted to do! I wanted to take a bath!"

"That won't be possible with that knee. But a footbath will warm you right up too." He takes one of her feet in his hand and squeezes it encouragingly.

"No, I don't want one," she cries. She wants to take a real bath, to smell nice again, and any minute now he'll see how black the bottoms of her feet are. She tries to wriggle free, and inadvertently kicks him.

"Now, now," he says, somewhat alarmed. He lays a soothing hand on her knee. The other one she can feel on her shoulder. His face is so close to hers that she can smell his breath, like the odor of rotten earth rising out of the cavern of his mouth.

Centuries of dampness and darkness must have held sway in that cave. She can see cobwebs, blanched bones and slimy fungi behind her uncle's smile and she lets out a scream in fear.

"Don't touch me," she yells, flailing around with both arms.

"What's all this?" Zwier asks loudly from the doorway. Slowly he enters the store, a blanket thrown over his arm. He glances from her face to her kicking bare legs and then to Uncle Gert. An expression that Mary Emma has never seen before comes into his eyes. "What's going on here? What's he doing to you?"

Mary Emma bursts into tears. Her shoulders shake, her nails dig into the palms of her hands.

"I don't understand," stammers her uncle. "From one minute to the next... And I just went out and bought a Christmas tree for her, on the square."

Zwier roughly pushes him aside. He clutches Mary Emma's face and grips it between his hands. He brushes the hair back from her forehead, presses her against him, rocks her. She can hear his heart pounding. "So, even here," he says, choking, "I can't leave you by yourself with an easy mind." He lets go of her, turns around.

Uncle Gert staggers back, knocking over the Colorsport collection. Uncomprehendingly, he raises his hands while the bright colored bottles around him roll across the floor. "Didn't I say I'd stop right away if you didn't want me to go on?" he pleads with Mary Emma. Zwier's fist encounters him in the middle of his stomach and he falls, knees buckling, among vials of Ocean, Peach, Magnolia and Avocado.

"I should tear your head off," Zwier hisses. He grabs her uncle by his thinning hair, pulls his head back and smashes his face with his other hand. Mary Emma screams. She slides off the counter, tries to grasp her father's arm. "His teeth," she wails, "Daddy, his teeth really hurt already!"

"I saved up samples for her," lisps Uncle Gert. Blood runs down from the corner of his mouth. His head bobs under the blows. "Little cakes of soap and perfumes... Revlon has a new line...in that pretty packaging." Something in his jaw cracks. Red foam appears on his lips. He babbles, "In those cute little boxes."

Panting, Zwier straightens up. His arms drop limply to his sides. "That I'm dirtying my hands on this," he mutters with disdain. Mary Emma bites her fingers.

"We're leaving," her father says flatly.

"But we haven't had anything to eat yet." She starts crying again.

"We'll eat somewhere else. And sleep somewhere else."

"But what am I supposed to wear? I don't even have any clothes!"

"Where are your jeans?"

"She threw them away. Now I don't have anything to put on!" she howls. She doesn't want to go away. She wants to play with those samples. She pummels Zwier's thigh with both her fists. He squats down, pulls her to him and lays his head on her shoulder. He is so heavy that she almost loses her balance. Almost inaudibly he says, "I'll make sure nothing happens to you anymore."

In confusion she shuts her eyes not to have to see her uncle any longer, still sitting on the floor, huddled up, a bloodied handkerchief pressed to his lips. Go away! In a minute he'll start up again! Tensely she whispers in Zwier's ear, "So, let's go, Dad."

He raises his head and looks at her like somebody waking up from a deep sleep. "My beauty," he murmurs. Then he abruptly gets up and takes her sneakers off the counter.

In the corridor behind the store it's dark, but there's a light on in the kitchen. On the stove a pot of kale and potatoes is simmering. A smoked sausage ready to be added to the pot is lying on the counter. The table has been set for four. A napkin decorated with holly boughs covers each plate, there's a wineglass beside each setting. Three tapers burn in the center of the table, and next to one of the plates there's even a candle in the form of a pot-bellied Santa.

Without a word Zwier opens the trash can in the corner by the kitchen door and pulls out her stained, torn pants and her wet socks. Mary Emma shudders as she wriggles herself into her clothes. She worms her feet back into her sopping sneakers. Then she trudges outside behind her father, across the dark courtyard. As he opens the gate, she looks back one last time, longingly, at the Santa Claus beside her plate.

Meanwhile, Meijken hauls herself up the attic stairs, pausing for a moment after each rise to collect her forces. Her breath comes in fits and starts, and black dots dance in front of her eyes from the exertion, but over and above all this Zwier's indignant words keep hammering in her head. Evidently without a second thought he has assumed that she has been set against him. He thinks her ears have been peppered with all manner of venom. Everybody knows sisters share all their secrets.

As soon as she has reached the attic she walks, without allowing herself to catch her breath, straight to the set of shelves that Gert has loaded with suitcases and overnight bags. The entire house has been booby-trapped with this kind of silent encouragement. Her husband still hopes that one day she'll step into the outside world again. She takes the shoe box from the top shelf and sits down on a big metal-edged trunk with it.

This box contains all she knows about Bonnie's life and her marriage with Zwier. And that is pitifully little. Answering for things has never been Bonnie's strong point. One day all allusion to Zwier simply vanished from her letters, just as abruptly as he had popped up in them earlier, without any further note or explanation. If she hadn't made off-hand mention that a marriage certificate had considerably facilitated travel in Islamic countries, Meijken wouldn't even have known that they were married. And in precisely the same way she herself later concluded that the bride had evidently picked up and left.

Meijken brushes aside a couple of stray strands of hair and then opens the shoe box. She lets her gaze rest on the stack of envelopes that contain all that Bonnie has ever been willing to admit to her—and not even that, because her letters, although addressed to Meijken, are intended for Mother. Since Mother's been having trouble with her eyes, Meijken has been receiving her mail and reading it to her over the telephone.

At random she pulls out a sheet of airmail stationery from an envelope. "Dear Mother," she reads aloud. You see, I don't even exist for Bonnie! How could it be otherwise. Since her birth I've done everything to create as much distance as possible between the two of us. Mother's the one with whom she corresponds so touchingly. Every five or six weeks she writes a letter home like an obedient daughter. But Bonnie has no idea what it really means to be an obedient daughter. Her whole life she has been able to come and go wherever she pleased.

Meijken allows her eyes to glide over the casual handwriting, but all at once she can't stop reading, pulled along against her will by the imaginative writing style. Before her mind's eye a primeval landscape unfolds, a gray expanse beneath a high vault of sky where insignificant people in dull, sandy-colored rags huddle around a fire to cook cornmeal mash. In that sepia-tinted tableau Bonnie's red shirt stands out brightly, as if she were the only figure in an old photo to have been tinted. Her dark blond hair sweeps from left to right while she roots in the dry earth with energetic movements. Then she suddenly lifts her head, her face almost perfectly triangular in shape, and looks, her dark eyebrows raised, directly into Meijken's eyes. Aghast, Meijken stares into the face of the woman they call her sister, until she realizes that she's looking over the edge of the letter at a newspaper photograph on top of the pile of paper in the box. She almost bursts out laughing from relief. After all, Bonnie's on the other side of the world: there isn't any reason to be afraid. Light-headed, Meijken cools herself off for several moments with a fan of envelopes on which exotic stamps have been pasted: Bonnie on the Amazon, Bonnie in Sudan, Somalia or at the Cape, Bonnie in Madagascar and in Mozambique, Bonnie in the Hadar Valley—where she met Zwier. Lord knows what sort of vegetation she'd had to study in the desert at that time, but it must surely have been something unusual. Bonnie has a passion for the exceptional. She's always on the lookout for plants that can survive three years without water, plants that eat meat, plants that mock everything natural. *Plants Without Roots* was the title of the book with which she made tropical botany popular a couple of years ago, referring to the Welwitschia Mirabilis from the Kuiseb River valley, a plant like an octopus that lives for two hundred years and barely possesses a root system. Bonnie not only ranks as an expert in her field, she also has a way with words, she knows how to present her findings in the realm of flora as true voyages of discovery. Her book has been snapped up by people who can't tell the difference between a stinging nettle and a dandelion and who themselves never undertake anything more adventuresome than jouncing over the speed bumps in their neighborhood. On the back cover of the hardback edition is the photo that also appeared in all the papers. Bonnie with a provocative smile: while you're all paying off your mortgages, I'm traversing rain forests and steamy swamps. The media was quite enamored of her when she was in The Netherlands briefly at the occasion of the book's publication. "So enterprising," commended prestigious Dutch talkshow host Adriaan van Dis, "and that, coupled with such beauty!" In response, Bonnie had laughed broadly into the camera. And Meijken, sitting in front of the television in Sibculo with a packet of Spritz cookies, torn between pride and revulsion, suspected that at that moment all throughout The Netherlands spoonfuls of sugar were landing beside cups of coffee; even though Bonnie's teeth aren't pretty, they're too long and pointy, like those of a rat. At van Dis' customary invitation, Bonnie had accepted a glass of red wine and was leaning back comfortably while he heard her out about her childhood. "Nothing spectacular," said Bonnie laughing again, the sound of a mountain stream. "Except that I was an afterthought and my sister married practically right away after I was born, so in fact I grew up an only child. Maybe I wouldn't have been able to go to college if the family had been larger."

No matter how concentratedly Meijken, at home in Sibculo, had studied her face on the screen, nothing indicated that at that moment Bonnie was being assailed by childhood memories, for instance, by the memory of those dreary little visits once a year. On Meijken's birthday Mother's feeling for decorum demanded that a visit be made. The outside world didn't, after all, have to know how deeply into disfavor her daughter had fallen. Mother made it a point to order a birthday cake at Sloot's and, with the help of a couple of neighbor ladies, sewed a new dress for Bonnie. With the cake in one hand and the festively dressed child holding the other she would make her way through Sibculo's streets, condescendingly nodding at acquaintances. "Go ahead," was her ritual opening as she bent down in the doorway of the living quarters behind Balm's Drugstore to tighten one of the bows in Bonnie's hair, "give your sister a kiss and wish her a happy birthday." With a stony, sharp little face Bonnie would enter the room and do what was expected of her. Meijken, who had by then already started overeating, would see herself through the timid eyes of the child: a gigantic sow bug, always hiding in the dark, pale and doughy, a goulish stranger to whom Bonnie was unfortunately related by blood. Throughout the entire half a second that her embrace lasted, Mother would look on tensely as if she feared Meijken would take advantage of the opportunity to whisper something in the ears of her little darling. Afterwards she would plant herself triumphantly in a chair and say, in a tone that defied contradiction, "No doubt you can see that Bonnie's grown again."

"Can't she ever come over to play after school?" Gert would ask cautiously, aware of unspoken family secrets, or sensitivities, or whatever it was that caused his mother-in-law to come by not more than once a year with her youngest daughter. She lived so nearby and his poor Meijken, incapable of leaving the house, could certainly use some distraction and company.

"Soon you'll have children of your own," Mother would say, reaching out for Bonnie, who would later appear on Adriaan van Dis' talkshow, watched by millions.

"But somewhere in your immediate surroundings you must have had a shining example?" Van Dis attempted, evidently incapable of believing that a woman could become a celebrated botanist on her own initiative. Bonnie nodded. She looked directly at her interviewer, turning her attractive profile to the audience. Sweetly she said, "Of course. The same sister who married when she was eighteen. I grew up with a living example of what I never wanted to become."

The sound of a door slamming somewhere downstairs rouses Meijken from her thoughts. She becomes conscious of how cold it is in the attic and how stiff she's gotten sitting on the hard trunk. It must already be high time for dinner. It must be around seven-thirty by now. She puts the letters back in the box, suddenly ashamed of the impulse that drove her upstairs.

When she puts the shoe box back on the shelf with the new suitcases, she feels her ankles buckle under her weight, and for an instant she thinks of everything she herself might have become if Bonnie had never been born. Then she switches off the light in the attic.

Downstairs it is peculiarly quiet, and for a moment Meijken is alarmed: she had expected the sound of voices. She had expected her guests and her husband in the living room, drinking sherry. Did Gert bother to think of buying some kind of soft drink for the child? With a feeling of amazement she thinks: I believe I'm even starting to *enjoy* it all.

She waddles toward the kitchen where the dinner table is set and waiting. On the counter there is a smoked sausage from which she cuts herself a piece on the sly. Buttery and juicy she can feel it melt on her tongue as she glances into the pot of kale and potatoes in which Gert has drawn decorative furrows with a fork. He does silly things like that with food. Meijken eats another piece of sausage while she pictures how her husband had stood there whistling softly while raking in his stew. He exudes a kind of innocence that's almost painful in a person who is almost sixty. While chewing, she notes that it's plain to see she's been nibbling at it. She cuts it up completely and arranges the slices as generously as possible on the cutting board. Her father, who used to derive pleasure from things like that, had made the board. Toiling and silent, and carving wood at night, those are the only memories she has of him. Seeing nothing, she stares briefly at her checkered gingham curtains. She never forgave him for not standing up for her. He idly stood by and watched, instead of protecting her from Mother. He didn't even once make an effort to talk with her. All those months of her nightmare he avoided her eyes, slinking around the house as if a little consolation or understanding were a capital crime. It is now, in retrospect, even harder to digest than at the time. Then, shame and confusion held her in their grip. Now her head is clear and her heart cold. Lucky, being a father in the era of one-guilder notes, clean underwear Saturday evenings, entertainer Lou Bandy, Faas Wilkes the soccer star, the Run-Of-The-Mill Family, the era of the coal-burning stove, the family board game of goose, and everybody wearing a duffel coat, just like the little princesses, Queen Juliana's daughters. In those days fathers weren't expected to concern themselves much with their children. Fathers were there to bring home the bacon. Mothers took on full responsibility as far as the raising of the children was concerned. And at eighteen you were still entirely under their jurisdiction. It was a completely different world, in 1955.

There was no such thing as rape, for instance. And people also lived, with some success, without fax machines.

Of course there were fallen women. But their lot was entirely their own doing. And any woman who didn't fall, who wasn't made to fall, set herself with society's approval to the bearing and raising of children, bearing and raising. The rebuilding of the nation after the ravages of WWII hadn't been completed yet by a long shot. All of us together, setting our shoulders to the task, was the motto. There was something odd and suspect about throwing in the towel after just one child. Moreover, what were you supposed to do with your time, your life, without children? What were you supposed to do, for heaven's sake, as an adult woman, brimming with nothing but tender loving instincts, without children, in 1955?

Say 1955 and you say Dr. Spock! Say 1955 and you say maternity dress! 1955! The General Synod of the Dutch Reformed Church rejects in a vote of thirty-two to twenty the entry of women into the pastorate. 1955! The Dutch Supreme Court has all the copies of *The Love Between Bob And Daphne* by Han B. Aalberse, reputed to be a pornographic work, confiscated. 1955! KLM orders eight DC-8 jets from the Douglas factory in the United States, the first exciting step toward the age of jet propulsion. In order to become a stewardess, one has to be young, slender and appetizing, otherwise the country won't ever take off into the age of jet propulsion. One is expected to marry a pilot before the first wrinkle can insult the passengers, and then get on with bearing and raising children, bearing and raising, just as women all throughout the course of human history have done.

In 1955, in other words, you had no choice but to sit in a boiling hot bath drinking a mixture of salt, vinegar and brandy.

The sweating walls quiver, vomit spatters in all directions. With an ill grace, then. Jump, Meijken, jump. Thirteen hundred eleven, thirteen hundred twelve, thirteen hundred thirteen, we'll make a decent girl of you again.

Sweat beads up on Meijken's forehead. She rearranges the last pieces of sausage on the cutting board her father made in the long-ago era during which they still quarried in Sibculo and she had unsuspectingly walked through woods and fields telling herself her own life. She'd become a pharmacist's assistant. Maybe even a pharmacologist. Brains galore. 1955: possibilities aplenty. 1955: Meijken Bentveld enters into matrimony with Gert Balm, druggist. "What more do you want?" Mother had asked. "You should be happy somebody still wants you. You'll just have to take him. Anyway, you wanted to sell pills, didn't you?"

"Meijken?" From somewhere in the house comes the voice of the man who made a decent woman of her. She can hear him approaching from the corridor and she snatches the last piece of sausage, not more than a bit of skin with a metal band around the end, and sucks it clean. "Meijken!" her husband calls. "Meijken!"

With the back of her hand she wipes her mouth. Only then does it occur to her how distressed he sounds.

"Come on, eat your pancake," says Zwier.

"I think it's a funny table cloth," Mary Emma responds in a subdued voice.

"It's called plush. Come here, your face's all covered with syrup." He takes a napkin, spits on it and, reaching across the table, starts scrubbing her cheeks and chin clean. From behind the bar the proprietress looks on suspiciously, as if she were regretting the fact that she ever let them in her café: skinny man with no socks on in a crumpled summer suit jacket, scruffy kid in torn pants. Some of the other customers also furtively size them up over the rims of their glasses.

"Everybody's staring," whispers Mary Emma.

"Looking doesn't hurt," says Zwier relatively loudly. He defiantly glares around, taking in the whole establishment.

"Why don't we just go back to Africa?" Mary Emma entreats. When Zwier doesn't respond, she adds threateningly, "Victor Hugo doesn't like it here much either."

Her father throws the napkin down on the table. He leans back. "What's he got to complain about?"

"He just thinks it's shitty."

"Did he learn that word from you? Tell him that that's no way for children to talk. And don't make such a mess with that pancake." He gestures meaningfully in the direction of the woman spying on them from behind the bar. "We're in the civilized world here."

"So?" She kicks the table leg.

He fixes her with a brooding look. Then grabs her hand across the table and says brusquely, "All in all, today wasn't such a good start, was it?"

"It doesn't matter," Mary Emma mumbles mechanically. She hopes her uncle agrees with her.

Zwier is silent for a long time while he studies her hand closely, first the back, then the palm. He pushes her thumb inwards and folds her fingers around it. "Did any of the girls ever have a serious talk with you?"

"About what?"

"About men and women and stuff like that."

A loud medley of Christmas carols suddenly cheers out of the jukebox. Raising her voice to make herself heard above "Silent Night," Mary Emma asks, "Can I have some more chocolate milk?"

"You've already had two. I asked you something. Did they explain, how should I say it, the facts of life to you?"

"No, nothing," says Mary Emma. "So I still don't understand anything about solifluction or anything."

"I'm not talking about our work, Emma." He shifts in his chair. "I'm talking about sex."

"Oh, that's what you mean." The direction the conversation has taken surprises her, but that's simply the way her father is. "That you can get pregnant from fucking without using the pill and stuff?"

After having stared up at the ceiling for a moment Zwier says thoughtfully, "Myself, I find making love a much nicer term."

"But that's different!"

He pats her arm. He looks relieved, amused. "Point for you. And don't shout like that."

"But what do you want to know anyway?"

"Whether they ever happened to tell you about complete strangers, men, that just grab you. That want to feel you everywhere."

"Well, most times that isn't how it goes, you know," says Mary Emma, wavering, thinking back of the mocking voices of the students, of their derisive talk. "They mostly just want to jump on and stick it in."

Her father coughs. He calls over to the woman behind the bar, "Another chocolate milk and a Scotch, please." Then he leans towards her and continues, "I'm talking about men who try and force women to make love to them. To fuck them, I mean. Men like that are called rapists."

"But there's sprays for that."

Zwier plants an elbow on the table. "Sprays."

"You can buy this spray in Germany. It makes them go blind." She bursts out laughing. "Or else you knee them. Stand up and I'll show you." She pushes her chair back and slips around the table, but instead of also getting up, her father pulls her onto his lap and wraps his arms around her. "No, Emmy, not here."

"And we never do the Zwierios anymore either," says Mary Emma, suddenly sad.

"You're getting much too big for games like that." He

clears his throat, as if this were just the beginning of a lengthy statement. Mary Emma is overcome by the feeling that he's just about to tell her something that she doesn't want to hear. Holding her breath, she leans against him.

Deep inside him it's rumbling and gurgling, like a swamp where they're dredging for a terrible truth. He sighs under the pressure. She almost expects to hear him say, "Go ask the girls."

Where are they, wonders Zwier, now that I can finally use them for something? Language is their ally, not his. When it comes down to talking they leave him far behind in all respects. His students find words, sentences for everything; nothing, as far as they're concerned, is unsayable or unnamable. Practice makes perfect, Professor! After all, we've been talking the situation over with each other since the beginning of history! What you call chitchat, Professor, is the thing that has allowed humanity to survive! From pure necessity, since the safety of offspring simply couldn't be guaranteed in a world where communication was impossible, suddenly one day hundreds of thousands of years ago meaningful sounds pushed their way up out of prehistoric women—precisely as in this epoch every two-year-old once again discovers that mystifying growls and impotent gestures can be replaced by something better. Exit the Neanderthal! Exit the Peking Man! Exit all speechless hominids, including Lucy! The curtain is now raised for Homo sapiens sapiens! And Adam calls the zebra, zebra, the cactus, cactus, and the boar, boar, and century after century after century soft voices complain, "Hey, *you* say something, too, for a change."

"Why aren't you saying anything?" asks Mary Emma.

"I'm thinking," Zwier says irritably. None of his students appeared to aspire to any offspring themselves, that was more like something for others, but for all that they considered themselves no less the bearers of life, and the possessors of secret knowledge on that level. A knowledge, Professor, they said with witchy expressions, that dates back to the dawn of humanity! For this, too, women obviously needed language: to tell each other about how they could gain control over their fertility. We, said the students from their primal feeling of unity with the universe, collected shells in Neolithic times and hung them around our necks to be able to be just as fertile as the inexhaustible sea. To bear a child we waded into the water during the waxing moon, we slurped up cormorants' eggs, we did whatever we could, and beat off the men if they came to disrupt our fertility rites in order to copulate with us. Countless centuries we whispered our knowledge to each other, we bound wormwood around our thighs, took stinging nettle seeds, drank birch sap and ate the wombs of hares. We enhanced our fertility with the finely ground testicles of a pig, the gall of a bear, lemon balm water, jenny's milk mixed with bat's blood, wild parsley cooked in wine, or the water in which a newborn had just been bathed. And at the same time we gathered the remedies to ensure that we wouldn't become pregnant, to this end wearing the finger of an aborted fetus around our necks, or a piece of burnet root, a pouchful of hare's droppings or the scrotum of a tomcat wrapped in muleskin. We ate from the tubers of the orchis, rubbing the sexual organs of a dead man into our menstrual bandages, drinking vinegar and gunpowder, or wine with little girls' earwax. We aborted by eating hawkweed and gray peas and drinking water in which a whetstone had been moistened and in which larch needles had then been boiled. We took salt and brandy, and a selection of herbal abortifacients: glycirrhizza glabra, tectonae grandis semen, asclepias rosea, oxalis, sesamum orientale, piper longum, red mangosteen, panicum dactylum. We applied distillations of tar, naphtha soap, stimulating poultices, glowing coals. We inserted opium into the vagina. We rid ourselves of unwanted children by taking hot baths, carrying heavy loads, by jabbing inside ourselves with sharp objects, by thumping and stomping on and kneading the belly.

And that, said the students, is the way we killed our time

while the men went about their business. They looked at Zwier with somewhat condescending expressions: it was all very well for him that he had accidentally fathered a child, but they were, by virtue of their sex, the experts on this subject. If only you knew, they would say straight-faced whenever he cursed because Mary Emma's needs and his once again weren't to be reconciled, if only you knew for how many centuries we've been cursing, Professor Zwier, for how many centuries we've been crying.

"One Scotch, one chocolate milk," says the proprietress, setting the order down on the table. She gives Zwier, who still has his arms wrapped around Mary Emma's waist, a look filled with mistrust. Then she asks Mary Emma, "Does your mother know that you're still up this late?"

The girl says firmly, "My mother's away on a trip." She feels warm the way she does when she's caught at a lie. In need of assistance, she looks around at her father.

"We'll be off to bed in just a little while," he tells her reassuringly, or perhaps especially for the benefit of the meddling woman who slowly sets the empty glasses on her tray.

"So where are we going to sleep?" asks Mary Emma. "Where are we going this time?"

"We'll sort that out in a minute," says Zwier. "Could I have the check now?" With obvious reluctance the woman moves away, half-looking over her shoulder once more as if she were hoping to catch them at something. "Anyways. Where were we?" Zwier continues, after downing the contents of his glass in a single gulp.

"I don't know," Mary Emma says on her guard. She drinks her chocolate milk. Close beside her, in the dark window, she can see both of them reflected under the words Café Binnenmars. Zwier's angular profile with the tangled curls and right below, leaning against his chest, her pale face, framed by medium length, straight blond hair. "I don't look like you at all," she says distractedly.

She wants to ask him if she looks like her mother, but instead she mumbles, "When you were as old as I am, what were you thinking the whole time?"

"Oh," says Zwier. Suddenly he laughs bemused. "I thought that the whole world had only one purpose, and that was to turn around me."

"Oooo," says Mary Emma duly impressed.

"If people on the street looked at me, I knew precisely why: I was that little boy for whom they took all that trouble, for whom they directed traffic, let trains, buses, trams and trucks drive, for whom they baked bread, cultivated potatoes, laid asphalt squares and alleys, put in water lines, made television programs—and when I lay in my little bed at night, they stopped and rested until I'd step onto the stage again the next morning." Again her father laughs. He gives her a quick pinch in the side. She is happy and proud that he has recalled such a pleasant memory because of her. Softly she starts to sing along with the song about the Christmas tree that is now thundering through the café.

In a very different voice, Zwier continues, "But that's not what we were talking about." He cups his hand over her mouth and says in her ear, "You have to listen for a minute. I'm trying to tell you something." She wants to pull free, but he's got a firm grip on her.

"Your check," says the proprietress who pops up from nowhere to toss the ticket on the table. Her eyes dart back and forth suspiciously. Then she quickly turns away and walks back to the bar as if she has suddenly reached a decision. She picks up the telephone receiver.

"Why don't you go pay her now, or else we'll still be sitting here till kingdom come," says Zwier. He pushes Mary Emma off his lap and pulls his wallet out of his pants pocket.

"But then where are we going? We don't even have our things with us."

"A couple of blouses is no great loss. We need warmer clothing anyway."

She can hear by his voice that impatience is again building up inside him. It had already been an unusually long time for him to be sitting around in Café Binnenmars, and that only because she'd had to have something to eat. Quickly she takes the check and the money over to the counter. The proprietress is busy dialing a number, but she can't be bothered to wait for that. "I'd like to pay," she indicates, nervously looking around to check whether her father isn't seizing the opportunity to leave without her.

"You should call the police," says Minnie. "You don't just stand by and let your husband be beaten to a pulp!"

Meijken doesn't answer. With considerable concentration, pressing the receiver to her ear with her shoulder, she carefully seats herself on the stairs. There's a draft blowing on her ankles. In the winter she should really bring an afghan into the hallway when she's going to be calling Minnie. She can hear the pendulum clock in the living room start on the first of its ponderous ten strokes. Where are they, Meijken wonders, where can they be at ten o'clock in the evening?

"How's it possible," her friend ponders, "for Gert to get somebody so angry? He never has that effect on me."

"But that's what I was just telling you. Zwier suddenly just went nuts, he says. Just like that, for no reason."

"All I can say is I won't say anything," Minnie responds. Why, Meijken wonders, was I stupid enough, once again, to call her?

"And where'd they go?"

"No idea."

"But that's absurd! They can't just disappear!"

"No," says Meijken. Dear Zwier, seeing as you're gone,

I'll write you a note. You'll have to forgive me if I sound a little clumsy. I'm not used to writing. You certainly did create a stir here, Zwier. My husband looks as if the devil himself planted a hoof in his face. His lower lip is split, he's missing a canine and two of his front teeth slant back even more than before. I should be at his side with wet cloths and camomile tea. He was terribly upset by your outburst. He himself wouldn't hurt a fly and so he sees nothing but good in others. Did you really think that he sees me as the monster I've become? He sees me more like a big fairy. For weeks already he's been tinkering in the basement to make me a Christmas present. I can't tell you how often I've been at the point of bashing his teeth in myself. With best regards and a kiss for Mary Emma.

"Are you still there? Meijken?"

"Minnie," says Meijken, "have you ever thought about what it's like to be loved without being able to make even the smallest gesture in return?"

"What are you talking about?"

Tired, Meijken says, "Never mind."

"Do you happen to know his date of birth? So we can get a better picture, astrologically, I mean."

"No," says Meijken.

"Well, in that case I could also work him out according to the Kabbala, of course," Minnie reflects. "If I knew his full name, that is. What's his first name?"

She knows, Meijken realizes, nothing about the man who calls himself her brother-in-law. She remains silent.

"Well, does he have one?"

"We can only assume so."

"Right, that's what you say! I just read about somebody in the paper, or was it in a book, that they'd forgotten to name. So scary, Meijken. His mother's obituary simultaneously served as his birth announcement. You don't have a clue about that kind of thing though, of course, but a lot of women have died in childbirth. But anyway, what with all the commotion, they hadn't thought to give the child a name."

"What child?" Meijken asks puzzled. But Minnie continues on her own train of thought. "That would obviously explain a lot. Can you imagine a worse way to begin life? Bringing about the death of your own mother. Wouldn't you agree? People become psychopaths over a lot less."

"I didn't notice anything strange about him, actually."

"Of course not! Nobody ever notices anything strange about them. You know my theory, don't you."

"Yes," says Meijken resignedly.

"Well then. You shouldn't expect that you can ever see or tell anything strange about them," says Minnie. The general lack of any kind of inner life, says Minnie, has gradually stolen from men as a whole the possibility of adopting facial expressions that could bring to light anything about their true natures. Innumerable little muscles, says Minnie, that we use every day to give expression to oceans of feelings and thoughts in their case became paralyzed on account of lack of use, thereafter to atrophy and finally, for reason of not being required, to disappear. That's just how evolution works. If you look at a man you see a merely functional face: it can hear, speak, smell and see; end of story. With some effort you might distinguish neglected beard stubble or a strange mole, but you're none the wiser for it.

Even her late husband, Minnie sometimes admits when she's had enough sherry, she'd look at after over forty years of marriage and, honestly, she still wouldn't know whether he were thinking of dinner or of the meticulous and inventive torture of tied up naked young women. A body has so many possibilities, says Minnie, amazing what all you can do with it. But nary the quiver of an eyelid betrayed him.

Meijken feels at the little wart on her upper lip and says, "I take it they'll be standing at the front door any minute now and since he'll be calmed down and feeling better, he'll offer his apologies."

"I wouldn't count on it."

"But their bags are all here, Minnie!"

"Oh," says her friend, reconsidering. "Then you could maybe work the dowsing pendulum over something of his, his socks or something."

"I don't think he wears socks."

"And you call that normal? So take something else, then. That way you can at least find out if he's often violent like that. You can ask the pendulum that straight out, Meijken. Imagine him slapping the kid around like that too. Because then you'd have to do something. Even if he's terribly astral."

"She seems crazy about him."

"But be realistic for once," says Minnie, "it's already almost ten-thirty and he's still wandering the streets with a little girl in tow. Is that what you call being responsible?"

"Oh my god!" Meijken starts. "They were supposed to go see Mother tomorrow morning, too! I promised! She's already furious because she's never seen Mary Emma!" A few streets down, in the nursing home, Mother, with her milky eyes opened wide in rage, must still be waiting for a phone call. After all, she's been at it all day to get Zwier on the line. To warn him about me, thinks Meijken, to lie to him, to tell him as if in passing that I can come up with the strangest stories, to make sure that he won't believe me if I were so rash as to open my mouth.

"Well yes, but we're talking about her grandchild, you know," Minnie glosses it over.

Not so, Meijken wants to say, suddenly, to her own horror. She has to clamp her jaws together in order to resist the centrifugal force with which the truth unexpectedly threatens to unleash itself. The words crowd in the back of her throat, no matter how much she tries to swallow them down. If she opens her mouth now, a whole lifetime of lies will irrevocably be gone. And then she'll have kept her silence all that time for nothing. The constriction around her larynx eases.

"Are you still there?" asks Minnie. She audibly splinters a peppermint.

"Where else would I be?"

"Well then, do something! Next week it's your birthday. You'll see that your mother will want to visit with a cake, just like she used to, now that those two are in town. She'll be expecting a cozy family circle, not just you. Do her that favor."

"It isn't next week by a long shot," snaps Meijken in the grips of the realization that she'll soon be fifty-five and still not leading the life she told herself about when she wandered through the woods. I'm grown up, she tells herself, her head about to split, she's got nothing to hold over me anymore. I'm from 1937, would you believe, from the year Princess Juliana married Prince Bernhard von Lippe-Biesterfeld, who took on the position of Royal Commissioner of the Boy Scouts. 1937: Catholic People's Party member Romme, Secretary of Social Welfare, presents the Executive Department of Labor his draft of a piece of legislation to prohibit married women from having jobs. 1937: In The Hague, Max Eeuwe loses his title as world chess champion to the Russian, Alekhine. The NSB, the right-wing national socialist party, holds four seats in the Second Chamber and is thereby the big winner of the parliamentary elections. The Feyenoord Stadium is opened. All schools get a milk allotment because the calorie is still deemed a number one necessity, preferably consumed en masse. But by 1937 they have already been combating for a long time the other darling of the universe, the virus. And in a remote corner of the province Overijssel, in Sibculo, Meijken Bentveld is born, the only daughter of the closemouthed, hardworking foreman of a gravel works.

"You have to find a way to bring them back," says Minnie. "So call the police to start with."

"But Gert's just sitting down there in the basement," Meijken protests, "with an ice pack. I don't think he'd ever want to press charges."

"I mean to report the child missing. Or kidnapped."

"But he's her father!"

"They can all say as much."

"Bye, Minnie," says Meijken, "I'll talk with you again tomorrow." All the time she has been talking with Minnie, Zwier, wherever he is, might have been trying to call.

When Mary Emma wakes up in the middle of the night in the unfamiliar boarding house, she doesn't know where she is for a minute, not even when her eyes have gotten used to the dark. While her gaze passes along the contours of the unfamiliar furniture, her bewilderment only increases. So much so that her own body, lying in a strange bed, becomes part of it. Whose arms and legs are these, whose sore knee is this? Mary Emma whose? And who's that supposed to be?

She flops onto her other side and sees her father stretched out in another bed, flat on his back, one arm protectively thrown over his face, the hand palm up as if in appeal: let no new day come after this night. She presses one elbow into her pillow and raises her head as other, new worries flood in: aren't grown-ups automatically supposed to be happy, over nothing? After all, they can decide for themselves what they're going to do and where they're going to go, when they'll go to sleep and what they'll eat, and they've got all the money, too. But even in sleep Zwier looks troubled.

A feeling of anxiety steals over her, seeing him lying there like that. His black moods don't just come out of the blue: it's always her fault that he loses his patience and then does things he's so ashamed of afterwards that he feels rotten and downhearted, and grinds his teeth in his sleep. Like that time she had a broken wrist. He went around for at least a week with a look on his face like he was all torn up inside and his heart was hurting him at every beat. But she mostly really pays attention. She'd do anything to spare him his rage. Except sometimes she'll make a mistake. And then he's left holding the bag.

Biting her lips, she runs through what she did wrong that day. Immediately the thought flashes through her mind of how she got him to laugh briefly that evening. In any case, she must get him to laugh more, that would already be a big help.

She throws back the covers and slips out of bed. She tiptoes across the linoleum, her arms hugging her bare little body. Just as she's about to loosen the covers at the foot of Zwier's bed with bated breath, his sleepy voice says, "Don't forget to put something on when you go down to the bathroom." He's still lying in the same position, but between the spread of his fingers she can see one eye sparkling.

"But you were asleep just a second ago!" she exclaims in disappointment.

"And will be again in a second," mumbles her father. He rolls over with a groan. For a moment she stands there indecisively, but then she walks around the bed, lifts the covers and crawls in against his hard, angular body. "Only if you lie still," he says with a sigh. He smells of the night.

"Yes, Dad," she whispers, carefully scratching at the edge of the scab on her knee. She's whole again. She's plain old Mary Emma Zwier, eleven.

And waiting for signs of life from her guests, Meijken dozes in her easy chair, glancing up hour after hour when the pendulum clock chimes. With the passage of time Zwier's return becomes more improbable. However, she can't bring herself to go to bed and remains half awake, half asleep, sitting there, occasionally starting out of sleep to fall back into the restless dream in which a young

Bonnie is crying and crying and crying from remorse and shame. But that's what you get, Bonnie Bonbon! You asked for it!

Bonnie nods, dismayed. Without protest, she watches as Meijken ties a pillow sewn up in an old apron around her stomach in front of the mirror and then puts on her dress again. Together they inspect her silhouette, then at the same time lay their hands on the pillow and push it down a bit. There. Like real. Around them, the house creaks and sighs. How strange the nights around Christmas are. Both dead and living matter go their own ways: between twelve and one o'clock the old people in Sibculo say that the cows stand up in their stalls, house pets can talk, the bees sing in their hives and all water turns to wine. When they were young, Meijken and Bonnie heard those stories, handed down from mother to daughter: these are the nights in which the dead rise up—the soothsaying maid still holding the fortune-teller's cards in her hand, the blasphemous stocking peddler, and the country girl with her greatest treasure as well as her greatest shame bundled in her arms. In silence they spread out over the field on their way home, on their way to the past, but the clock is already calling them back with one short knell, the hour of the dead is past: "Co-om-me!"

Meijken gives herself a shake and lets the time sink in. It's two-thirty. She staggers to the kitchen to drink a glass of water. On the table there's a forgotten bowl of peanut brittle clusters that she empties in a single scoop of her hand. Cautiously she sits down on a hard kitchen chair in order not to doze off again. She says to Bonnie, swollen Bonnie with her red-rimmed eyes, "Not a soul needs to know. You just give it to me. And go answer the phone." Suddenly she registers the ringing of the hall phone. She grabs the edge of the table and kicks the chair out behind her. The phone keeps jangling shrilly as she hurries out of the kitchen. Her hand trembles as she takes the receiver off the hook. In staccato bursts a hoarse voice starts panting in her ear, "Am I hard enough? Am I hard enough for ya? Ya wanna gimme a good screw?"

She slams the phone down, goes back to the kitchen and

drinks another glass of water. She spreads jam on two slices of bread and while she's stuffing her mouth she asks herself perplexed whether the breather was part of her dream. Slowly she lets her head sag into her hands, repressing a shiver as the images come back to her one at a time. Even her subconscious distorts the facts. I'm losing track of myself, thinks Meijken with a start. Soon, I'll die without knowing exactly what was reality and what was a figment of my imagination. Then the phone rings again.

She squeezes herself into the corridor, grabs the receiver and immediately recognizes the hard-pressed voice. "Ya nice and wet? Ya nice and hot? Ya gonna come? Ya gonna come? Say you like it!" With a shriek of horror she drops the receiver. Dangling on the cord it knocks against the wall a couple of times and then hangs still. At the height of the baseboard she can hear the rhythmical, "C'mon honey, c'mon, let yourself go, just enjoy it."

Any thought of sleep is now far away. Wide awake she forces herself to breathe in and out deeply to allay the panic. Not again, thinks Meijken. Not again.

When, after breakfast, they leave the boarding house early in the morning, Mary Emma skips at Zwier's side holding his hand, down the wet sidewalk that shines in the light of the street lamps. Her thoughts are full of new boots, a hat and a scarf, and real Levis and a jackknife to hang on her belt. "Wait a minute," her father mutters, patting himself, "my wallet must still be on the bedside table. You go on ahead to the bus stop. I'll be there in a minute."

By the yellow sign on the corner there is nobody as yet. Mary Emma wraps her arm around the pole and swings around it. Tights with a matching sweater, shiny shoes with buckles, colorful woolen mittens. Seven pairs of underwear. Seven undershirts.

And a dress with puffed sleeves. She slows down. Puffed sleeves, she didn't even know she knew that word in Dutch. Puffed sleeves of fine gabardine, for a flowing effect. She sees the picture before her again, the one in Aunt Meijken's ladies' magazine: a girl under a Christmas tree in a red plaid dress with a white collar, an angelic smile on her face, holding a candle in her hand. In her mind, Mary Emma turns the page. She starts swinging faster again. A puzzling sentence spins with her: "The battle against cellulitis is a lifelong battle, and therefore it makes no sense to treat the skin only during the summer months—paying constant close attention is advised."

"You're an early bird, too," a voice nearby says suddenly, so she dizzily comes to a standstill and looks up, right into the face of the woman from the shoe store, not the cake, but the other one. Constant close attention is advised. Mary Emma wants to disappear into the ground. The woman catches her by her arm in a flash of red-polished nails. She must read that magazine too, her hands look so pretty. The best sequence to follow when putting on nail polish is: first apply a nail hardener and a foundation polish, then two applications of colored gloss and finally a protective transparent coat of finishing gloss. If you want your nail polish to last longer, rub egg whites on your nails once they're dry. "I...I didn't have enough money with me yesterday," stammers Mary Emma.

"Those socks won't run away," the woman says pleasantly. "Do you want to have a nice raisin roll, dear? Here, they're fresh. My word, what I just heard at the bakery! It just gave me the jitters."

"We're going to Ommen. On the bus," says Mary Emma, relieved. "We're going to buy some clothes." She scratches her head while she takes a bite out of her raisin roll.

"That's nice," the woman nods. "It was because Mrs. Binnenmars, who came to pick up her Christmas wreath cake, since they happen to have the best pastries and cakes at Sloot's, says she had such strange folk in her place last night. She says:

there was something wrong, you could tell by everything, by how they looked and how they acted. It's just that we've never had a child molester in Sibculo, otherwise you'd fear the worst right away, she says. She called the police just in case, but then again they've got Christmas coming up too, so you be very careful and make sure you don't go into the woods by yourself. And don't talk to strangers, hear?" She shifts her grocery satchel to her other arm and starts walking, on to Huisman's Butcher Shop.

Mary Emma eats her raisin roll. Only now that she's standing still does she feel how cold it is. Even though yesterday's snow has melted, an icy wind is blowing and it cuts right through her torn pants and bites into the scrape on her knee. She's stamping her feet by the time Zwier finally comes running up.

"What took you so long?" she complains.

"I wanted to call Meijken," says her father as he straightens her collar, "to tell her that she shouldn't be expecting us for a while. There's no need for her to be getting worried. But the line was busy. Or maybe something's wrong with their phone. And then on second thought I went and paid for our room, that's why it took a while. Where'd you get that raisin roll?"

"Aren't we coming back here?"

"Answer me."

"From a lady. But where are we going tonight?"

"This lousy hole in the wall was no good, right? You desperately wanted a room with a bath."

"We stink," says Mary Emma soberly. She's sure she won't be allowed to try anything on in the stores. Again she has to scratch her head.

"You know that you shouldn't accept anything from strangers."

"She wasn't a child molester, honest!"

"So you're familiar with the idea. Put it into practice then. Oh, here's the bus."

They get on. The large back seat is completely empty, but

Zwier, who quickly falls victim to motion sickness, prefers to sit in front. After some consideration it's an arrangement to Mary Emma's liking: at least she won't lose track of him this way.

Out of Sibculo there is a road that runs straight for miles, as if drawn with a ruler, through empty meadows and fallow fields. At an intersection with a highway Mary Emma jumps to her feet: on the other side is a digging machine company; there are at least ten imposing yellow monsters in the parking lot. She'll have to bring Victor Hugo here some day. Surely they'll let a nice little boy like that clamber up into the cabin and touch the controls. She can already see him pulling at the throttles while making growly noises. And she'll be standing a ways off waving at him, in her puffed sleeves. A frown clouds her face. Puffed sleeves are more like something for that doll with the candle. She stares at the diggers until they disappear in a curve in the road. Out of habit she signals Victor Hugo: *"Come in, come in battleship two. We've only got fourteen hours to save the world."* But she can't seem to lose herself in the game as usual. Her mind just isn't on it. In cadence with the wheels of the bus phrases keep running through her head: "Actually, depilatory cream in the form of a roll-on is the most logical solution. Now Roll-On Depilatory is here. For a bathing-suit shave, for normal and sensitive skin types. Smoothes the face in six minutes, the legs in eight minutes, and the bikini line and underarms in a quarter of an hour." Puffed sleeves won't get you very far. You need a bikini line too, and cellulitis. And the only one who presumably knows about such things, her uncle, has been beaten to a pulp by her father.

"You look so angry," says Zwier when they get out at the end of the line.

"You're no help at all."

"Oh, are we going to start that again. So, just get another father why don't you?"

"You don't even buy enough underwear for me!"

110

"But that's exactly what we're going to do now, Emmie."

"And if I suddenly get my period? I wouldn't even have another pair!"

He looks sheepish, rakes his hands through his hair. "You're still too little for that."

"Like you'd know!"

Zwier catches her by her shoulder. "Now, just look at all those decorated stores. Does it look like it's going to be Christmas in a couple of days or what, warrior?" he asks, pushing her ahead of him towards one of the coffeehouses on the square.

"I'm not a warrior!" He holds the door to the coffeehouse open for her. "And I don't want to drink anything!"

"OK, we won't," he says curtly. He sticks his hands in his pockets and with large strides walks into the pedestrian mall.

Angry, Mary Emma slaps her arms across each other and turns her back on him. If he looks around he'll see she means business. She stares straight ahead across the square. There's a raisin fritters stand and an old-fashioned music pavilion there. Nearly all the parking spaces are already occupied despite the early hour. People are dashing back and forth with full shopping bags. It's Saturday, the last chance to shop before Christmas. After some time Mary Emma sneaks a glance over her shoulder. She turns around. The human mass veers past the stores. Her father's tall form is nowhere to be seen.

At first she doesn't believe it. He wouldn't just leave her behind all alone in Ommen. With all her might she tries to keep her thoughts in check. But inevitably the terrible message gets through to her: finally, the moment has come.

Against her better judgment she runs into the busy street. She bumps into passers-by, squeezes in between couples. Her tongue sticks to the roof of her mouth, she has to tear it loose. Her vocal cords are paralyzed, she can't use them. This is what she has seen coming out of the corner of her eye her whole life. As long as she can remember this day has cast its shadow before it in her subconscious, from the moment a soft voice in the dimness of the tent said, *"About three months. At most a half year."*

"But just now when she's starting to talk? You won't be able to recognize her anymore."

"Otherwise I'll have to wait another year for the right season. She's still so little, she really won't miss me. And besides, you'll be there with her, won't you? Besides, you'll be there with her, won't you? Be there, won't you? Won't you?"

Mary Emma hears somebody screaming. People slow their pace and stare at her. She throws her hands up to her face, cringing, she buries her head in her arms and clutches at her hair. The hairstyleshairstyleshairstyles this winterwinterwinter are full at the crown, the tones, warm, blond is outoutout, styling foam works best when the hair is still damp, but gel can be applied to dry hair. *"What would she specially need me for that you can't give her? And it's only for a little while. It's only for a little while. For a little while. A little while."*

"But in two months we'll be breaking up camp and I don't even know for sure if we're going to Samburu or to Koobi Fora."

"When you go, you can just leave me word. Leave me word. Leave me."

With buckling knees Mary Emma crosses the last part of the brick street and ends up at a three-way intersection. In confusion, she hesitates, runs into a narrow alley, thinks again, races back. She's just about to take the widest street when a few yards back in front of a window display she spies a piece of paper lying in the street. Her gaze constricts itself. Farther down, there's another one. By the newspaper stand at the entrance to the bookstore, still another one. Together they form a dotted line through Ommen, just like the trail she and Zwier have left across continents.

Her heart pounding, she squats down over the first one. It's stuck to the pavement and covered with footprints: Zwier was here. What are the earliest traces of humans, bunny-rabbit? The footprints of three hominids near Laetolil, Dad. In the museum in Nairobi one day they had looked at the plaster casts of them. Actually, Mary Emma thought Lucy was nicer. She could never get enough of Zwier's version of the creation myth, in which Lucy lived in a tree with her children and fed them nuts and fruits, and played Stone Age games with them.

An irresistible itch on her crown makes her dig all ten fingernails into her scalp for a second. Then she picks at a corner of the paper with fingers stiff from cold and pulls it free of the pavement. It's a flyer from the Ommen Dry Cleaners with a special Christmas offer on dry-cleaning trousers.

"*Come on now, Emmie, come and say goodbye to Mommy.*"

"*Let her be, Zwier, she just started playing. It's a good moment for me to just slip away unnoticed. Slip away unnoticed. Slip away.*"

Mary Emma's throat is pinched shut. She didn't watch either one of them as they left. Without protest she gave both of them the opportunity to sneak out of her life. From now on whenever people on the street nudge one another and point at her, she'll know why. She's that little girl that managed to chase away both her parents. She's too worked up to cry. Zwier's image, too, will fade and disappear from her memory, just like her mother's, and even his name will finally be lost to her. She's nobody's child anymore, just Lucy's great-great-great grandchild, and not even that, because Lucy wasn't a Homo sapiens, Lucy couldn't even talk, never mind write, nobody expected any letters from Lucy. The students who, from one class to the next, passed on everything of use to one another, always hid their mail from Zwier with compassionate looks.

"*Still, after all those years?*"

"*Sure, a person happens to want a written explanation.*"

"*It would've been different, of course, if there'd been an accident. You can at least make peace with that. But somebody that just disappears!"*

"And in the beginning he had no clue. It was only when she didn't get back from Mexico that he sent her family a telegram."

"Turned out she'd already moved on to the Kuiseb a long time before that, for her next project, without a word of explanation."

"And only a general delivery address."

"But still, he could've found her a long time ago that way."

"Yeah, well, too proud, of course. She has to want to get in touch."

"But she really isn't going to. She's smarter than that—after all, she knows him."

Mary Emma lets the paper, heavy with rain, fall to the ground. Pushing passers-by aside she runs to the next sheet. She already recognizes the bold print before she bends down: have a second pair of trousers cleaned for only ƒ5. She zigzags past bags and legs to the entrance of the bookstore and picks up the last of the flyers.

When she stands up again, she sees Zwier in the store by the check-out counter.

He changes his mind and walks between stacks of books to the magazine section because it suddenly occurs to him that a single newspaper is too obviously a mere pretext. A lucky grab produces a comic called *Penny*. His daughter will think that he's bought it especially for her, as a peace offering. A chocolate bar to go along with it? He isn't sure whether she prefers milk or pure chocolate, and only after he's been standing near the wall full of shelves displaying colorful magazine covers thinking this over for a while, does it dawn on him that he's looking at splayed sexual organs. "Hot prep school girls," one cover promises. One shelf down there's a nymphet of about thirteen, naked except for a pair of white knee socks, kneeling down by a pony that she's giving head to with posed relish. He bends down, snatches up a fashion magazine from a pile on the floor and places it in front.

At the check-out counter he lays his acquisitions beside the cash register. "One *Volkskrant* and one *Penny*," says the cashier, routinely punching up the amounts. She looks up to take the money and instantly her businesslike expression vanishes. Her eyes light up. She smiles as if she's been looking forward to seeing him all morning. He attempts to compose a friendlier expression on his face, then suddenly notices that the comic book he's bought for Emmie is about girls in a pony club. "Can I exchange it?" he asks, cursing himself for the senseless impulse: in so-doing he is wasting even more time, only to ask a simple question.

When he lays a *Donald Duck* on the counter moments later, her expression is even more expectant than before.

"Are you sure, sir?" she asks teasingly, only to shake her long hair down over her face as if she were startled by her own forwardness. Red hair, shockingly red hair. She is wearing childish clips in it.

"Yes I am," he says, holding his irritation in check: what on earth is it that makes him so attractive to completely unknown women? It insults him to be considered, right off the bat, without any further acquaintance, as most desirable. His students are the worst—they aren't out in the sticks standing behind a cash register, they think it's totally normal to make advances to him openly. No first-year student will ever resist taking a shot, to withdraw thereafter, insulted, in the ever growing chorus of lamenting women's voices. Huffing with indignation they hiss amongst themselves, "Somebody who lets herself be hit over the head with a club and then lets herself be dragged by her hair into his cave, that's it! Somebody who likes Cro-Magnon manners, that's the one for him!"

"For my daughter," Zwier opts by way of conversation, holding the *Donald Duck* in front of himself like a shield. For my little chaperone, whose bed stands safely next to mine, everywhere in the world. Too late he realizes that he must stay on good terms with this willing cow, and quickly adds, "We're here on vacation together, for Christmas."

The cashier can't resist, "Just the two of you?"

"I'm raising my daughter by myself," he says.

"Oh, right," she laughs, "this is the age of fathers. The age of the new man." Slowly she slips an elastic around the rolled up *Donald Duck*. The newspaper is too thick to do anything with, she can't stretch the time with it.

"May I ask you something?" Zwier queries in a pleasant tone.

She blushes. It is becoming to her and he feels like an animal. He's not going to offer her a cup of coffee, he's going to disappoint her.

"You have such a good assortment here. This must be the best bookstore in the area."

She looks at him expectantly. Hope is still glowing brightly.

He coughs. Then he asks, "Would you mind telling me when the new book on tropical plants by, what's his name, Bentveld, is coming out?"

"Her name," says the girl. "It's a female author." She blushes again. Her face is turning into an illuminated headline: Am I Being Too Caustic?

"You're familiar with her work," Zwier surmises.

"Yes, I'm pretty interested in nature."

"Then you must enjoy living here," he says with a feeling that he's wading through syrup. "The woods. The heath."

"And the sand-drifts! They're unique here along the Vecht. The river-dune landscape is so beautiful. Except you do have to know where the nicest spots are."

"The title's slipped my mind," he says, ignoring her modest initial move, "but evidently you know exactly which book I'm referring to."

"Well yes," she shrugs, "that's also because of the fact that Mrs. Bentveld comes from around here. Her last book she came and signed here, straight from the tropics." She darts a glance at him. "You're pretty tan, too, by the way."

He's beginning to sweat. Taking a stab in the dark he says, "Sounds like fun, getting an autograph."

"Maybe she'll come this time, too. Would you like me to check on the computer to see when that book's expected to come in?"

"Please."

She disappears into the office and he breathes a sigh of relief. Behind the open door he can see her confidently punching keys. He turns away and studies the drizzly street through the store window, while in his thoughts he tries to formulate a parting phrase. Mary Emma, he can see, is standing across the street leaning up against a store front waiting for him. How long already, for god's sake? He holds up the *Donald Duck* and pulls a questioning face. His daughter takes her hands out of her pockets, makes little cylindrical cases of them, and holds them up in front of her eyes. Her bony wrists stick out of the wide sleeves of her jacket. Then she lowers her binoculars and nods seriously. It's OK, Dad.

Tenderness overwhelms him. He grabs a candy bar with a red wrapper from the rack beside the cash register and holds this up as well. Now she shakes her head in an emphatic no. He holds up a blue one. With his eyebrows raised, he holds up two fingers. Without smiling, she holds up three. He motions with his head: oh come on, now. Four, Mary Emma signals back, unmoved. She drills her big eyes into his. Every day she looks more like her mother.

After her night's wake, Meijken has the feeling that she could disintegrate any minute. Waiting, without knowing exactly for what, she spends the entire morning motionless in her chair. The familiar chiming of the pendulum clock hurts her ears, it brings back memories of confused dreams and hoarse voices and sporadically she places both hands instinctively over her stomach until the clock has chimed its last chime. Each time she starts up a healing exercise: in your mind, plant a circle of rose bushes around yourself to safeguard yourself from intruders. But she doesn't succeed in rounding off the visualization to completion. After several attempts, she gives up. I'm really not the type for that hocus-pocus stuff, she thinks, so irritated all of a sudden that it revives her. Every day reality's already complicated enough without getting into esoteric realms. She has let herself be swept along by Minnie.

"Meijken!" Minnie calls out. She barges in so unexpectedly that she practically seems an apparition, the more so because it isn't at all close to her usual time yet. It's only the end of the morning.

"What?" asks Meijken, both unfriendly and fearless. After all, she is familiar with ghosts—there isn't a room in her mind not inhabited by one; she is her own walking haunted house—but then her eye falls on the balanced combination of Minnie's red dress and matching lace-up boots: this is reality, this is Minnie. In the flesh.

While pacing around, Minnie, without having removed her coat, has come to the conclusion inside of ten minutes that it was a cosmic coincidence that made her end up in Huisman's Butcher Shop this morning of all mornings just as the last person to see Mary Emma alive and well was coming in to pick up her Christmas rolled rib roast. "Because, how often do I go to Huisman's?" she chirps rhetorically as she finally lets herself flop into one of the chairs: Minnie is a vegetarian. She's always saying, you've got hamburgers and world burghers, on top of which she doesn't trust all those hormones animals are shot up with. Hormones! Minnie says appalled. As if without that a person isn't already sufficiently exposed to violations of her spiritual integrity. Torture-eggs she obviously won't eat either.

Meijken debates whether she should slide a newspaper under the Huisman's bag before the frozen heart for Harold starts to leak on her carpet. But she doesn't have the foggiest how she'd ever manage to get to her feet.

"Anyway," says her friend, "at least we know where they went. To Ommen. And this morning in any case the child had a raisin roll."

"As long as she eats," says Meijken mechanically. She gives her head a shake, but the image won't let itself be routed. She keeps seeing a column of calories descending into Mary Emma's throat by rope ladders, clamping themselves to the rungs with mitten-shaped hands, crooked grins on their round little faces. She squeezes her eyes shut. What's happening to her? It's not like her to let something get her all hysterical.

"You look frazzled," Minnie observes. "Just pull your aura more snugly around you. Come on, Meijken. We're going to have to make a plan."

Meijken manages to control herself. "Because they went shopping? They simply didn't bring anything warm with them. Yesterday Zwier was already saying that he wanted to get some things today."

"Yes, but in Ommen?"

"Distances don't happen to mean anything to them."

"What I mean is," her friend says with a sigh, "is that from there you can easily catch a train to Germany."

You don't have to tell me that, thinks Meijken. Long before Bonnie became a world traveler she herself had covered that trajectory. To cut her thoughts off she blurts, "Don't be so dramatic! What're they going to do in Germany? The man's just gotten a job here. I'd like to know what all's going on too, but one thing's for sure: he's not going to leave the country."

"But his job doesn't start till after Christmas. That still

gives him four days!"

"To do what, for heaven's sake?"

Minnie says nothing, nettled.

"Let me first just go and make some coffee," says Meijken in a conciliatory tone, but she helplessly remains seated. In the train to Osnabrück, Mother had been wearing a jaunty straw hat and she herself had received a new coat, the wide style called a swagger coat.

"Don't bother," Minnie says dryly. "I don't need any coffee."

"And to start with, take off that coat why don't you," says Meijken, herself almost fainting in her far too heavy swagger coat, in the hot train coach. The coach. They didn't say compartment yet back then. All those other words, those other concepts: another reality—it's hardly conceivable nowadays.

Gazing at Mother's figure one of the other passengers said that a woman due any day really shouldn't be traveling anymore. Everyone's attention was instantly directed at Mother. Perspiration was running in rivulets down her neck, too, even though she had taken her coat off. She said sharply, "It's not for another six weeks yet. Otherwise I wouldn't be going all the way to Germany now." That's what the neighbors and acquaintances had also been told. Everybody made a fuss over Mother; she wasn't so young anymore, she wasn't to take any risks. The entire village felt that she should spare herself. It wasn't that often after all that you met women of her age who had still been touched by God's blessing.

In the train, too, she was looked at fondly. The woman sitting across from her peeled her an apple. Another opened the window for more fresh air.

"My sister-in-law had her baby too early because she sat on the bus for ten minutes," somebody remarked with concern.

"M-hm, the jiggling," a second confirmed.

In her corner by the window Meijken suddenly felt how

each irregularity in the rails rhythmically reverberated in her body. Beneath her wide coat the movements rippled on. In her belly a vague cramp made itself noticeable. For how many more railroad ties would she be able to stand it? Stomach acid rushed up into her throat while with wide eyes she looked at Mother who said undisturbed, "This isn't a bus." Her expression was cool and disapproving beneath the rim of her jaunty hat. Beside her, Meijken felt like a dishrag, an old woman. She made an effort to relax. Looking at the landscape flashing by she told herself as consolation that she was now farther from home than ever before. Even the trees along the tracks seemed exotic, different from those in the woods where she, wandering through the twilight, had told herself her own life. Who would be so stupid as to wander all alone at night outside a residential area? Wasn't that simply asking for trouble?

Beside her, Mother brushed a lock of hair back under her hat. A smile played around her mouth. When they were back a week later, she told everybody that wanted to hear, "It came on early from all that bouncing around on the train. Of course I shouldn't have gone, I just shouldn't have let myself be persuaded. We could easily have postponed that trip, but those girls these days just have to have their own way."

"Meijken, Meijken," the maternity visitors had sighed, "where was your common sense?"

"All that time she was at home helping Mother for the most part," her father suddenly put in a good word for her. "She hasn't been out in months, had no time for her friends or her schoolwork. She's gotten pale from it all." But as always, he spoke too softly, nobody had heard him.

"So wonderful," Mother said dreamily, "to have my own figure back." Like a godmother she leaned over Bonnie's crib, that prodigy from whom you couldn't tell, no matter how hard you tried, that she had been driven out of the womb weeks too soon, that little angel who had come into the world far from home because of Meijken's irresponsible behavior, and she foretold a future full of love and happiness for her.

"Minnie left awfully quickly," says her husband while cutting the crusts off his bread before cutting it into minuscule pieces. It sounds like: Vinnievef offy kicky.

"She had to put her heart in the freezer," Meijken explains tersely. "It was starting to thaw."

He brings a hair-thin slice of bread to his mouth and grinds it with slurping sounds. His upper lip is swollen and there are bloody scabs stuck on his lower lip. Blessed are the meek, thinks Meijken.

"They're in Ommen," she says. "Out shopping."

"Oh," he says. He always takes her words at face value. So ask me something, thinks Meijken rebelliously, as if back then she hadn't taken him precisely because he didn't ask questions.

"Oh," she mimics. "Is that all, oh? It so happens you can easily cross the border from there!"

He lowers his fork and looks at her anxiously. "Yes. Yes, that's true, of course."

"So, there you have it!"

Her husband reflects for a moment. Then he asks by way of distraction, "Do you want some buttermilk?"

"There isn't any."

"I'll go get some in a minute," he shushes. He always stays closed a half hour longer than the other shopkeepers in order to do the shopping. In a minute, everybody will see the gap in his face.

"And what did the customers say this morning," she asks viciously.

An expression of alarm appears on his face: he's still in the process of trying to digest the Ommen business, he doesn't understand what she's driving at.

"About your teeth!" she almost shouts.

"Oh, they asked if it hurt."

"Oh, nothing else? Didn't anybody ask: hey, how'd that happen?"

"No," says her husband.

"I'll be. And what did you say? Oh, it's nothing?"

He shrugs.

"How discreet everybody is," Meijken comments. What tact all of a sudden. As if the folks in Sibculo didn't follow your every move with a magnifying lens! Suddenly she could weep with rage, because of then, because of now, because of the fact that she could hammer on her husband's face every evening without anybody's being the wiser. "And that's what they call the caring society!" she exclaims.

"OK, I'm going to go get groceries," says Gert, pushing his chair back.

She broadens herself. "Sit down. You've only had one slice of bread."

"Eating's a bit painful," he says apologetically.

"That's nothing new. My whole life I haven't heard anything else from you," she snaps. He drives her to it. One day he'll drive her to do terrible things. "You're going to eat at least two more," she commands. She slides the bread basket towards him.

He capitulates. He takes a slice of white bread, cuts off the crusts, spreads butter on it, lays cheese on one half, ham on the other. No doubt he thinks she'll fall for that. The thought is so childish, on his part as well as hers, that Meijken downs four slices of spiced honey-raisin bread one after the other. She should have let him go right away just now. He should just have left. Her anger is building up again. *"You* say something!"

As if he's been waiting for her permission to voice something, he asks, "Was Mother pleased with Bonnie's letter?" Vazuther heezdith Vonniezetter?

"What was that?"

"The letter that arrived this morning."

"Where is it?"

"Where I always put the mail."

Meijken lifts herself out of her chair. "So now you finally mention it!"

On the little table in the hallway she finds the letter. When she bends to pick it up, she hears the telephone beep. She sees it dangling just above the baseboard. It's still hanging there off the hook! They've been unreachable the whole morning! She jerks the receiver up by the cord and slams it back on the hook. Simultaneously, in her mind, she can hear the voice again, "Say you like it! Say it!" She seeks support from the doorjamb. But it's impossible that it's him after all these years! How could he have found her and why should he, she's old. But what's more important, she has built a fortress around herself; she should finally be safe, shut up in this body, shut in by these four walls—it can only have been a coincidence that last night she had been made to break into a cold sweat.

In the living room the decorated Christmas tree stands all alone. In between the baubles and the tinsel Gert has used red ribbon, tying pretty red bows to hang up little chocolate wreaths. Meijken swipes a couple of them off the tree before slumping in her chair and ripping open the airmail envelope. The previous one came only three weeks ago. Would Bonnie have found out that her daughter and her husband are here in The Netherlands? But so what. Her letters never show that she ever even thinks about them.

Meijken unfolds the thin blue sheet of paper. Only a couple of lines are written on it. She can feel her pupils expand as she begins as usual with the sign-off, "See you soon, then—Bonnie."

3

Intergalactic Wars

From the moment they leave Ommen, loaded up with packages, the wind is against them. Zwier has to implore, threaten, plead with his daughter. She can just barely reach the pedals of the bicycle he has rented for her; tears run down her face and snot hangs from her nose. She grips the handlebars, her knuckles white. He is angry with himself because he forgot to buy her mittens. In annoyance, he pedals faster, holding her by the collar of her jacket, half dragging her along, half pushing her ahead down the endless road through the dead silence of the forest park.

A fine, icy rain is falling, making the trees drip drearily and the leaf-strewn path dangerously slick. Out of the pulp rises an odor of rot and decomposition, a smell that reminds Zwier of what has deteriorated and decayed in his own life, what is irremediable, past, what has died for always. And as a living reminder, a walking souvenir, the child that is straining on beside him uttering soft sounds from exertion, the child that innocently chatters at him day and night unaware of what's hanging over her head.

"Dad," she complains.

"Yes?" he asks, as if he can't guess her thoughts: I'm cold. I'm tired. I'm wet. And Victor Hugo doesn't like it one bit either!

"Are we almost there?"

"Sure," says Zwier. The mire sputters under his tires.

Wistfully she says, "At Grampa's I was always allowed to sit on the baggage carrier."

"Yes, sweetheart," says Zwier, his teeth clenched, "but now you'll have to bicycle yourself. Because I've got your new underwear on the back of my bike, and all those sketchbooks and boxes of colored pencils we bought." Instantly he realizes that he will also have to try to stock up on foodstuffs for the weekend somewhere so late in the afternoon. She'll automatically expect bread and eggs and tea in the morning. It isn't her concern where it's all supposed to come from. Just then the handles of one of the plastic bags suspended from his handlebars gives way and its contents land in the wet leaves and squashed pinecones on the bicycle path.

"My sweater!" his daughter yelps. She drops down from the seat. Clamping the bicycle between her legs she looks at him reproachfully. "You lost my new sweater."

He gets off his bicycle. One of his shoes leaks; he can feel the wetness seep into his shoe, chilling his bare foot. He snatches the torn bag out of a mud puddle and crams it into his bulging pannier.

"Man, that way everything's going to get dirty," says Mary Emma leaning forward disapprovingly, so wet strands of hair fall across her face.

"Why the hell didn't you put your hood on," he snaps.

"Oh," she says, feeling her head, surprised, "I forgot about that." She reaches back to the collar with both hands, pulls out the hood and obediently slides it over her head. She pulls the drawstrings so tight that half her face disappears behind the red fabric. "Yeah, that makes a difference," she says happily.

"Your father knows what's good for you," Zwier wants to say, but the words die on his lips. What will she think of him later? What will she tell her girlfriends when she's talking about her father? Helplessly he thinks: but I was your slave, from the day you were born.

"Are you coming?" Mary Emma calls, bicycling off.

In a bend in the road, just as the tourist information office had predicted, Rose's Campground comes into view at last. The grounds look desolate, lying there by a muddy slough of the Vecht. The rolling fields that must be full of tents in the summer, are empty and there's no light on by the entrance to the store. "There's nobody there," Mary Emma observes.

"They're expecting us," says Zwier. "That guy at tourist information called."

"But why couldn't we just go to a hotel?"

"All the hotels are full because it's Christmas. Or closed because it's Christmas. And besides, this is a lot more exciting."

She looks at him, speechless. In an imploring tone he says, "And on top of that, at least we can stay here in a cottage until we get our own house in Sibculo. We have to live somewhere. You can get to school and I can get to work easily by bike. Or else I'll rent a car. Would you like that?"

"I want a real house," says his daughter mournfully. "These are only for vacations. And then, only when it's summer."

To Zwier's relief, farther down on the path between the cottages he can see a figure approaching them. Guiding his bicycle with one hand and pushing his daughter ahead with the other, he goes to meet the man. The latter quickens his pace, flips back the hood of his rain suit and from still some distance away yells out in greeting, "You must be the party they called about this afternoon from Ommen."

Zwier hurries over. They shake hands. The manager appears uneasy with the situation. "To be honest, I never rent cottages in the winter," he informs them. "I turned off the water in all the cottages already a long time ago. I've only got one cottage with a heater, but I can't get the water running."

"Fine," Zwier says airily. "Fine, fine. We'll manage."

"I left some jerry cans with water in there."

"Great," says Zwier. "Wonderful. Do you want me to pay now?"

"No, that's all right," the man says. Zwier's exuberance reaches a new peak: in this cost-conscious, penny-pinching, tight-fisted country, such a laconic attitude is rare: he struck gold in choosing this campground, they couldn't have done better. Practically bowing in gratitude he accepts the key. The first right. The cottage is called Rose Red, that can't be all bad. When he makes motions to get his outfit moving again, the manager asks, "How long was it again you were planning to stay?"

Before Zwier can respond, his daughter interjects, "Only till the end of Christmas vacation." Beneath her red hood her face is set, obstinate.

"So, till the beginning of January?"

The man looks questioningly from Mary Emma to Zwier, so that Zwier almost comes out with, "That's according to the computer. But at this time of year we'll simply have to take the possibility of a delay into account."

The wooden walls of the cottage have been painted a dark red. On the terrace in front of the cottage garden furniture draped with tarps stands out in the rain. French doors lead into the living room and adjoining kitchen. Four chairs stand around a table, there's a wicker chair and an armchair with velour upholstery. Set out on the shelves above the kitchen counter are glasses, dishes, bowls and cups: four of everything. Plus a kettle, a frying pan and a colander. Behind the kitchen area is the bathroom, the toilet separated from the shower by a plastic shower curtain whose edges are black with mold. On the other side of the cottage there are two bedrooms: one with a double bed, one with a bunk bed. In her mind, Mary Emma chooses the top bunk for herself. The prospect of sleeping in it somewhat compensates for the cheerless forest and the deserted campground. Who would've thought that such desolate places existed in The Netherlands?

When Zwier comes bicycling back an hour later loaded up with provisions, Rose Red's lit-up window can be seen from afar through the bare branches of the trees. His heartbeat quickens. He mustn't forget to instruct Mary Emma to keep the door locked at all times. And to arrange a code of knocks or rings on the doorbell with her. Does a summer cottage have a doorbell?

He leans his bicycle against a tree and takes the box of groceries off the baggage carrier. A raindrop falls down his neck and runs, cold, down his back. When he straightens himself up, he sees his daughter, a couple of yards away, standing in the middle of the room, dressed in blue tights over which she has put one of his new shirts. She is looking straight ahead while her lips move. Then a smile appears on her face and she makes an elegant bow. Before he realizes that she evidently can't see him in the dark, he has raised his hand without thinking to wave at her. In the room, Mary Emma pirouettes and strides towards the left, a hand on her hip. She circles once again towards the right, before disappearing behind the bedroom door. A few seconds later she reappears, this time sporting a jersey and matching skirt. She has boots on over bare legs. She walks over to the window, gives her head a thorough scratch while looking at her reflection. The she pulls another face. "Our Chantal," Zwier lip-reads, "is now showing a design from the gabardine-collection." His daughter makes a kind of curtsy, whereby she spreads out the hem of her skirt with both hands. He can feel a lump forming in his throat, but just then he notices she has lipstick on.

"Emma!" he calls out.

Behind the window, Mary Emma freezes in her pose. "Who's there?" she calls loudly.

"Your father," shouts Zwier. Cursing, he bends down to pick up the carton of milk that has slid out from under his arm.

His daughter opens the door. "Did you bring chips?" she calls out.

"What's that on your face?" yells Zwier. "What is it?"

She backs away. "Nothing special. Lipstick. For the fashion show."

"Where'd you get it?"

"In Ommen. Didn't you say I was supposed to go to the drugstore while you were at the tourist information office?"

"Yes, for toothpaste and soap! Not for that crap!"

She slams the door in his face and turns the lock.

Through the glass she shrieks, "And I went and bought Tummy Tone too, so there!"

"Emma!" shouts Zwier. "Mary Emma! Open up!"

"Do it yourself!" She turns around, her skirt flutters. Resolutely her legs, so skinny now they're in the boots, carry her out of view, into the bedroom.

Beside himself with rage, Zwier jiggles the doorknob. Only now he notices that a piece of paper has been pasted on the inside of the window. In large capitals it reads:

DADDY,
MARY EMMA AND
VICTOR HUGO
ZWIER

Through the steadily falling rain he strides around the house in the hopes of finding another door at the back of the cottage. In the dark he knocks into a garbage can. He fights his way through wet shrubbery, one foot sinks down into a rabbit hole or mole burrow. He's soaked to the bone when he reaches his daughter's bedroom window. A narrow strip of light slices out between the closed curtains. He bonks so hard on the pane that it rattles in its frame, and in spite of himself he looks around guiltily. But he could smash the glass and no one would turn a hair. They are, it's true, miles from civilization. Nowhere among the trees are there detectable signs of human habitation. If something out of the ordinary were to occur, no one would grab the phone in alarm to alert the police. I still have to call Meijken, thinks Zwier with a pang of guilt. He wonders where the manager lives and if he might be able to use the telephone there. Could he at the same time ask in an off-hand manner for a second key. Which would do him no good as long as his daughter leaves hers in the lock on the inside.

"Emma," he bellows after renewed pummeling on the window, "there'll be hell to pay if you don't open the door this instant!" He can hear how menacing his voice sounds. You have the gift of persuasion, sir, his students always mocked. Without a hitch, Zwier thinks: love me. It is no more a quick flash that lasts just long enough to throw him off-balance. All of a sudden he doesn't have a clue as to what he should do. During the course of several minutes the rain falls on him. Then, he slowly sets himself in motion and walks back to the front of the cottage where Daddy, Mary Emma and Victor Hugo Zwier live.

The groceries are no longer on the terrace. Only the carton of milk is still lying on the gravel. She has picked her moment to get the provisions inside unnoticed. In the brightly lit kitchen she stands with her back to him near the counter strewn with the things he has bought. She performs an invisible task, chopping or slicing, and her movements are so self-assured it's as if she hasn't done anything else her whole life. As if, he thinks taken aback, she has always had a kitchen, and somebody in it she could watch and learn the art from. Bonnie won't believe her eyes. Will it hurt her or please her? You never know with Bonnie. That's what'll make the whole enterprise so complicated. He'll have to proceed with caution. We don't want to see you cry, Mamma, now we've almost got you.

Just then Mary Emma turns around and intuitively he steps to the side. She carries a tray with the entire weekend's supply of cheese, cubed, a glass of genever and a glass of cola to the table. It takes her some time to display her cocktail trappings as attractively as possible. Then she nervously moves toward the door, causing Zwier to withdraw even farther into the darkness. She turns the key. Afterwards she quickly sits down at the table and opens the comic book he bought for her. As she reads she raises one hand and scratches her head.

Zwier brushes his wet hair back. He knows exactly what he has to do. He's supposed to rap-a-tap softly on the door and cheerfully roar, "Wilma! Open the door!" This time he'll control his temper and keep his hands to himself, and tonight they'll let the dinosaur out together and walk through the wet woods giggling, and she'll lift up her face covered with smeared lipstick, under which her mouth will scream, "No, Daddy, no!" when his fist strikes her.

That night Mary Emma dreams that she's still very little, she can't even walk yet, so she still isn't a Homo sapiens by a long shot, she isn't even a Lucy. Drooling, she crawls in the semidarkness of the tent, pushing all objects aside, plowing her way through disorderly piles of clothing, rooting along the side where the ground sheet and the wall come together. Her parents continue to breathe regularly when she loses her balance, rolls against the side of the tent and the next minute finds herself in the hard white light of the desert. Beneath her, right through her clothes, she can feel the heat of the sand, and the afternoon sun falls on her like the blow of a sledgehammer. Blinded, she propels herself forward again, crooning softly.

"One time," the students whisper to one another, "she managed to crawl out of the tent in the middle of siesta-time. It wasn't until hours later that they found her, all but dead. Which, of course, would have been the best solution. Not an accident either that the kid could get out of the tent so easily. But anyway, her tracks were visible in the sand."

Luckily, thinks Mary Emma, luckily: she left tracks, she can't be lost. She tries to open her eyes. Immediately all the joy in the fact that she's still alive leaves her: one eye, stuck shut reminds her that last night, once again, she went and spoiled everything. The new day lays heavy on her heart.

After a while she bends over and whispers from the top bunk, "Victor Hugo?" At once her gaze falls on the tray by the door. On it there are two glasses of orange juice and two plates, with a slice of bread and an egg on each one. There's a note. She slips down from her bunk so high up. Excitedly she unfolds the piece of paper. The new day smiles at her: Good morning Vic and Emmie! Daddy's written.

As long as he doesn't get down in the dumps because that

stupid eye's a bit gummed shut.

Meijken's dreams do not recognize the bounds of her house or the burden of her weight. Every morning, when she feels her shackles again, she falls victim to several minutes of bafflement: how did she end up here, in this flesh, and between the walls of this tiny square room imbued by a strange glow from the exclamation point on the storefront?

Merry Christmas And A Happy New Year!

In the bed beside hers, her husband is still sleeping. The alarm clock says it's only seven thirty. This whole long Sunday will somehow or other have to be tackled and endured before it's Christmas and people reach the conclusion that it's just another day like all the rest.

On her way to the bathroom Meijken passes the guest room, its door ajar. She pushes it open and, after a moment's hesitation, switches on the light. She looks at the new pale blue wallpaper with the friendly little sheep and at the neatly made, unslept beds. Dear Zwier, I'm so worried—please let us finally hear something from you! P.S. What do you want me to do with your luggage?

Suddenly the sight of the still not unpacked bags hurts her deeply. Her guests didn't even want to stay under her roof long enough to put away their clothes in the closet especially emptied for them. You open your home and your heart and in return you're discarded as easily as a bunch of shabby bags. Am I, thinks Meijken, not worth even the teeniest bit of respect? Will literally everybody always just go ahead and walk all over me, as if that were the most commonplace thing in the world?

She slams the door shut and makes a beeline for the

kitchen.

Reflected in the window above the counter she sees herself coming closer, her hand already reaching toward the refrigerator, her body billowing under her nightdress. The thin fabric is spanned tautly over her breasts that roll on the mountain of her stomach with every movement. She turns her eyes away, lets her hand drop down to her side, overcome by a disconcerting thought: had Mary Emma possibly looked at her the way Bonnie used to? She again recalls the expression on Zwier's face when he saw her sitting in her chair that first evening. Had the revolting sight of her driven her guests away? A shudder runs over her flesh. It is cold in the kitchen. But the knob on the gas heater, right above the baseboard, is out of her reach. She can't even bend over to turn the heat up. If, without a second thought, she sat on any old chair, it would splinter to bits; should she shift her feet, the drone would make her pots and pans clink and clatter on their shelves. And as an added bit of mockery, leaning up against the zwieback tin, is the pale blue fleck of Bonnie's airmail letter from yesterday.

She picks up the letter and walks over to the cold heater with it. According to the postmark from Kenya, this disturbing piece of news took over three weeks to reach her. She pictures the envelope passing through countless hands, how it was transferred from one mailbag into another and then transported by mule, bicycle, train and plane around the world to land on her doorstep in Sibculo. That somehow makes Sibculo the hotbed of all things, the hub of all concerns, the midpoint of the earth, as if burning arrows pointed at this cluster of houses, the surrounding feeder sheds, the Stormvogel Carrier Pigeon Association and the SVV 56 soccer team, roads and streets like Eighty Bunderweg, Schoolstraat, Church Street and the Monastery Dike—with Meijken Balm, the addressee, at the epicenter.

And what do I do? thinks Meijken. I do what I've been doing all my life: I sit here and wait. Everything and everybody is on the move, except me. I've been condemned to Sibculo, a place that isn't even on most maps, and of whose existence hardly anybody knows, besides a handful of botanists: Bonnie, in order not to sow any confusion among her international colleagues concerning her nationality, always signs her publications with Bonnie Bentveld, 1955, Sibculo, The Netherlands. Once, an American botanist, as is mentioned in one of her letters in a hilarious vein, inquired after landing at Schiphol Airport about the next plane to Sibculo: the little lie about where she was born had made an old gravel quarry in an unknown Dutch province as renowned among botanists worldwide as Amsterdam.

"The little lie about my birth," Meijken had read out loud to Mother over the phone. She had allowed a silence to fall before reading on. No reaction on Mother's part. Mother was, as she herself said conspicuously often, not a woman to rake up the past. One did what one did honorably and in all conscience. One acted when necessary and as one thought fit. So, one sewed a pillow in an old apron, if nothing else would do. This, Mother had said at the time nodding at the apron she was tying on with a faint smile, you'll just have to consider as the proverbial cloak of charity. Mother, pitied by all! Killing two birds with one stone!

Only once had she said she was sorry. But Meijken had misunderstood her. She was sorry that they had been forced by sheer necessity to go all the way to Germany, so that Bonnie had taken in something of foreign soil with her very first breath. And that sort of thing simply avenges itself: that's how a person gets fleeing fever and road-hunger, resulting in needlessly chasing across borders. Otherwise Bonnie would simply be where she belonged: in Sibculo.

Bonnie in Sibculo—that thought, for so many reasons, is suffocating, or maybe Meijken's breathing is labored because she finds herself on the forbidden terrain of the past. A person can't live in the past, she's been telling herself that her whole life.

But Bonnie in Sibculo is unfortunately a reality that is fast-approaching. Over three weeks ago she announced her arrival from a tiny village on Mount Kenya: roundabout the holidays, in time for the appearance of her new book. At any moment the telephone can ring: "Listen, I'm standing here at Schiphol waiting for the next flight to Sibculo."

In revulsion, Meijken tenses her muscles. If the phone should ring soon, it'll only be Mother, naturally, as always. But that thought, too, is unbearable. She feels sick at the thought of having to cheer Mother with news that a visit from Bonnie is near at hand. A minor consolation in Meijken's life has been that Mother, on account of all that traveling and trekking in the name of science, has derived little pleasure from Bonnie, the adult, at least.

Meijken turns around and glares at the telephone hanging quietly on the wall in the hallway. If the thing should ring, it can only mean misery. Then her breath catches in her throat. For, what are Mother and Bonnie compared to the other greater horrors that the instrument still has in store for her? If the phone rings in a little while, who'd you think was going to be on the line, Meijken Balm? What a short memory you have, all of a sudden! You haven't forgotten my voice, have you? Did you really think I wouldn't find you, hidden away in your cold kitchen? I know you're there anyway, that you're always there, that you'll never get away from me! Soon, when the phone rings! When the phone rings, Meijken Bentveld, then it'll be me, and I'll pant, "C'mon, baby, let yourself go! Just say you like it! Go on, say it!"

Meijken fights the impulse to run out of the kitchen—she can't go anywhere anyway. Cornered! At someone else's mercy! Just like before! But that isn't how it is. That really isn't how it is at all. It's nonsense, getting all out of joint like this. She isn't out in the gloomy forest all alone, far away from any habitation. She is safely at home, nobody can bother her. How come, she thinks distraughtly, I'm getting so unhinged? I have to watch my step. She hears her husband coming downstairs and can already smell his after-shave from a long ways. He is whistling between his teeth, a sound as normal as the whistling of the teakettle. It's a day like any other. Nothing to get worked up about. In a while she'll lay out a game of patience or read a magazine and the time will pass slowly but inevitably, so that a night will automatically follow this day, after which a new dawn will break, in the dependable rhythm in which Mother Earth has already been rotating for countless, countless centuries.

And during all that time in all the remote regions of the planet, at every moment and in every imaginable place, women are always the disinherited. That's what Minnie always says anyway. They shouted, they cried, they prayed, scared to death they gave in. Unforgettable acts were performed on them, unforgettable. That, too, is part of the natural order of things. But of course that's only Minnie's theory.

Certainly the history of humanity has more interesting aspects! In the meantime, wasn't the other half, from the moment that they had gotten up on their hind legs, amazing the world? Hadn't men piled up gigantic, ponderous stones to form monoliths and pyramids? Hadn't they earned everyone's admiration by inventing writing, the wheel, money, the drawbridge, the boomerang, gunpowder, typography, plastic, root extraction, the electric chair and the birth control pill? They had discovered blood groups, streptococci and new continents, along with gravity and electricity, had formulated the law of communicating vessels and developed the Magdeburg hemispheres, they had split atoms, tread on strange planets and fought wars. Where would we all be without them?

"You're early," says Gert Balm with surprise on entering the kitchen. He rubs his hands: no customers with shingles, hemorrhoids or corns today. He'll be able to spend the whole morning in the basement, with his jigsaw and his little jars of enamel paint to put on the finishing touches. While he sets the teakettle to boil he asks, hopefully, over his shoulder, "Did anybody call this morning?"

It's so cold in the shower stall that Mary Emma can see her breath. There aren't many people that can breathe out a whole sheep, and for a moment she is absorbed in the art. But soon her teeth are chattering, so that her sheep start looking like they've come from the slaughterhouse: a smashed head here, a tattered bit of rump there. Behind them, in the mirror, shimmers her half-closed black eye.

    The water in the jerry can is covered with a film of ice that she has to break up with her toothbrush before she can brush her teeth. Then, suppressing a shiver, she pours some water into the basin near the toilet and starts washing herself. Only half soaped up, she already has to dry herself off, so badly is her body shaking from the cold. Her new clothes feel chilly and rough on her skin. Stamping her feet, she pushes buttons through buttonholes, pulls at stubborn zippers. Now, her hair. Dubiously she touches the snarls. She tips her head forward, shakes it from side to side a couple of times and then starts brushing the hair forward from the nape of her neck with the new hairbrush. In front of her eyes, grains of sand that escaped the shampoo at Jomo Kenyatta International Airport fall out of her hair into the washbasin—except they have little legs and move. She screams in horror.

Zwier parts her hair, shoves his glasses higher up on his nose and inspects his daughter's scalp. Behind her ears and in her neck is the worst: on each hair follicle clusters of nits are clumped together, and all over the white skin of her head it's swarming with lice. "It isn't so bad," he says, shocked. Her scream brought him out of bed where he had lain for hours, after he had set the placating breakfast down in her room, wondering how he could show his face to her today.

In the mirror, she looks at him, pale and horrified. The discoloration of her eye socket contrasts darkly. He can feel himself cringe under her gaze and inadvertently he touches the knuckles of his right hand. "I'll go heat up some water and give your hair a good washing," he suggests briskly.

She says nothing. She looks at him in desperation, with her one eye, a hand pressed against her throat in a matronly gesture of despair.

"C'mon, Emmie, it isn't the end of the world," he says awkwardly. "All kids get little bugs in their hair sometimes. You must've brought them from Africa. But at this temperature no new eggs can hatch at least." Lighter fluid, he thinks, kerosene, canola oil? Act, don't dither. He can't bear to look at that little face any longer.

After two shampooings the lice are squirming around among Mary Emma's hair roots no less than before. He draws a part above her ear. The nits, too, are still there. "That's already made a big difference," he lies. "Now all we need is some hair tonic."

"The stores aren't going to be open again until Wednesday," she moans miserably.

Zwier lowers the comb. He suddenly realizes that he didn't take the Christmas holidays into account when he was shopping. They don't have enough food for three days. He walks into the kitchen and opens the freezer. Two pizzas.

From the shower his daughter follows his movements with curiosity. To conceal his uneasiness, he bends down and also looks into the cupboard under the counter. "Just what I was looking for," he says with relief, producing a can of methylated spirits, a cleaning fluid that a previous resident must have left behind. "This kills them.'

With drooping shoulders Mary Emma comes closer, "Says who?" she asks, suspicious.

He studies the container, not able to accept that she won't

take his word for it anymore. Without answering he throws a towel around her shoulders. He unscrews the cap, pours a goodly amount of the fluid in the palm of his hand and starts industriously massaging her head, small and breakable under his fingertips. "Honey," he mumbles over her bent head, "I still love you, even if your head is covered with lice. And I'm really sorry about yesterday."

She wriggles out of his grasp. "It doesn't matter," she says, eyes averted. Her lip trembles. Lost, she stands there in the middle of Rose Red.

"I think it does matter," says Zwier. "I'm offering you a sincere apology."

Her face contorts, so that the shiny skin, pulled tight over the swelling, looks even tauter. Silently, she starts to cry. She blubbers, "And I wanted to look *nice* for Christmas."

"I understand that," says Zwier with a dry throat.

"I never look *nice*. I always have nothing but old clothes on." Now she's crying so hard that he can barely understand her.

"Emmie," whispers Zwier. He squats down and pulls her to him. "You look lovely. There's nobody I like looking at more than you. Besides, isn't that a new blouse I see you've got on?"

Again she wrestles out of his embrace. "Yes!" she exclaims, incensed. "Finally I've got pretty clothes, and now this!"

"That'll go away by itself," he says, hoping she's referring only to the lice.

"And it itches!"

"That'll only last a minute. Hey, bunny-rabbit, that's not the girl I know. You never let your spirits flag, right?"

"Today I am," she says, in total misery, jutting her nose in the air. "And we don't even have a Christmas tree."

"Aren't we sitting in the middle of all kinds of Christmas trees? The ranger won't notice one less, for sure."

His daughter shakes her wet tangles back. Uncertainly she

asks, "Well, do you have a saw?"

"Sh!" sisses Zwier feverishly. "Or I'll get fined."

Mary Emma nudges him in the shoulder. She fiddles with his shirt collar. With downcast eyes she says, "And after, are we going to wrap everything up again that we bought yesterday, so we'll have packages under our tree for tomorrow?"

"My idea exactly," says Zwier.

"And can I put nail polish on my nails?"

He stands up. Guardedly he asks, "Why do you want to do that?"

"Because I bought it specially!"

"Yes, but why did you do that?"

"Oh, Daddy," she says, pitying him, "you wouldn't understand anyway." She trots to her room and returns right away with two tiny bottles of nail polish. Animatedly she starts to explain something about alternating applications, now and then interrupting herself to scratch her head with a pained expression on her face. The cleaning fluid has made her beautiful hair, that always reminds Zwier of toffee, dull. "And then you're supposed to put egg whites on after, so it'll stay longer," she says, as if she were revealing a secret.

He eyes her as if from a great distance: Mary Emma Zwier, eleven. Other little girls have Barbie dolls to practice on, or each other. He can't keep his daughter from growing up. He'll just have to get used to the idea that she isn't the picture of unsullied innocence anymore. Prep school girls her age do it with ponies, and men are already stretching out their greedy hands towards her as well. With keen satisfaction he thinks of the beating he gave his brother-in-law. If only he utilized his fists so well all the time.

"And you have to leave a rim free to provide oxygen for the matrix," Mary Emma concludes.

"You make a real science of it," says Zwier. Unless he chains her to her bunk bed, he won't be able to protect her from everything nature holds in store. Nor from himself. He runs both hands over his face. Then he reaches out a peremptory hand toward the vials of nail polish.

Timidly Mary Emma clutches them to her chest. "Soldier," he says with a frown, "come here with that crap. Do you want me to do your nails for you, or not?"

"Of course," Meijken promises for the third time, despondently, "as soon as I hear, right away...," but the line has already gone dead: Mother hung up on her.

Meijken goes to the kitchen, opens the refrigerator and eats a piece of cheese while standing there. She lays a pile of Huisman packets on the counter and systematically works through the slices of smoked and roast beef. When she notices that the third packet contains ham, she gets a jar of pickles from the cupboard and wraps the contents in the slices of meat. At that moment, there's a thumping on the cellar stairs, and an instant later her husband pokes his head around the corner of the kitchen door. "Did I hear the phone just now?" he asks eagerly.

"Mother," Meijken shrugs, her mouth full. No matter how much Mother wheedles and threatens on the phone, this time she won't succeed in stealing something from Meijken: this time, Mother's too late, the bird has already flown the coop. For all I care, thinks Meijken, suddenly discovering a new aspect to the circumstances, for all I care we won't ever see Mary Emma again, for all I care Zwier can have taken her to the ends of the earth—that's what Mother deserves.

"Did she have any news?" asks her husband.

"Mother?" snaps Meijken. "What news could she possibly have?"

"Well, they might have called her."

"She'd like that, yessir." Meijken pops a wrapped pickle in

her mouth. No more Mary Emma looking at her like Bonnie used to: she can keep stuffing herself, until she finally has the girth she had to hide back then for all those months. She lays an inquisitive hand on the bulge of her stomach.

"Oh," says her husband, disappointed. Then he asks, "Were you planning to make some coffee or shall I? It's past eleven already." With him, the spirit of rationality, of common sense, of normalcy has entered the kitchen. Meijken screws the lid back on the jar. It isn't clear to her anymore what happened halfway through the morning to bring on this eating binge.

"I'll do it," she says.

"You look so pale," he says frowning. "Are you all right?"

"Yes," she says tersely. This morning she completely forgot to ask him how his mouth was. His lips, in any case, look a little less mangled than yesterday. "You just get back to whatever it was you were doing," she says.

"I'm done."

"With what?"

"In the basement I've got, as a surprise, I've been doing a little tinkering, I was thinking, for Christmas...so if you just, then I can, I mean, is it all right if I close the kitchen door for a sec so you can't see what I'm, then I can go ahead and put it in the living room."

"Now that," says Meijken.

"Of course it isn't...I could've bought one, too, but I thought, well, but they only had small ones." He waves his hands to indicate dimensions. His face has become red. Even his ears are flushed. He starts backing out of the kitchen. "To be honest, I'm pretty pleased with it. It turned out rather nicely. But you'll be able to see it for yourself in a minute."

With throbbing temples, Meijken spoons coffee into a filter. Whatever she does, she has to make sure to curb her irritation. She'll smile, and maybe even give him a kiss. She should consider herself lucky, because her husband already content with so little, can be made happy with hardly anything. A thimbleful of encouragement and appreciation, she thinks, I ought to be able to give him that much? Then she hears him clambering up the cellar stairs and her heart sinks. Why me, she thinks, why not somebody else?

When she has poured water over the coffee grains a third time, he calls her from the living room. "Just a minute," Meijken calls back. But there is nothing with which she can put off her going to the slaughter. She dries her hands. In a surge of inspiration, she fixes her hair in front of the mirror in the hallway. Then she goes in.

Her husband is standing beside the Christmas tree. His face is beaming in expectation. He looks like a younger version of himself—this is the way he used to look at her in the days when he still hadn't realized that his marriage would never be consummated, when he still didn't know that Meijken's body was absolutely untouchable.

Several moments pass in silence. Then he asks, "What do you think of it?"

Meijken is unable to utter a word. Stiff as a board, she stands in the middle of the room.

"All the doors and windows open," he says as he leans over the dollhouse standing on display on the sideboard. He demonstrates with the door to a balcony from which planters with minuscule geraniums hang.

"And the lights really work, too," he illustrates, sticking the plug in the outlet so that everywhere in the house all the lights are switched on at once. There's a kitchen with a stove covered with miniature pots and pans; a living room with a cuckoo clock, a sofa and an antique Dutch sideboard with decorative Delft blue plates on it; a bedroom with a double bed, covered by a checkered bedspread, and a second, smaller bedroom in which, amazingly, there's a microscopic scaled-down model of the dollhouse. In the attic there are suitcases; in the basement, a workbench. A real stairway with painted portraits on the wall connects the floors;

there's a portrait of the father, one of the mother and one of the child, each one the exact likeness of the father, the mother and the child sitting on the sofa in the living room watching television.

Meijken finally regains control over her muscles. She steps closer and snatches the mother doll from the cushions. "What's she supposed to make of this," she barks, "that girl doesn't have any mother, she isn't used to one."

The joy on her husband's face vanishes. He glances from the little doll in her hand to the dreamhouse, the materialization of all *his* unrealized dreams, and then at her. "But children want to play Mommy and Daddy, don't they?"

"Like you'd know," says Meijken. "What gives you that idea! What would you know about that?" Her own cruelty shocks her, but she can't stop. "Or do you happen to have a child, somewhere? One I don't know about?"

"Well, no," her husband replies. He shakes his head in a way that indicates both disavowal and incredulity. Gert Balm, pitied by all; who helplessly watched life pass him by while everybody around him just kept on bearing children and raising them, bearing and raising!

"What're you babbling about," she exclaims. She has to restrain herself from throwing the mother doll on the floor and pulverizing it under her weight.

"Well, I was only thinking…"

"That a kid who's almost ready for high school still plays with dolls? That goes to show what an expert you are."

"But maybe she never had any toys, with that odd life they've led," he says softly. A muscle quivers in his jaw.

"Well," says Meijken, trembling, "I suggest you just go and ask her yourself. If you happen to know where she is, since you drove her away."

Her husband makes motions to say something, but instead with a bowed head pulls the plug out of the outlet, so that the interior of the dollhouse disappears into darkness. He briefly lays his hand on the red roof, right by the miniature chimney. "First, I better get us some coffee," he says.

But, at the door, he whips around. His face is contorted. "You! Can't you ever share in the pleasure of something?" he shouts unexpectedly.

This is too much for Meijken, as if she has been slapped in the face. Aghast, she stares at him.

"You always manage to spoil everything," he whispers almost soundlessly. With his hands balled into fists, he approaches her and for a moment she thinks he's going to hit her at last. "You never consider anybody but yourself, Meijken. As if you didn't have a goddamned heart," he says right in her face.

For a long time after he has slammed the door shut behind himself, Meijken just stands there, stunned. In thirty-seven years she hasn't ever experienced this. Is she supposed to feel guilty now because she spoiled his fun? Well, he'll be waiting a long time: she and guilt have been cellmates already for so long that they've learned to stop paying each other any mind. In a little while he'll be deeply ashamed of his outburst. He won't be able to make amends fast enough. She can be sure of that. Absolutely sure.

Still holding the doll in her hand, she starts pacing back and forth, seeking support from the sideboard and the back of the couch. But the furniture feels remarkably fragile to her touch, as if it had shrunken. If she opens the living room door, she'll see the portraits along the stairway. Upstairs, her little bed, not much bigger than a matchbox, awaits her, the miniature dollhouse beside it, with the real kitchen, the red roof and the attic full of suitcases the size of the nail on her little finger. Attentively, Meijken takes in all the loving details. Hadn't Gert Balm saved her life? Hadn't he freed her from having to live under the same roof as Bonnie and Mother? She rubs her forehead. You simply can't keep a marriage going on gratitude alone.

Filled with anger, she continues to pace back and forth.

What can she do about the situation? *He* had been dead set on having *her*! Their marriage isn't *her* responsibility! "I've gone through enough misery already," she mutters: she can be excused from new ordeals. Anyone who suffers as she does is relieved of further obligations! Just then the realization flashes through her mind that her kind of grief might well be addictive. It demands so much anesthesia that mercifully you don't feel the rest of life either. Except—doesn't that change something about the fact that at eighteen she had to give up all her chances at happiness?

She goes over to the dollhouse and sets the mother back in her place. She sticks the plug in the outlet. Everywhere the lights switch on. Motionless, as if startled, the doll family sits on the sofa: father, mother, child. Who's doing this to us? Who's making us visible to the outside world? We were just fine in the dark! Is our dirty wash safely inside? They don't have to know everything about us!

Meijken checks the windows and doors, all closed by tiny, securely mounted latches. In any event, nobody can get in. They are safe. They are ensconced behind solid walls. They are locked in. They have no choice but to wait, imprisoned, buried alive and well, for the danger that is creeping up on all sides. At any moment somebody can loom up in front of one of the windows. Meijken shuts her eyes. But, ineluctably, on her retina, like a computer photo reconstructed by the police, the dreaded face with its almost perfectly triangular shape appears, the eyes hidden beneath heavy eyebrows, a damp lock of dark blond hair stuck to the forehead and the animal-like sharp teeth exposed in a grin: "Go on, say you like it!"

By early afternoon a watery sun has broken through, lengthening the shadows it casts of the trees over the bicycle path. While he pedals through the bare, wintry landscape with his daughter, Zwier worries about his frozen pizzas. Hopefully he'll still be able to reserve a table somewhere for tomorrow's Christmas dinner.

"That way we'll leave the forest," Mary Emma remarks.

"We'll do the tree later, on the way back," he answers.

"And that's the road to Sibculo!"

"But we aren't going to take it. We're turning left here." He bicycles in the direction indicated by the familiar blue road sign with the knife and fork. He hopes Mary Emma won't start in again about her uncle and aunt.

"I know that because of those bulldozers," she chatters, pointing at the yellow digging machines on the other side of the road. "Victor Hugo's hoping that he can go in one of them some time. Can't you go ask that for him?"

"There isn't anybody there, honey. It's Sunday."

"But when they're open again!" She takes one of her hands off the handlebars and scratches her head.

"You'll wear off your nail polish that way," says Zwier.

Dismayed, his daughter studies her nails, first those on one hand and then the ones on the other, while her bike swerves.

"And now that we're on the subject," he continues, "aren't you really getting a bit old for Victor Hugo?"

She throws him a baleful sidelong glance, leans over the handlebars and pedals on in silence.

In the distance, the inn promised by the sign looms up. The parking lot is empty and there are no lights on anywhere behind the windows. Nevertheless, Zwier gets off his bicycle and tugs at the door, until his gaze falls on a small card behind the glass pane: Closed until January 4. Backwards hicks. He doesn't even have enough bread at the house.

"Where are we going, anyway?" asks Mary Emma, balancing her bike between her legs.

"We're scouting out the area," he says. "We're on an adventure."

Half a mile farther on, the road forks. Zwier follows the

side along which a couple of campgrounds are located, while he pushes Mary Emma along by her neck. Her hair feels dry and stiff, like beach grass. "Scratch me," she says, rubbing her head up against the palm of his hand.

"You aren't giving them a chance to die." He pulls his hand back.

"Are you scared you're going to get infected?" his daughter inquires in a shrill voice. "You probably think I'm dirty!" Zigzagging, she spurts ahead, her shoulders hunched up. He quickens his pace. "Hey, Emmie! Did you see what a funny name this road has? We're bicycling on the Grote Beltenweg!"

She slows down. When he has caught up to her, she asks, scowling, "What does that mean?"

"What? Belt?"

"Slug, right?"

"No," says Zwier. "Yes, that too. Sand hill, dune in Dutch."

"You see!" Her head tucked down, she pedals on down the winding road.

"Emma! It must mean something else here!" Cursing himself, he labors after her, registering in passing that every single one of the campground stores along the Grote Beltenweg are closed. He catches up to his daughter. "So, shall we go find a Christmas tree for tomorrow?"

"You don't even have an ax, man," she snaps.

"A little one, I mean, that got knocked down by the wind. Or else we'll take loose pine branches to decorate our house."

"You said a tree!"

"I said a tree," says Zwier.

"Besides, I'm hungry," says his daughter sourly. "Did you take any bread along?"

"In a bit we'll go eat some French fries somewhere."

"But where?" she asks. Where'll we go? What am I going to eat? Do I have any underwear even? Where are we going to sleep this time? What are we doing here anyway? Then his eyes drop to her bruised eye again and he says nothing.

They bicycle side by side for a couple of minutes in silence, until Mary Emma says querulously, "And I suppose of course I can't dig a hole, huh?"

"Where?" asks Zwier. "Here? Do you want to play here?" He brakes. On the other side of the road is the charming rise of a dune. Among the trees the blond sand slopes up, only sparsely covered by underbrush.

Mary Emma has already gotten off her bike and tossed it by the side of the road. He crosses the road behind her. At the foot of the dune she drops to her knees in the sand. "The sand is cold here," she mumbles to herself in surprise.

He turns his eyes away from her. How in heaven's name is he ever going to manage what he has decided to do?

"I'm just going to the top to have a look," he says hoarsely. His legs heavy, he starts climbing up the loose sand. Halfway he has to catch his breath near a crooked pine whose roots have been exposed by the wind. When he looks over his shoulder he sees his child, small and insignificant, crawling around in the expanse of sand. In the strange wintry light he can even follow the tracks of her knees. She traces her furrows on the face of the earth. Mary Emma was here.

Zwier trudges to the top that is overgrown with scrub oak. Pulling the new scarf from around his sweating neck, he looks out over the landscape that rolls away beneath him: fallow fields, stands of conifers, here and there a farmstead.

He tucks his scarf in his pocket. This must be one of those famous sand-drifts about which that red-haired girl in the bookstore yesterday was so excited about. In his thoughts, Zwier lets her soft voice say ecstatically, "And this is my absolute favorite of favorite places." That naive neck and her Dutch bovine look. And that's what he's supposed to fall for. For some docile cow, dripping with adoration. Able cook, in possession of twelve sheet sets and pillowcases, and missing but one thing in life: somebody she can shower all her wonderful talents on. Pearls aplenty! Now for the swine! You can bet that this one's not the kind to jump on her motorcycle one day and disappear without a trace! This one's got downy slippers, practical aprons and naughty babydoll chemises. This one knows what a man longs for. He knows her kind perfectly. When it leaked out via the jungle tom-tom, by means of which Europeans in the tropics exchange their own bits of news, that Bonnie seemed to have disappeared for good, the wives of his colleagues would lure him away from digs, symposia and conferences in order, during countless dinners and cocktail parties, to lobby incessantly on behalf of their sister, the neighbor lady, their best friend, such a different personality, vital and still feminine, somebody who, in short, had much to offer. At airports, meetings were arranged, stacks of airmail letters arrived—the most desperate wrote him even when he was out in the field, as he usually was, to mention, transparently, safaris they'd always wanted to undertake.

He saved their letters for the weekend he'd take off once a month to get drunk in Addis, or Nairobi. In a dingy bar, a bottle of whisky within arm's reach, he would skim the closely-written sheets and throw them, one by one, crumpled into wads, on the floor, not interested in who would pick them up and, snickering, make fun of them. Meanwhile, the black prostitutes would slink around his table, making crude jokes about him to one another in glib Swahili, assuming he didn't understand them, patting the wallet in his shirt pocket over his shoulder and whispering their price in his ear. Most of the time he'd wake up with a hellacious hangover the next morning in his jeep, his means of escaping their witch-ring.

When he returned to the dig, sweating alcohol, sporting a two-day beard, the students would nudge one another, rolling their eyes. Professor Zwier, the older students would pass down to the newcomers at the beginning of each season, is very, um, macho, in the most primitive sense of the word.

The newcomers, without exception, found that to be a romantic notion. The older students' expressions were mocking. "Primitive," they would say again, as if only they could fathom the incredible implications of the word. In chorus, bursting out laughing halfway through, they would recite Zwier's most famous quote: "Stone Age man wasn't any different from us. He ate and drank, worked, loved and hated and beat his enemies to death." They wore meaningful expressions: thus, complete identification with the age when beating to death and that kind of masculine behavior was still the order of the day. Just ask him, said the older students, just ask him what, according to him, the cultivated modern-day person represents on the clock of eternity!

A cool seminar room during Zwier's famous summer school. Benches full of obedient daughters who know the recipe for cherry pie by heart and the twelve steps to prevent nail polish from prematurely chipping. Zwier doesn't understand what they do with their lives. He says, "It took millions of years before man developed from a dark being with a stone in his hand, or hers [laughter], namely Lucy's hand, or rather, Australopithecus afarensis from Central Africa, into Homo sapiens. But," and he pauses for effect, "it took less than twenty thousand years before Homo sapiens became a scientist, a reader, a traveler, a researcher and an inventor."

He briefly paces back and forth, until he is sure that they aren't thinking about their recipes and their hairdos. Then he continues, "And it was less than six thousand measly years ago that humans learned to write and that the historical period commenced. We tend to overrate the significance of that period a great deal." He looks around provokingly. They stare back blankly, the eighteen-year-olds who think that the world was created the moment it opened for them. To be eighteen in the age of Madonna, the ERA, AIDS, protection orders, fast food and an affordable CD player for everybody! They think, the ignoramuses, that it makes a difference in which age you're eighteen.

"For us to imagine the significance of the course of time," says Zwier, "we must think of a clock where each minute constitutes a hundred years. If it's noon now, then on our clock the United States barely came into existence two minutes ago. Columbus discovered America five minutes ago. Twenty minutes ago Christ hadn't been born yet. The pyramids aren't even fifty minutes old and the first real civilizations in Egypt and in the valleys of the Euphrates and the Tigris were born just an hour ago." His eyes move down the seminar seats and he continues with diabolic satisfaction, "But the prehistoric people, to whom we pay so little attention, lived a full 168 hours, according to this clock: in any case, an entire week. The dinosaurs are at this point in time 694 days old: almost two years old. And for those who want to look this up: on my clock, the art of book-printing is only five and a half minutes old."

In the white, barren landscape, the older students would pass around the bottle of vodka. Certain of their business, they would say to the pale, blonde girls who had had to move heaven and earth, just like them, in order, just like them, to spend at least one season on a dig with Professor Zwier, "So as far as his wife, who walked out on him about a hundredth of a second ago, is concerned: as soon as he gets the chance at least, it'll be a bashed skull, twisted arms, well, prehistoric scenes." As if by chance, they would be tossing a stone hatchet from one hand to the other as they spoke. Myeah, Mesolithic, for sure. Ideal weapon. There's six hundred or so of them lying around here. They're right at his disposal.

The incoming students, without exception, found that to be a romantic notion.

So intent is Zwier on his own thoughts that only when he has trudged halfway down the dune does he notice that his faithful chaperone isn't at his side. Many yards below he sees her crawling around in the sand. "What are you doing?" he calls out.

His daughter looks up, so that the light falls on her discolored eye. "I'm building a boat, Dad," she calls back.

Dad. The way she says it—it makes his heart melt: he is the one in whom she places all her trust, in that unpredictable, uncertain life of hers.

"A sand ship, Daddy!" she cries enthusiastically.

Now he sees the mounds around her and can make out the vague contours of a ship. Irrational rage wells up in him: why doesn't she make sand castles like every other child? Why is she, like her mother, so contrary? He runs down the dune. He grabs her by the collar. "Just look!" he snaps. "Just look for one second at your nails. Did you want to be a lady, or not? Is that why I went to all that trouble?"

Perplexed, she glances from him to her construction. "But wasn't I allowed to play in the sand?" Fear is written on her face.

But if she thinks that this is fear already, then her father's got a nasty surprise in store for her. Down to the very depths of her soul, she'll know fear. Breach of trust. But she should know better by now. He gives her reason enough, after all! She won't be able to claim later on that that dirty trick of his just came out of the blue! Can he help it if the kid still doesn't know any better? Furious, Zwier strides over to his bicycle.

"But I didn't do anything, did I?" she whimpers, her eyes filled with tears.

"You?" bellows Zwier. "You supposedly never do anything!"

"Really I didn't, Daddy!"

"Just plain fed up with it, that's what I am, I'm telling you!"

"But with what?"

But Zwier doesn't let himself get cornered by her inexhaustible rationality. "With those whims of yours!" he shouts.

Without end the long Sunday afternoon stretches before Meijken. The sounds from the kitchen, where her husband is handling the kitchen utensils louder than usual, do nothing to improve her mood. She doesn't understand why he didn't already come in a long time ago to offer his apologies, along with a tasty treat. By the time Minnie comes, she feels more agitated than she would like to admit to herself.

"I've got PMS tea with me today," her friend announces as she sets the pot and the cups down on Mother's side table, "to lessen premenstrual tension."

"We aren't premenstrual anymore," says Meijken caustically. "We are postmenopausal." Naturally he has made his complaint to Minnie while preparing the tea. He has fully aired his feelings, for once. And she, no doubt, will feel a great deal of sympathy for him.

"We, on the contrary," says Minnie with satisfaction, "are personally getting better and better every day and in every way." She smiles and pours the tea. Today she is wearing the white-speckled blue pumps from her collection and a turquoise suit, underneath it a shell with a nonchalant shawl collar.

The sight of her gives Meijken overtly hostile feelings. As she studies Minnie's crisp profile, she wonders how much she actually cares for her. If she doesn't watch out, she'll get into a fight with her, too. "I don't have any premenstrual tension to release," she repeats nonetheless in a surly tone.

Minnie clicks her tongue. "You shouldn't say that," she reckons. The point is, says Minnie, men don't menstruate either, never even, and yet they really do have a kind of emotional cycle. It has been scientifically proven. With her index finger she sketches a large circle in the air by way of clarification, but it is also as if, secretly, she wants to get the stale air in the living room behind

Balm's Drugstore to circulate a bit. Ebb and flow, Minnie continues mysteriously. In short, it's nonsensical to believe that the rhythms of emotions should exist purely by the grace of estrogens and whatever they're called, I can never remember those terms—if you'd continued your education like you always planned, then at least you'd be able to tell me now what those things are called. Not that I ever understood why you stopped so all of a sudden, says Minnie reproachfully, but anyway, a person can't understand everything. Where was I? Oh yes, says Minnie: considering that men manage somehow in spite of the complete absence of ovaries to be entirely unpredictable beings full of irrational urges, we'll have to assume that all that ovulating we do is merely a side effect of something larger, and not an end in itself—so if that stops with menopause, then it doesn't definitely mean that the machinery that runs our emotions has also come to a standstill. "Drink your tea," says Minnie. "Even if it doesn't do you any good, it won't do any harm."

Meijken brings her cup to her lips. Then she puts it back on the saucer. "You and your endless theories."

"Excuse me?" says Minnie. "If only it were just theory! I'm talking about what happens in practice every day. Suddenly they're in the throes of an irrational *mood* and then they start raping and murdering." Aggrieved, she adds, "While we vent our PMS by doing a little shoplifting." She pours herself another cup as she continues, "I just want to say, Meijken, they aren't all like Gert, believe me."

"And what's that supposed to mean?" Meijken asks belligerently. I did it, she thinks, I really did it, I managed to get into a fight with him.

"You know," says Minnie. "Someone else would have been hacking somebody to bits in that basement, and he goes and builds a dollhouse." She gets up and moves over to the sideboard. She studies the amazing piece of work tenderly. "By the way, what's he going to do with himself all day long, now that this is finished?"

"He'll cook, as you were able to see for yourself just now. Christmas dinner. Tomorrow. Preparations. Whatever."

"Somehow you certainly struck it lucky with that man," sighs Minnie. She touches the dollhouse gutters. "A shame," she says, "that he can't give that child her present, now. Or are you still expecting them back?"

Meijken shrugs her shoulders. She fingers her wart.

"I can't see it happening," predicts Minnie. "But maybe that's for the best, now that Bonnie's on her way. You could hardly have put all of them together in that guest room."

Appalled, Meijken blurts, "But she isn't staying here! She never does! I mean, the last time, she stayed in Amsterdam on account of those journalists and those other people that had to see her."

"But she'll want to visit your mother. Speaking of whom, isn't she excited?"

"I haven't told her yet," confesses Meijken.

"What's that?"

"I mean, a surprise seems like more fun, to me."

"Oh," says Minnie. "Well, anyway, if she's in Sibculo, she'll stop by here, too, of course. And then you'd have cut a pretty odd figure, what with Zwier decorously seated on the couch."

Meijken keeps her mouth shut. The recollection of Bonnie's previous visit dampens her spirits even more. What on earth were they supposed to talk about, considering that the only thing of any real importance was absolutely unmentionable? And nothing has changed with respect to that. She received a life sentence, although before, a long time ago, she had thought: maybe soon, once Mother's dead. But Mother will be around forever—Meijken will have to die another thousand deaths before she's rid of her.

Minnie has sat down again and is drinking her PMS tea. Then she picks up the thread of her argument again. "But really,

Meijken, those things I was just talking about honestly happen." She pinches her lips together for a moment. "Not everybody leads a protected life like you do."

Meijken almost screams because of this new offense. She manages to squeeze herself up out of her chair without feeling her weight. But at the same instant a mechanism she spent a lifetime cultivating takes over and in seconds she is back in control. She walks to the dollhouse, as if that had been her intention, and sticks the plug into the outlet.

"Gee," sighs Minnie, "how ticklish that must have been, with all those tiny wires. But are you listening to what I'm telling you? Even here in Sibculo they're on the loose! Yesterday I heard at the butcher's that a child molester was spotted in the village. You honestly shouldn't think that nothing can happen to us here."

"A child molester?" Meijken gasps.

Minnie nods. "That's what I just said, didn't I? They're everywhere. That you're still alive doesn't mean a thing anymore these days. Even children aren't safe. And what's the government doing, I ask you?"

Meijken stands as if she were nailed to the spot. Might this be the cause of her inexplicable fear and the feeling of being hunted? Had her instincts been warning her? Had her sixth sense wanted to let her know that an actual, tangible danger was imminent? After all, this concerns her own flesh and blood! Out there Mary Emma is unsuspectingly wandering around, ignorant of the violence that plays itself out with the same indomitable regularity as the rhythm in which the earth turns! Meijken wrings her hands. How can she, from inside her living room, ever prevent history from repeating itself?

As if that would even be possible. For, since the hour zero, it has never been any different! At least that's what Minnie always says. Was there ever a generation that was spared? You can be old or young, ugly or pretty, it can be your husband your neighbor your father your friend your colleague or a stranger, but they'll get you, they'll get you. That it still hasn't happened means nothing. After all, tomorrow's another day.

"Say, is one of your planets in the wrong transit that you're so quiet today?" inquires Minnie testily. When Meijken maintains her silence, she gets up. "Then I might as well go have a little chat with Gert," she says.

"Go ahead," says Meijken, shattered by the realization that she is utterly powerless. There really isn't a single way imaginable to prevent her granddaughter from coming into contact with the world.

From time to time when her father turns the page of his paper, Mary Emma cringes. Sitting across from him at the kitchen table, she hides behind her *Donald Duck*. She doesn't dare stir a hair. Even her eyes don't have the nerve to wander from the picture, in which all three, Huey, Dewey and Louie, decide to go out fishing, to the next one. On the way back, Zwier didn't say a word, not even when he suddenly got off his bicycle very close to Rose Red, strode to the verge, seized a small pine with both hands and uprooted it in a single, horrible wrench. At the cottage, he stuffed it crookedly into a bucket and put it in the corner of the room, near the rattan couch. Afterwards, he had picked up the paper.

Now and then his hand appears from behind it to reach for his tumbler. "Let's go fishing," cry Huey, Dewey and Louie in unison, their words contained in a shared balloon. Mary Emma imagines that a little funnel like that is leading up out of her mouth to a balloon inside of which is written: Sorry, Dad. It was just for her that Zwier rented this cottage and she doesn't even want to live there, for her that he stole a tree from the forest and she doesn't even thank him. And instead of taking a nice walk with him, this one time they're on vacation together, she goes and builds a sand ship with Victor Hugo. Guilt feelings render her immobile, even though her head itches like hell and she's sure that the lice among her hair roots are busy bearing young and raising them, bearing and raising. But she won't be a crybaby. Lucy didn't even have cleaning fluid or any shampoo, and Lucy had hair everywhere, she must have almost died from the itching, and yet she brought forth all of humanity. She musters all her courage. "Dad?"

From behind is newspaper he says, "What?"

"Sorry, Dad."

Nothing happens for a moment, but then he puts the paper down and reaches out to her. "Come on over here." She gets up and approaches him, hanging her head. He spreads his knees apart and pulls her in between them. He lifts her chin, so she has to look at him. His eyes are right near hers, brown with flecks of green in them. His gaze is searching, "About what?"

"About my whims."

"Oh," says Zwier. He gets that tormented look again. "Do you always have to take what I say so literally?"

"Sorry."

He heaves a sigh. "You shouldn't keep thinking you're to blame for everything. What does a real warrior do, Emma?"

"He hopes for nothing. He fears nothing. He is free," she mumbles.

"Exactly. At least you learned that much from your old father."

What's he saying? She's so happy, it's incredible: his dark humor has somehow or other passed! Maybe she has finally learning how she can avoid his moods. "And marking out a three-dimensional grid with stakes, I learned that from you too," she says adamantly.

"Or would we sometimes rather use a theodolite to do that?" he asks pensively.

"To measure vertically," she says quickly.

He gives her a kiss on the top of her head. "As far as I'm concerned, you're already eleven and a half."

She screeches gleefully, "No, Daddy, not by a long shot!" Then the grin on her face fades: her father's eyes look so sad. "Do you want another drink?" she asks timidly.

"Since you're up anyway."

Quickly she gets the bottle out of the refrigerator and fills his glass again. She feels his arms around her waist, he pulls her to him.

"Sometimes I'm just mad at myself," he says. "And then I start yelling at you instead of at myself. Actually, Emmie, you should just yell back. Got it?"

"No," she says, bewildered.

"Sometimes," he says, "you're a girl who asks to be slapped, did you know that? No, forget what I just said. Tell me quick: do you really like your father?"

"A hundred million," she pipes up.

"Stones?"

"Stars," says Mary Emma. She takes both hands and pushes his hair back so his forehead is laid bare, wide and broad like the sky.

"Oh yeah, right, the stones are mine. If you pluck the stars out of the sky for me, then I'll shower you with what?"

"With jade, onyx, aventurine, aquamarine and tourmaline."

"Or would you rather have a black morion or a red zircon?"

"Inscribe my likeness," says Mary Emma dreamily repeating the familiar mystical words, "in the face of the earth, in gray Nysted granite, in Finnish porphyritic granite, in Vanevik granite, in Vislanda granite, in Revsund granite, in Haga granite, in Uppsala granite, in Bothnian aplite granite."

"And then I've got basalt, slate, chalcedony, phytolith, chalk and flint for you," he says. "And later, much later, you'll remember that and suddenly you'll know that your father was the guy with the stones, and then maybe you'll laugh a little." He picks up his glass and empties it in a single gulp.

"Why are you crying, Daddy?" Mary Emma asks anxiously.

"You going to get me another one?"

The bottle is as cold as ice in her hand. She spills a good portion when she fills his glass.

"Whoa," says Zwier, "you, sit down. You have to console your father a little bit. Victor Hugo'll clean up the mess, that way he can make himself useful for once."

The lump in Mary Emma's throat turns into a stone when she finally catches on: so he thinks that she loves Victor Hugo more than him. He thinks she's just like her mother. If one person can simply stop caring about you, if that's possible, if that *exists*, then another will do the same, sooner or later. One day they hop on their motorcycles or their sand ships, and you're left behind in a cloud of dust. Like mother, like daughter!

The shock is so great that she can barely think. Not true, her brain snivels, not true! She is the most faithful, the best—he can always count on her. He doesn't have to cry for her in that awful way grown-ups do: with sobs that shake his whole body and with that raw sound that she remembers so well from Africa. What are you doing, Daddy, she asked once, whispering in the charitable darkness of the tent and he didn't respond, but a moment later he laid a warm, moist hand on her forehead: nothing, bunny-rabbit. He still does it once in a while, and then his bed creaks and squeaks even though he isn't making a sound, except suppressed panting. When you're as big as Zwier, your grief is naturally huge too—there just isn't any end to it.

Mary Emma glances up. "I thought of a surprise for you," she says with determination.

"You," says Zwier, "are a surprise yourself. You're my lifelong surprise."

She strokes his hair softly. "Can I go outside for a little

while?"

He takes her face between his hands and presses his forehead against hers. "What do you have to go outside for? In an hour it'll be dark."

She can see herself reflected in his eyes. "I'll be back long before then."

He lets her go and takes a sip of his genever. "Only if you're careful. Promise?"

"I'm always careful." It hurts her that he doesn't know that. And also, she wants him to go with her. She wants him to see with his own eyes what her surprise entails, so he'll know she's serious. But he has picked up his paper again. She lingers at his shoulder. She longs for a kiss. "OK, bye," she mumbles at last.

He puts his tumbler down and, once again engrossed in his reading, waves absently.

It takes her a moment to muster her courage. Then she signals, fast and clear: *Come in, come in, Battleship Two!* For a long time she hears only static, but then in her head she hears Victor Hugo in a tinny voice saying, *"Roger, Captain!"*

It's slightly misty outside, just enough to make everything look different. The trees reach gnarled branches out to her, they want to catch her and shut her up in the secret hollows in their trunks. Mary Emma keeps her eyes glued to the bicycle path. As long as you don't leave the path, nothing can happen.

In the pale moonlight, the Grote Beltenweg has become almost unrecognizable. The desolate campgrounds spread out along the edge of the forest like gaping maws, ready to swallow up any passerby. Even the tiny twinkling lights on Christmas trees in the yards of a couple of farms seem like the restless eyes of hungry night creatures on the prowl.

When she finally reaches the sanddrift, she is sweaty from

head to toe. Out of breath, she leans her bike against a tree trunk and squints to glimpse her sand ship, hidden among the folds of the slopes. It turns out the deckhouse has caved in. But she has to rebuild the ship from stem to stern anyway. She quickly kneels down to knead the remains into shape. She has no watch with her, but it's at least a half an hour later when she allows herself a moment to rest and assess her progress. The most important thing, the cockpit, is done at least. Now she can scratch. Feverishly, she gives her scalp a going-over with her fingernails. Then she signals Victor Hugo. Nonchalantly she says, "That's where the ignition is, see? Don't touch it before you're ready to take off." She has to swallow a couple of times: he already has his shiny helmet on and is wearing his best silvery space suit. He looks great. If only he doesn't forget to keep an eye on his oxygen. She puts on her headset. "You OK in there?" He gives her a thumbs-up sign.

Now the whole back hull. She draws the outline in the sand and starts at the tail fins, equipped with laser torpedoes, in case of intergalactic wars. Yielding to an impulse, with a pointed branch she carves the name of the ship on its tail: WARRIOR I. Just so that bloody space rabble knows who's coming. "What do you mean, WARRIOR I approaching? Ready arms! Open fire! Launch more ships to bring his body back!"

"Holy moly," mumbles Victor Hugo, "it's them crazy Martians again!" At that moment there's a shout, something whizzes through the air, and Mary Emma throws herself forward in the sand. The hairs on the back of her neck stand on end when, right above her, she can sense something fly past her and the same hoarse voice utters another cry, a satanic laugh. Then, only a couple of yards away from her, a seagull lands.

Mary Emma laughs nervously and sheepishly sits up. Chortling, the bird flies off.

She shakes the sand out of her clothes. Only now does she notice that it is almost completely dark. Mistrustfully she looks around. It must be much later than she thought. She sticks her cold hands in her pockets. All right. There's no time left. She can hear herself say in a small voice, "Ready for take-off?"

With almost floating steps Victor Hugo approaches, as if gravity already doesn't have a hold on him anymore. He holds out his arms toward her. "I'm not going," says Mary Emma sadly. He stands still right next to his spaceship. He has never been anywhere alone yet. He thinks it's no fun, all by himself. Without her, he'll feel lonely and unhappy. But she can't turn back now. "Well, get going!" she explodes. "You've got the fucking universe to save. So go do it!"

She turns brusquely and marches over to the control tower taking big steps. "Five minutes to go after the beginning of countdown," she barks into the mike on her headset as she plods uphill through the sand. On top of the dune she turns around. At first she can't see anything of the spaceship anymore, and her heart starts pounding. When she finally thinks she can make out the drawn-out shape among the other darkened mounds of sand, she has already forgotten all the things she still wanted to say to Victor Hugo. She sits down in the oak scrub and wipes her nose on the sleeve of her jacket. For some reason she has to think of the white envelopes that together form a dotted line across the continents. She understands something now that had always been a mystery. It's much easier not to say goodbye.

"Commencing countdown," she whispers, wiping away her tears. "Here goes!" Now she really has to start counting down, or else there'll be an accident. She braces herself. Numbers whirl through her head. Five minutes to go. An eternity! Anything can still happen before Victor Hugo's spaceship lifts off the ground and disappears for always among the nebulae. Out loud she stammers, "Three hundred, two hundred ninety-nine, two hundred ninety-eight, two hundred ninety-seven, two hundred ninety-six." And now she has also neglected to ask Victor Hugo to say hello to E.T. But it's too late for that: launching-procedure cannot be stopped or interrupted. Or else the fuel will explode and Victor

Hugo will end up in the ozone layer in a million pieces. Mary Emma counts. The roar of the jet-engines gets louder. Miles away, in Rose Red, Zwier must be able to hear it. In surprise he'll lower his glass of genever and suddenly smile, because he understands what that sound means. She'll be able to sit on his lap the whole evening and for just this once he'll let himself be persuaded to do the Zwierios. Climb, Mary Emma, keep going, you're almost there, finish what you started! And he laughs and she's shouting too that... Mary Emma pricks up her ears while she continues counting. Another gull that sends shivers down her spine. One might even go ahead and sit on her, in the dark. One hundred eighty-one, one hundred eighty, one hundred seventy-nine, one hundred seventy-eight. Now she hears it again. Suddenly anxious, she crawls halfway out of the bushes, to duck back right away.

  At the bottom of the dune the three boys on mountain bikes are circling around. As they let out bird cries, the beams of light from their headlights veer back and forth. They dance around one another in complicated patterns. Stinging nettles and putty! Up on top of the dune Mary Emma crawls way back into the bare thickets and slaps her hands over her eyes. In a minute, when she looks up, they'll be gone. It's Christmas Eve and their mothers are waiting for them with Christmas wreath cake! Ninety-three, ninety-two, ninety-one. Full of hope, she opens her eyes.

  One of the lights has separated itself from the ballet below. Rapidly it surges uphill, almost immediately followed by the other two fiery eyes. Sand spurts in all directions when the bikers turn at the top of the dune and zigzag back down. The one reaching the bottom first whoops and makes a figure eight before, once again, riding up while standing on the pedals. He veers up just missing the bush behind which Mary Emma hides trembling. Sixty-four, sixty-three, sixty-two, sixty-one: just one more minute to go, WARRIOR I.

  All three boys careen down the dune together, they thunder

downhill, pitching over each bump, so that now and then they appear to be hanging in the air for an instant, before jouncing back down without ever losing their balance. Mary Emma rattles off the seconds that separate Victor Hugo from his safety—you have to take good care of a small child, you can never walk out on one, never, even though you'd like to take off yourself, or else the kid'll explode and end up in the ozone layer in a million pieces—nineteen, eighteen, seventeen, sixteen, fifteen, fourteen, and she starts to moan in fear when suddenly the three beams of light come straight at her.

And all over Sibculo it is slowly getting to be bedtime for the littlest ones who are still barely aware of what the morrow will bring. The older children are making a ruckus in their excitement and outdo one another in risky endeavors with melted candle wax. Over their heads, their parents give one another meaningful looks:

Merry Christmas And A Happy New Year!

It is going to be a cold night with bright stars—just like the eyes of children winking at Sibculo from the farthest reaches of the universe. Anybody looking up out the window will be overcome by a humbling feeling of insignificance. Beside the firmament, the festively lit wishes of the merchants' association all but pale:

Merry Christmas And A Happy New Year!

But from seven o'clock in the morning on, from the moment the news bulletin is broadcast, the lofty thoughts of the residents of Sibculo and environs transform into terror and dread. Gradually, an anxious silence settles over all the houses. No model train fresh from the box rattles, no offensively unwrapped vacuum cleaner zooms, no computer received with cheers bleeps, no single-mindedly yearned-for blender grinds, no drill given as an obvious hint roars. The only audible sound is the monotonous voice of the newscaster repeating the shocking facts every hour.

Behind the exclamation point on his storefront, Gert Balm rearranges the almond paste-filled Christmas stollen and inspects the breakfast table. On Meijken's plate lies his gift, wrapped in golden foil. Soon they'll be sitting here together by his candles and he'll unwrap the shirt she ordered at Wehkamp's and then she'll start on her little package and she'll say, "Can't we turn on the light?"

Broad, his wife stands in the doorway. "I'm just about to break my neck," she grumbles.

Gert Balm switches on the light in the kitchen. The teakettle whistles. From the oven comes the smell of burned rolls. "Merry Christmas," he says. He can hear how reproachful he sounds, although he intended it as a reconciliation. "Sweetheart," he tacks on hesitantly.

"The same," his wife says coolly. She has sloppily tossed a shawl over her nightdress. Her hair still hasn't been combed.

"To start with, why don't you sit down."

"Where?" asks Meijken.

"Over by that little package."

"Oh, that." She remains standing. "Did you happen to put something in the oven? I smell a kind of singed smell."

"Just go ahead and open it, now," he says, pouring the water into the teapot.

"Do I really deserve a present?" she asks sarcastically.

"Oh, Meijken," he says, "for pity's sake, let's not keep on squabbling."

"I was just starting to find it interesting."

"But I wasn't."

"Besides, you started it."

"Then, may I put a stop to it as well?"

"Why should you?" she asks in utter amazement. Her face, pale up till then, has turned red. "Why don't you let me hear the awful truth? Get it all off your chest. It'll do you good."

"Few things are worth fighting over," says Gert Balm.

"Not even me?"

Awkwardly he turns the oven off. Can he make her happy today only by giving in to her provocation? "Maybe we're a little tense because of the whole situation," he makes an attempt to relativize.

"A situation we have you to thank for," she retorts.

After a moment he admits, "Yes. Indeed."

"Oh!" she exclaims. "Limp rag that you are."

Powerlessness mounts to the back of his throat like gall. What does she want? What more does she want from him but that he should say she's right? Does she really want him to scream and yell at her? Does she maybe want to be dragged through the kitchen by her hair?

At that moment the telephone rings in the hallway. In confusion they stare at each other for a couple of seconds. "That'll be them," Gert Balm whispers at last, slowly getting up. The riddles with which his wife has confronted him lose their oppressiveness for a brief moment: his heart leaps. He knew all along that Zwier would call sooner or later and there's nothing he would like to tell him more than that everything has been forgiven and forgotten and that there is a surprise for Mary Emma standing by the Christmas tree. Peace on earth. You have to start with your immediate surroundings.

He coughs, picks up the receiver, "Balm speaking."

"Oh, Gert!" says Minnie. "Merry Christmas, of course."

He needs a moment to swallow his disappointment. Then he answers, "You, too."

"Not that the circumstances are very merry," Minnie's

voice continues. "And then to think that it was only yesterday I was saying to Meijken…"

Through the open kitchen door he can see his wife tear the paper of his carefully wrapped gift. She opens the manicure set and looks at it with her head bowed. He can't see the expression on her face. "She isn't here," he interrupts Minnie in order to be done with her as quickly as possible. He immediately realizes the enormity of the remark. "I mean, she's still asleep."

"Asleep?" Minnie exclaims. "But didn't you two hear the news, then?"

With automatic gestures, Meijken spreads butter on a slice of Christmas stollen while her husband, stumbling over his words, acquaints her with the facts. The facts are simple and definite. There is nothing more to be said. Meijken lays the butter knife back down beside the butter dish and looks at the raisin bread on her plate as if it were a new and unfamiliar kind of food. Then the message finally reaches her brain. She can feel the blood drain out of her face, all her weight seems to sag down to her feet and in her ears a thunderous roar starts up. "Did they say how old?" she stammers.

"No, only that they didn't know, how do they call it, not yet identified."

Seeing nothing, Meijken stares at her slice of raisin bread until it takes on the form of the province with its expanses of forest, its desolate and remote corners, its windswept dunes. She doesn't want to think what she's thinking.

"Out in the dunes!" ponders her husband shaking his head. "On Christmas Eve!"

"Gert," says Meijken. She clutches his arm, "Call the police just to make sure."

"What?" he says. "But what for?"

"To find out what she looks like. Her description."

"But what do we have to do with…"

"Just to make sure!"

Startled, he looks at her. "But you really don't think…"

Meijken avoids his gaze. "Just call." She clasps her hands together. She says, "It could very well be her."

"But we don't even know at this moment where, if she's in the area, she could just as well be somewhere else, safe and sound!"

"Let's hope so," says Meijken hoarsely. The sight of the raisin bread suddenly makes her sick to her stomach and she pushes the plate away.

Plaintively her husband asks, "But what am I supposed to say, Meijken?"

"That you have reason to believe that it concerns a member of your family who was visiting in Sibculo," she says staring ahead, uttering the words one by one like lead bullets. When she has reached the end of her statement, exhaustion overpowers her like deadweight, as if she has just performed a superhuman feat. "Oh my god," she whispers as she starts to rock back and forth; Mother will have to be told. She presses her fingertips against the roots of her hair. Above her left eye the throb of a blinding migraine kicks in.

"Now let's not draw premature conclusions," her husband suggests in a reasonable tone, "You'll see that soon we'll…"

"You'll have to go there to identify her," Meijken interrupts him. "After all, we're the only ones that can do that."

"Yes," he says. "It's true. Of course." His face has become ashen. With a dazed look, he gets up. "Do you think I should call the emergency number?"

"Try it," says Meijken numbly. As she hears her husband dial a phone number, she gets up and starts mechanically clearing the table. She piles the plates on the counter. She fills the sink with water. She is about to pick up the dishwashing brush, but instead takes a couple of steps in the direction of the telephone. With each step it's as if she has to drag herself up a steep incline, and at the same time she is practically weightless. The least breath of wind could blow her away. At that thought, she forces herself toward the kitchen door and flings it open. The December cold bites into her bare legs, but she isn't lifted up, she doesn't blow away, she stays upright in the doorway as if she were nailed to the spot—no power in this world will ever get her to cross this threshold: after all, an everlasting curse has been laid on her. "You'll stay indoors," Mother's voice intones out of the distant past, but so clearly, as if she is only now pronouncing her sentence, and just as unrelentingly, as if Meijken were standing before her this very moment in her torn clothing, "You'll stay indoors until this is all over."

Meijken balls her fists: this will never be over. For, how can this ever become the past when already two generations of her descendants walk the earth? The faces of Bonnie and Mary Emma stare at her, questioning, incredulous. Aren't you mistaken? Aren't you terribly mistaken? Come to your senses!

Meijken gasps for breath when the reality of the moment crashes in on her, like somebody smashing open a door: the truth is, there aren't two faces any longer. Since last night there is only one left.

From the hallway she can hear her husband's voice rising and falling, yes, he says, yes, no, then of course I'll come right away, and an instant later he pokes his head around the door and says that right away he'll, aren't you catching cold, Meijken? And she says no, you go on, and she can hear him fiddling around for his coat, his car keys, and then the slam of the front door.

Before Meijken's mind's eye a face appears, contorted in a grimace of deadly fear, the blue eyes are frantic, opened wide, the caramel-colored strands of hair wisp through the sand, one cheek is swollen, blood dribbles out of the nose. Soundlessly Meijken screams, "Don't struggle! For god's sake let him have his way! He'll let you go afterwards! He promised he would!"

Her lungs fight for air, as if she had suddenly landed in a

strange and hostile element—and she discovers she is no longer standing in her kitchen, but outside in the courtyard, beneath the dizzyingly high, free sky. Tottering, she shuffles her feet. I don't have any shoes on, she thinks from afar, I'm walking in my slippers. Her hand finds the latch of the gate. "Just hang on a little while longer," she implores in her thoughts. "Just a little while. I'm coming."

4

Safe on Mother's Lap

When Zwier wakes up on Christmas morning, his head is one large slurping morass in which air bubbles slowly well up. Sitting up, he notices that he has been lying fully clothed on top of the blankets. The walls of Rose Red's little bedroom are spinning and it seems like the floor is tipping sideways from under his bed. He hears himself let out a groan under his breath, and sinks back down. He closes his eyes hoping for a few more moments of benumbing slumber. From a faraway planet Mary Emma calls out: "Daddy!"

"Yes, bunny-rabbit?"

"Daddy!"

"Not so loud."

"Are you awake? It's ten-thirty already."

With his eyes still shut he says, "I'll be there in a minute. Go play some more with Victor Hugo."

"But he isn't here anymore! C'mon, wake up sleepy head!"

"So where is he?" Zwier asks, all hope fast fading. With difficulty he focuses and looks at his daughter. Her puffy eye has now discolored to a brownish blue. She exudes the penetrating odor of methylated spirits. A look of astonishment is written on her face.

"He went to Mars," she says. "I told you all about that yesterday, man."

"Oh, right," he lies. His tongue is a dehydrated mass in his mouth. He places his feet on the floor and has to rest for a couple of seconds. "I think I drank a little bit too much yesterday," he says.

"The bottle's all empty," his daughter replies with an undertone of amazement. "You said you were going to keep going until there wasn't a drop left."

Zwier wraps both hands around the edge of his mattress. "Did I say any other words of wisdom?"

"That it was OK for me to eat your pizza too." She looks like she had a good time last night. No new traces of rupture, thinks Zwier. He holds his arm out to her. "Hey, that's my girl. Merry Christmas."

"I made Christmas breakfast. Fried eggs."

"Great," he says, as his stomach turns. By way of experiment he stands up. Cautiously maintaining his balance he totters after his daughter into the kitchen. It is totally beyond him what brought him to drink yesterday. Maybe it was just his time of the month to go on a binge.

Mary Emma's already sitting on her chair at the table which is set. He tries not to look at the two plates on which fried eggs are lying in pools of congealed fat. Sometimes greasy things can stabilize the stomach somewhat, but he doesn't dare risk it. "Can I start with juice, Em?"

"Oh," she says. "It's all gone. I was so thirsty this morning."

"The whole carton?" He immediately checks himself. He is the only one to blame for the state he's in.

"It was a good thing we sang Christmas carols," his daughter says with a meaningful look.

"Carols? Oh, those carols," Zwier fruitlessly searches the cavity of his memory.

"Or else Father Christmas wouldn't have come," she says.

He follows her gaze. Under the tree that he ripped up out of the woods yesterday in a blind rage lie lumpy packages. "Mother Christmas," he says.

She laughs elatedly. She slaps both hands on the edge of the table so that the dishes rattle, and pain shoots through his head.

"Not with your mouth full," he snaps. He taps her on the arm. "Sorry, I've got a bit of a headache."

"Your eggs are getting cold," she says with concern. "Did you know the fridge is empty now?"

"Yes, I know." Just leave that to your father.

"Oh, Daddy," she says brightly. "I've guessed your secret! Tonight we're going to eat at Uncle Gert's!"

"Christ," says Zwier.

"Yesterday," Mary Emma starts, as if confessing. She glances down. She clatters her silverware. "I mean," she says. "Well, when I got home so late? Because I had to hide from those boys? I was still scared you'd be mad." Shyly she looks at him. Then all of a sudden, she laughs, Bonnie's sunny laugh, "And then it turned out to be really fun!"

"Yes," says Zwier. "And?"

She is visibly disconcerted. Under her dull hair her forehead wrinkles as she hunts for words that are beyond her. So, after all, Emma, your father isn't so bad, is he? He turns his eyes away. How did that kid get to be so generous? Practically a damned saint! Saint Mary Emma, eleven!

She has found the solution. "So," she exclaims, "Uncle Gert doesn't have to worry that you're still mad at him."

"Doesn't he now," he says, infuriated: if it hadn't been for her he would have been able to keep his hands to himself and then he wouldn't have been sitting with an empty refrigerator in Rose Red. "Which boys were they?" he asks sternly.

"The ones with the bikes. The mountain bikes, remember?"

"So," says Zwier. "Am I to understand that you aren't happy with the bike you got? You want a nicer one?"

"No," says Mary Emma. "'Cause then you wouldn't be able to keep up with me." She has finished her plate and is now eyeing his. "Aren't you going to eat them? They're only burned on the bottom, you know. But if you think they're icky, I'll eat them."

"Do you know what you're never supposed to do?" Zwier threatens. "Sacrifice yourself. It makes a very unpleasant impression, you see. Like you feel superior to everybody."

"But I'm hungry," she exclaims. "And you're not."

"You already had my pizza, too, yesterday."

"You weren't hungry then, either!"

"And when," he bellows, "is your father allowed to be hungry, then? Could you tell me that?"

She slides her chair back. She is screaming with laughter. Strands of her hair swing in tangles from side to side. With a flushed face she manages to say, "Do that again, Dad."

"What?"

"You were just...you were just like a baboon!"

Zwier feels like he's deflating, as if she'd unscrewed his valve. Feebly he says, "Ung, ung," and drums his chest.

Now his daughter's almost crying with joy. She has wrapped her arms around her stomach and is wobbling around on her chair. "Oh, Daddy," she splutters, wiping the filthy strands of hair out of her face so that her black eye reappears.

"Yeah," says Zwier. "That was a good laugh." He wants to caress her cheek, he wants to do everything for her, because she has managed to reestablish equilibrium just in time. Mary Emma Zwier, savior. He reaches out a shaky hand and gives her a tap on her nose. "And you don't even know what my Christmas present is."

She leaps up. She looks at the packages under the tree. She looks at him. The corners of her mouth start quivering.

"What you always wanted to have," teases Zwier, "but were never allowed to touch."

"Oh, no," says his daughter, shrinking back from the thought he has planted in her brain.

"Yessiree."

"But how are you supposed to...?"

"That's none of your concern. It's Christmas only once this year, kid. And probably in our whole life we'll only be here at Rose Red one time. Don't you think that under those circumstances you deserve a special present?"

Mary Emma nods, wordlessly.

"Of course it isn't wrapped."

"No," she says.

"Here," he says, pulling the cartridge pen out of his shirt pocket. "For my grown-up daughter."

She sighs heavily. She takes the pen with her thumb and index finger and studies it, the way she did so often on his knee. Zwier can see only the top of her blond head. Now at least she'll have a tangible memory of him.

When Gert Balm parks the car in front of the drugstore following his visit to the morgue, the light-headed feeling still hasn't entirely disappeared. Stiffly, he steps out of his car and sucks in the refreshing air, but his nausea doesn't go away, nor does the irradicable image just now, in the morgue's cooler.

He shuts the car door and takes a few more deep breaths, thankfully tasting the slightly frosted air that sends tingling sensations throughout his body. For a second he is very clearly conscious that his blood is flowing, his heart is beating. He straightens his back. If this beautiful weather holds up, he'll soon be able to skate into the wind on the Vecht, with long, sure sweeps, along the frosted banks glittering under a bright winter sun. Ice is his element. On the ice, something in him that is otherwise dormant comes to life; he is known for this throughout the region, it's a metamorphosis witnessed eagerly by most. On the ice he has complete control over what he is doing, he neither trips nor stumbles, he skates like an angel, an archangel, with regularity, elegance, tirelessly, sparks jump out from under his blades. Children cheer him on and their mothers nudge one another as the indulgent expressions with which they usually observe him make way for wonder. To be able to skate like he does. That's the way skating is meant to be! Too bad Meijken never gets to see it.

With his head thrown back to drink in the intense blue of the sky, he crosses the street. Everything is clearer, brighter, after the cooler. He beholds the familiar housefronts along the street as if he were noticing them for the first time. In front of his own store there's a woman dressed in blue jeans and a down vest, looking at the window display; she's wearing a red hat from under which blond hair shows, and she's stamping her feet from cold. The sight of her, so full of life, gives Gert Balm the feeling that she was placed there by providence to remind him that those who end up in cooling units are still the exceptions, and that life should be embraced. "Merry Christmas," he exclaims.

She turns around. "Ah, hello Gert," she calls. "Finally!"

As if he were veering past thin ice, "Bonnie!"

She is standing right in front of Wella's Sanara Intensive Care Cream, containing cellulose KC and betaine. Standing there, she looks like she never left, standing on one leg, the other nonchalantly crossed in front of it, her chin provocatively raised so that the winter sun shines on her tanned skin. Her face is, as always, a closed book: expectant? reserved? or just friendly? She promptly sets the canvas bag she's carrying on the ground and spreads her arms in welcome, as if he were the one returning from a long trip. "Boy am I happy to see you! I was almost freezing to death." Her voice sounds nasal, as if she's got a cold.

"Bonnie," he repeats. He can feel one shoulder hunching forward while the angel in him swiftly takes to its heels. In his astonishment and confusion, he doesn't know whether he's supposed to embrace her or not.

She bursts out laughing. She lays one hand on his chest and gives him a quick peck on the cheek. Her dark eyebrows arch.

"What's wrong? You look like you just saw a ghost. Didn't you get my letter?"

"Yes, but you didn't mention a date, I mean, good lord, we thought you were dead."

Bonnie takes the red hat off, shakes her hair loose with a fierce toss of her head and pulls out a kleenex. "What was that?"

"I just went to identify you. I just came from there. So I already knew it wasn't you, but just as well."

"What kind of morbid story is this?"

"Somebody was murdered here last night," he wheezes.

"But why should I be that person?" she asks. She has crossed her arms. She looks at him blankly. Then her expression becomes cold. The corner of her mouth curls disparagingly. Welcome home!

"That's because Meijken thought," he starts up, immediately realizing that the ice beneath him is about to crack irrevocably.

"What was Meijken thinking?"

"That it was you."

"Yes, you already said that." She bends down, picks up her bag and prods the kleenex into it.

"No," he interrupts nervously, "no, just come on inside. I've got Christmas spice cake."

"Meijken will have a cardiac arrest if I've suddenly risen from the grave."

"But you misunderstand, that is, I'm explaining it so badly, they said on the news that an unknown woman...we knew that you might very well be in the country already, and just think if it had been you."

"I was thinking," says Bonnie to the blue sky, "why don't I drop in for coffee Christmas day."

"But imagine," Gert Balm says again, "imagine if it had been you, Bonnie. Who would ever have identified you? Then you'd be lying there for all eternity and, believe me, you wouldn't have wanted that."

She brushes her hair to the side and puts the bag down again. She asks curtly, "Was it unpleasant, what you had to see?"

"Crushed skull," he says. "So how are you doing? Did you have a good trip? When did you get in?"

"Yesterday afternoon."

"And now in Sibculo already!"

"Where they seem to be bashing skulls in these days."

"No, but it was very nearby, in Rheeze. I can't tell you how much good it does me to see you standing before me alive and well."

He can feel he is gaining ground. The trick is not to be impressed by the fact that she's so intelligent and famous—certainly not a person to come to her end some night out on the dunes: whoever wants to bash in that skull will have to be of distinguished stock.

Evidently unsure of herself, she says, "I just thought: today I'll stop by and first see you folks ..."

"So that'll be over and done with at least," he understands. Actually, she hasn't changed in all these years, she still has something of the girl that used to come over for birthday visits, with bows in her hair, wearing a dress with a starched collar. In those days he had always had to try his very best to put her at ease. Reassuringly, he pats her on the arm and smiles at her, conscious of his swollen lip.

Bonnie doesn't seem to notice anything. She blows her nose. "I never should have flown with a cold. My whole head's buzzing."

"Bonnie," says Gert Balm, the ice trustworthy and solid under his feet, "we've got excellent drops for that nowadays. Against that, of course. In short, we can do something about it. But why didn't you go right in if you're not feeling well?"

"I'm not standing out here in the cold for the fun of it, you know," she exclaims indignantly. "I rang the bell until I was blue in the face. But nobody's home."

With slow, heavy steps, Meijken maneuvers herself through the empty streets of Sibculo. In all those years, surprisingly little has changed. As fast as she can, she shuffles down the sidewalk, forcing her body to move ahead from one step to the next. She holds her arms akimbo and mows her way through the freezing cold. Her breasts bounce, her legs stick to each other.

At a street corner, she cringes: the open space rushes at her, broad and wide, and above it, the vast sky. With her head scrunched down between her shoulders, she starts crossing the intersection, to drown halfway in the emptiness that is limited by nothing. For seconds, her body refuses to cooperate, her blood pounds in her ears, the road surface billows under her feet, the other side is oceans away from her. A car honks. Very close, brakes squeal.

Meijken regains control over her mass. She covers the final yards. She heaves herself over the curb. Her ankles crack and her thighs burn from rubbing against each other. She quickly retreats into the shelter of a portico. She is looking straight at a display window in which a reindeer of bacon fat is pulling a sleigh full of meat products. Old portions of her brain awaken as she stares at the saveloy sausage and the larded braised veal in Huisman's Butcher Shop window. As a child she had looked at this display, with a shopping list in her hand: generations of Huismans and Sons have served generations of mothers and daughters. Meijken pictures the familiar shopping basket and the wallet with exact change in it. She sees it, filled with packets, being lifted over the counter, a piece of sausage loose on top. Two child's hands receive it, carry it out of the shop and set it down by the doorway for a moment to pull up a sock or pick a pebble out of a shoe. She can feel the tiles move under the thin soles of her slippers: her daughter had been here.

In confusion she feels at her stomach, swollen as if all

those hours of pain and effort still lay before her. So push, Meijken, keep going now! There's the head, you can't keep it inside any longer, just once more and you'll be rid of it forever. And don't squeal so like a stuck pig! Control yourself, you really aren't the first one. This is simply what every woman has to go through sooner or later!

Panting, she extricates herself from the entryway. She has no time to lose: if she gets there too late, she'll never forgive herself. Past the well, from which monks in the middle ages used to draw their water, she plods on, past the tipping tombstones under which it is suspected that there is a crypt. Bushes rip the skin of her bare legs as she fights her way across the green, up the hill, among the junipers lying in wait like ominous figures, ready to attack. All the god-fearing citizens are holed up in the protection of their houses: going out alone is asking for trouble.

Somewhere up ahead twigs snap with a dry, sinister sound and instantly Meijken stands still as if she were paralyzed. Between her raw thighs blood drips down, flesh chafes against flesh, and stop that goddamn screaming or I'll wring your neck, do you really think you're the first woman on earth who got laid, most of 'em think it's nice, say you think it's nice, say it or I'll break your neck.

He has stepped out of the shadows of the trees, barring her way. "A little late," he drawls, "to be out by yourself."

Meijken looks at his feet, not more than a half a yard from her own. Her throat becomes dry. "I walk here most every day," she babbles, startled, hoping that with these words the woods will again take on the old familiar demeanor of which this intruder has stripped them. Among these trees on endless walks every day she tells herself her whole life, and nobody has ever put the slightest obstacle in her path.

"Don't you know," he says, "that that can be very dangerous?" He has hooked a thumb in one of the belt loops of his pants. Blond hair falls in damp tangles over his forehead. Sweat is beading up on his upper lip. She doesn't know him, he isn't from around here, she has never seen anybody with a face that is so triangular.

"Not at all," says Meijken, "I come here every day."

Without another word he steps closer and pulls her coat open with a rapid move of his hand. She tears loose, teetering for a second on powerless legs, then turns around and runs flat out. With her coat flapping around her she races down the narrow path, low-hanging branches sweep down to meet her, her hair comes undone, she trips over a bared tree root and falls down. The next minute his weight lands on top of her. Her breath is cut off, pine needles poke into her face and pierce her open mouth. He punches her in the neck, jabs his knees down on both sides of the base of her spine and jerks her head backwards until she can feel the bones in her neck snap.

When she comes to, it's as if she's been flung down stone steps, or dragged out from under a truck. Her entire body is throbbing. She's lying on her back. She attempts to free her arms, and something sharp pricks her left wrist—the buckle of a belt—she's been tied up—she's lying on her bound arms—and he holds her struggling body fast with his knees, he has torn her blouse open and is kneading one of her breasts while sucking on the nipple of the other, his saliva running over her skin, she screams in terror and gets a smack on the side of her head as pointy teeth bare themselves right above her face, between her legs a groping hand pulls her underpants down, fingers work their way into her body, he has planted one of his knees on her chest and slaps her across the face again, with hot breath hisses commands she doesn't understand, she tries to turn her head away from the clump of flesh, limp and pale, suddenly dangling in front of her eyes until a slam against her chin makes her mouth gape and the mass fills the hollow of her mouth and rams and rams and she's never yet seen a naked man, besides the one time that she saw her father in the shower and he'd looked at her kindly in the mirror, lathered up with shaving cream, and said, "Don't be frightened," but she was already gone, alarmed at the paleness of his buttocks and the mysterious shape between his legs, as if he was always hauling something big and awesome around in secret, something that women were spared, and she gags from the flesh in her throat getting bigger and harder, bigger and harder, God our Father who art in heaven, God our Father God Almighty God, the only sensation she can still recognize and comprehend is that of pins and needles in her arms, she concentrates on her sleeping arms when her breasts get pressed together and he slides his thing back and forth between them, we don't use words from the street, we don't have to know what everything is called, that only makes us improper, then the unspeakable forces its way into her mouth again and a voice shouts that he'll kill her if she doesn't make him come and her arms are asleep, she almost pukes but then suddenly it's over, so she's done a good job, a very good job, because he's drawn back out of the hole in her head, he'll let her go now, that's what he promised, he promised it while he was pummeling her but he works his way down her body, he shoves her legs apart, he spreads her open, he drives the unnamable into her insides and bucks and bucks it deeper into her, she'll split, red-hot swords run her through, God Almighty, God who art our strength, who art merciful, don't permit this to happen, God, but the cleaving continues, grinding and grating it goes on, her deepest hollows threaten to burst asunder and then he's sitting on her face again, but his fingers keep rooting in her body while he wedges that pulsating piece of meat between her lips again and with his other hand he gropes for her breast, he pulls and twists on the nipple, he grunts something and saliva spatters into her eyes and she can't feel her arms anymore, only stiff wiry hair scraping against her nostrils and the clamminess of his stomach against her cheek, but then the thing bounces by her chin, Lord have mercy, she'll never ask anything again, now it's over, this time she's evidently done it well and he won't harm a hair on her head, he promises that while he wallops her in the side and pulls her legs to one side and forces her onto her stomach and sticks a scorching poker between her buttocks, God God God, right away he shouts for her to keep her trap shut and he presses her face into the sand, then tosses her on her back again and slings her legs over his shoulders and her spine's going to crack and she feels him inside her again while he's panting cunt, cunt, filthy cunt and keeps moving back and forth inside her and clawing at her breasts, just as long as she realizes that for her there isn't any God at all, not if He lets this happen—if He tolerates this He is merely the God of those who stick their thing in women to keep on ramming without end while they moan and grunt, on them He looks down with favor, He lets them have their way, that's how Creation was meant to be, after all He created woman especially for them after first having created the whole earth for them, with its expanses of uninhabited forests and dark, desolate spots: made to order.

Shivering, Meijken gets up. Careful not to think of anything, she wipes at the stickiness between her legs with her torn underpants. She stuffs the remains of her stockings into her pocket. She finds one shoe in a ditch, the other under a bush. She smoothes the wrinkles in her coat and buttons it over her ripped clothes. She picks the leaves and pine needles out of her hair, combs it with splayed fingers and mechanically arranges it as neatly as possible around her face. As long as nobody notices anything. Stumbling, with bloodied thighs, she sets off. But where to? The junipers cut off her path. They hem her in. They grunt and snort. Once isn't enough, it will go on and on and on as long as she lives, it will repeat repeat repeat until she has finally learned her lesson and doesn't venture onto the terrain of those to whom the world belongs, and finally realizes that there's only one place where she'll be safe. Swaying, Meijken starts to run, to where she'll be safe. She loses a slipper and leaves it behind in the bushes. Mother already won't have any idea where she's been keeping herself for so long.

By the noon hour Zwier finally trusts his stomach enough to risk eating a sandwich. He cautiously moves to the kitchenette, where the meager remains of the bread he bought yesterday are lying on the counter. Incredulous, he opens the plastic bag. He can't understand where the kid puts it all. With a sigh he lays the bread back and drinks a glass of water from one of the jerry cans. It tastes tepid and dank.

At the kitchen table Mary Emma is singing "Jingle Bells" while she scratches her new pen over a sheet of paper. Zwier lies down on the bench that's too short and studies the notes he made on the monastery well. The local ecosystem isn't entirely reliable, the aerobic circumstances could create difficulties. First they'll have to do a soil probe to make a profile before they can dig test pits, never mind scrape or actually dig. Endless numbers of features will have to be oriented and recorded. The thought of all that work makes him yawn. But soon, when they start burrowing in the mud here in Sibculo, he himself will have long-since flown the coop. He tucks his notes back in his pocket. He smokes a cigarette. He sneaks a peek at his watch. He picks up Saturday's paper that he has already read, with the exception of the classifieds. Routinely he reads the columns. Somebody's looking for a lost black tomcat that answers to the name of Mohammed Ali. A collector is looking for Marilyn Monroe photos, to be picked up at the collector's expense. Attr. fun-lving gay-boy seeks BDM older friend. Sl. act. sks fr. same. "Everybody's looking for something," says Zwier.

"What did you lose?" asks his daughter, looking up from her work.

He wasn't aware that he'd spoken aloud. Lamely, he comes up with, "Something to do the crossword puzzle with."

"You can have one of my pencils, if you want."

"Thanks," says Zwier.

"They're in my room."

"You aren't chewing on that pen, are you?"

She takes the pen out of her mouth, wipes it off on her sleeve and blushes.

He gets up. He reels to her bedroom. He opens the door and swallows a curse. The floor is strewn with plastic tote bags and the wrapping paper from the packages that were lying under the tree that morning. On the lower bunk, all the new clothes have been left in a ball, the sweaters, the underwear, the skirt with the flounced hem, the tights. Her jacket is lying on the floor beside it. On the top bunk, between the twisted sheets, he finds a box of colored pencils, a little bag with elastic hair ties, a bottle of shower gel and half a sandwich. Standing on the windowsill are her sneakers, with a grimy pair of socks sticking out. Something grinds under his feet and he bends down to pick up a little bottle of nail polish. The other one, he notices, has ended up on the floor in the folds of the jacket. "Emma!" he shouts. "What kind of a pigsty is this? All your things are lying all over the place!"

From the main room his daughter calls back, "That way at least I can see them all!"

"Spare me," mutters Zwier. Never before did his child have enough things to leave scattered about, never mind having a room of her own to make a mess of. Is this the way other girls of eleven live? But he isn't prepared to be content with that. "Come over here," he calls.

She appears with a questioning look on her face. There's a smudge of ink on her cheek, right under her black eye. The collar of her blouse is crooked under her sweater. "What's the matter? Can't you find the pencils?"

"I just wanted to educate you about something," says Zwier. "That is, if you have a minute."

"No, I don't," says his daughter. "It's Christmas now."

She turns on her heel.

He almost goes after her, almost grabs her by the shoulder and shakes her. Do you know who else was such a goddamned unbearable slob? With a feeling of defeat, he bends down and starts to sort out the clothes. He lays the underwear in a pile, folds the sweaters up, rolls the tights into fat balls. He has no solution for the skirt. He neatly lays it out on the bottom bunk. At some point in time a totalitarian brain concluded that summer cabins don't need storage space. Zwier thinks of linen closets with piles of towels and sheets in them. Rods from which shirts hang. Shelves on which books are kept in formation. A desk with well-organized papers. You, Bonnie always said, will even organize an orange crate.

I'm just methodical, thinks Zwier. As if that were an aberration! His work simply happens to demand precision, being systematic, and that's become second nature to him. He effortlessly tolerates dirt, heat, physical discomfort, but he can't tolerate disorder. OK, so he's distracted now and again, but it doesn't cause him to make a mess of things. He shakes out the jacket, lays it next to the other clothes on the bed and starts collecting the wrapping paper and sticking it into one of the plastic bags.

Come on, man, Bonnie would say, it's the other way around, you chose this field because it's so deeply satisfying to your obsessive nature! All day long you arrange layer after layer in sequence! Not one grain of sand is allowed to get mixed in with a grain from another age! Only a pathological case like yours can stand the complete senselessness of that!

Only a slovenly pig like you, Zwier had shouted, raking together her shirts and throwing them into a corner of the tent, followed by her hairpins and notes, after them her underwear and her shoes, and everywhere there were still clods of earth full of interesting root configurations, tubs with messy labels on them, only a slovenly pig like you refuses to accept that science is order!

And life itself no less, Bonnie had sneered. Just say it,

Zwier! Just say that you're pissed off about my forgetting that blasted pill! Don't blame it all on science!

Don't say that word in vain, Zwier had said. You'll never get beyond the level of botanizing. Even your labels are unreadable. Do you know how you got that research grant?

Because of my beautiful eyes, no doubt, Bonnie had said. I dare you to say it.

It couldn't have been for your brains, Zwier had said, up there it's got to be just as tabernacular of a trash-out as what you've made of it here, that just happens to go together.

Maybe, you pitiful piece of work, Bonnie had said, your rules only apply to your particular kind of science, the kind that busies itself with what's past, dead, what's unchanging—sure, I can draw up dippy little statistics on that too. Personally, Zwier, Bonnie'd said, I am interested in living matter, which happens to be unpredictable, and therefore, full of chaos—take us, for instance, Bonnie'd said, did you think we'd be fighting day and night, that we'd do nothing but go for each other's throats: isn't that a mess?

You can say that again, Zwier had said.

That's a point for me, Bonnie'd said. She had taken a cigarette out and thrown the pack heedlessly on the ground.

Zwier had smashed their camping stove.

Shouldn't you, Bonnie had said sardonically, be checking up on your personnel instead? Those Ethiopians are very lax, you know. Right in the middle of a stratigraphic probe they'll suddenly go lie in the shade for half an hour and when they wake up a couple of grains of sand will have shifted. That could make centuries of difference to you! By the way, do you have a light?

Etcetera, etcetera, thinks Zwier, tired. He places Mary Emma's sneakers under the bed. He stuffs her filthy socks into his pocket for the time being and arranges her hair ties, her shower gel and her nail polish on the windowsill. When he straightens the sheets on her bed, he once again encounters the half a sandwich lying amongst the bedcovers. His stomach juices promptly start churning. They want more than a piece of bread. They're longing for potatoes, vegetables and meat, or else a plate of pasta, a couple of tacos running with grease, a lavish rice table, or whatever the menu of the world has to offer. There are, Zwier says to himself, still a couple of trifles here that urgently need to be settled.

"Can I have your empty bottle?" he hears Mary Emma call out.

He enters the main room. "What do you need it for?"

"For my letter," she says. She's holding a rolled up piece of paper.

"A message in a bottle?"

With downcast eyes she nods gravely. Zwier feels all his force ebb away. My father's a drunk. He beats me and doesn't give me enough to eat. Help me. He picks up the genever bottle standing beside the refrigerator. Overwhelmed, he says, "I'll soak off the label for you."

"And then I'm going to throw it into the river."

"Into the Vecht?"

"Yes." She has come over to stand beside him by the sink and is looking up at him.

Zwier clears his throat. "What all did you write, honey?"

She doesn't answer right away. Then she says evasively, "Just a letter."

"Growing up," says Zwier, "is a big job, Mary Emma. Nobody thinks it's fun all the time." He lays his hand on her head. Her hair is plastered to her skull. Under the palm of his hand her scalp feels crusty from scratching. My father lets me walk around with a head covered with lice. My father only thinks of himself. Zwier has the feeling his heart is about to burst. He leans forward. With difficulty he says, "While we're at it, might as well ask Uncle Gert for a hair tonic tonight, don't you think?"

Sitting in Meijken's awe-inspiring chair, Bonnie Bentveld contemplates her sister's apparent return to the world. There is something alarming about the thought of a Meijken walking around out there like everybody else. But hadn't Meijken, imprisoned between these two immense arm rests, always been disturbing? Bonnie presses her back into the cushions on which her sister has spent the better part of her life and makes an attempt, though not a wholehearted one, to imagine how Meijken got through all those hours. You'd think a person like that would be happy if a visitor showed up, but Bonnie never noticed anything like that.

Abruptly she gets up and starts meandering around the room. If only she'd never come up with the wretched idea of this surprise visit, just because it happened to be Christmas. As if half a day with Mother wasn't bad enough by itself. And now she's trapped: her brother-in-law has posted her by the telephone while he himself, wild-eyed, left to comb the streets of Sibculo. Briefly, Bonnie wonders how he got that cut-up lip. In what kind of strange, singular hell do those two live? She isn't sure whether she'd like to know the facts. She sits down again, as a familiar feeling of claustrophobia takes possession of her: she never wanted to know anything about her sister's life. Whenever, as a child, she had heard her parents arguing in low voices about Meijken, she'd cover her ears with her hands in order not to overhear anything about that frightful being they called her sister, that gigantic pig, that blob of blubber, that pudding. Once in a great while her father would say, much to her disgust: you're just like Meijken when she was your age, but then Mother's look was fortunately enough to make him keep his mouth shut. At night, in bed, Bonnie prayed with her eyes squeezed shut that her father's words didn't mean that she would have to turn out just like Meijken later. She didn't want to weigh a thousand pounds and sit in a stuffy back room, with vampire eyes like that, that looked like they wanted to suck you dry. What she wanted the most was to forget Meijken existed. In silence she often told herself that they weren't really sisters, one of them had been stolen, or switched, it happened often enough, after all since they didn't resemble each other in anything, the same blood couldn't be flowing in their veins; Bonnie would escape the curse. Mother never had to look at her with raised eyebrows because she'd uttered the forbidden name, it wasn't on her account that Mother would go lie down in a darkened bedroom and refuse to speak. It was her father who stirred up all those bad feelings. One night Bonnie had heard him shout, "We don't have the right. It's immoral! She's pining away before our very eyes!"

"Pining away?" came the sound of Mother's voice, as piercing as an icicle. "You call that *pining away*?"

"I should never have let you have your way!"

"But now it's too late," said Mother.

"I can't live with this. I can't."

Mother had fallen silent.

"And only because you always wanted another one!"

Then another silence had fallen, so long this time that Bonnie'd been sure that something unforgivable had been said. "That," Mother finally retorted, "would have happened if I'd at least had a *man*."

Bonnie had pulled her pillow over her head and even though she could no longer hear her parents, she could still feel their words coming straight through the wall, they droned with dull sounds, as if each word were the post of a fence that was being slowly and inevitably built up around her. She shot out of her bed, down the stairs, into the dark yard. Without knowing what she was doing she started pulling the petunias out of the flower beds. She had been grounded in her room for a week.

Her father, who was to blame for everything, brought her her food in the evening, still dressed in his gritty, crackly clothes. He had sat on the bed for a little while. But she didn't even bother to look at him. Not even when he said, "Princess? May God forgive me for everything I've done." That was to be hoped—she wasn't prepared to do it herself.

The chiming of the pendulum clock makes her leap to her feet. In the living quarters behind Balm's Drugstore you might forget that the world was turning, but it does turn. Bonnie gives herself a good stretch, flexing her muscles one by one. Then she kneels down next to the dollhouse under the tree. She opens all the doors and windows wide. "Are we running the heat for the whole street?" she mutters with Mother's intonation. Yes, Mother, we're running the heat for the whole street. Going along with her has always been the best strategy. Agreeing until you were ready to burst. Even as a child I was already an opportunist, thinks Bonnie and the thought gives her a strange, almost perverse, feeling of satisfaction. If you aren't good at what you do, you'd better leave it be. She takes the dolls off the couch and places them in different rooms, as far apart as possible, while she wonders disinterestedly for whom this toy is meant. It's difficult to picture a child ever coming here to play. In this cave. Bonnie lets herself roll at full length on the floor and sprawls out on the carpet. She looks at the ceiling and considers what all there might be on the first floor—she never got further in this house than the living room. Up there, there's obviously the conjugal bedroom. There, at the end of each day, Gert spinelessly lets his teeth get knocked through his lip. Bonnie sits up and crosses her legs. Strange that she never noticed before that her sister is married to the spitting image of her father. Whereas she had gone to great lengths to find his exact opposite. It suddenly occurs to her that the two scenarios aren't so dissimilar. She lets out a sigh. She picks at the broken heel of her boot while letting her last lovers pass in review. Maybe she should try a really young guy once. The question is whether she really feels up to undressing for a twenty-year-old. It's not going to get any easier in the coming years, that much is certain.

The silence in the house is starting to get on her nerves. Here she sits, on her sister's carpet. It is rather exotic. She might as well get up again. In the kitchen, she opens the refrigerator. She drinks some orange juice from the bottle. Her gaze falls on the packets from Huisman's Butcher Shop. Huisman's Butcher Shop! Say Sibculo and you say Huisman's Butcher Shop. With the reindeer! Bonnie grins. Without a doubt, the reindeer will be in the window display again this year: after all, nothing ever changes here. As a child it used to drive her nuts. The predictability of each new day, of each new week sometimes made her frantic. Endive on Wednesdays, cauliflower on Sundays. A new dress for Christmas, a new dress for Easter. Never any deviation from the scheme of things, never anything unexpected. And Mother, who watched over all her comings and goings—keeping things under control, it was called. Mother also had the Sibculo-syndrome, that desire for everything in its place and don't move. Mother had a way of pulling you to her that was absolutely suffocating. Mother possessed tentacles: I just get worried when I don't know where you are, Bonnie, you could take that into account sometimes, I just can't understand how you can go chasing after your own amusement when you know I'm sitting here waiting for you, all alone at home. And your father already dredged up and buried! I released you from being grounded in your room then, didn't I, I measured you for a black dress then, sewed it myself, and weren't we a handsome pair at the funeral?

Bonnie flings the refrigerator door shut. She goes back to the living room. It's just for a little while, she thinks, soon you'll be walking around free again, come on, be nice to your neighbor for once. But being nice has never been her strong point.

She takes a little wreath from the tree and bites into it. Before, when she came for birthday visits, she had never dared eat or drink anything. She wouldn't drink a drop of her pop, she'd leave her cake untouched—pastry, as Mother would say—and she even avoided the bathroom: anywhere in this house she could pick it up, that virus that had sentenced Meijken to steadfastness, like an old oak. She'd jiggle her little feet in order not to have to sprout roots on the couch and end up just like her sister, that immobile mountain of flesh, for always riveted to Sibculo. Anybody who stayed in Sibculo turned out like Meijken. Anybody who was like Meijken would always have to stay in Sibculo. She was a specter of unchangingness, a symbol of the hidden significance of Sibculo: Sibculo was the terminus of the world, anybody who found themselves in Sibculo could let their hopes go up in smoke, Sibculo was stagnation, Sibculo consisted only of the same faces, the same voices, the same rhythms, routines and rituals.

"Luckily, I'm a gypsy-child," says Bonnie in a low voice, as if she were once again the little girl who had almost suffocated in the stifling atmosphere of the living quarters behind Balm's Drugstore. She turns around and half-expects to see Meijken sitting in her colossal armchair. "I escaped," she exclaims. By way of challenge, she crosses her arms. But there is no Meijken, and thus, no contrast. With reluctance, Bonnie admits that she doesn't know where to begin with a Meijken who isn't to be found in her armchair. For, with that, hasn't the greatest difference between them fallen away?

With the unpleasant feeling that an extremely precarious balance has suddenly swung around to her disadvantage, she closes all the windows and doors of the dollhouse again. Wrapped in her thoughts, she sits down on the edge of the couch. An important point of reference is threatening to slip away from her. Her sister, wherever she might be, could well decide never to come back home and to her husband. That, thinks Bonnie, definitely runs in the family. The thought does nothing to improve her mood. She jumps up again. How can a live being stand it between these four walls? And what is she doing here for Pete's sake? What had she come here for? What causes her to come back to Sibculo time and time again? Does a pathetic part of her subconscious, entirely independently, have a need to see the puzzles of the past resolved, to be made privy at last to the secret that would explain everything? Now that she's finally old enough, is her curiosity winning out over her fear? She has to restrain herself to keep from stamping her feet: she doesn't like being at the mercy of ulterior motives, the way a marionette is of its strings. And besides, what could Meijken ever have to reveal to her that would be worth listening to? Won't the family secret turn out to be just another bagatelle of some kind?

In the hallway, unexpectedly nonetheless, the phone starts ringing. For the first time, fear grips Bonnie's heart: her sister might well have met with an accident—and then it would for always be too late. She rushes into the corridor, grabs the receiver and breathlessly speaks her name. Then she holds back a sigh. She studies herself in the mirror while she says in a welcoming tone, "Oh, hello, Mother. I got here just ten minutes ago—I was just about to call you."

There are children playing on the sidewalk, two little girls that hop from one colored square to another as they sing a little rhyme. They are so involved in their game that they notice Meijken only when she tries to squeeze by them, huffing and puffing. The smallest of the two immediately scoots off between some parked cars, while the other girl stops dead in her tracks, one of her legs still up in the air. Meijken can feel the child's eyes pierce her as if they were burning holes in her. She doesn't know how she's supposed to protect herself from those stares, she almost trips, she utters a stifled shriek. Don't look at me that way! She pulls the shawl tighter around her nightdress. Crossing her arms over her stomach to cover her shame as best she can, she stumbles right over the hopscotch figure, so that the little girl darts away with a howl. Ahead of Meijken she runs around the corner, while at the same time three boys on mountain bikes turn into the street. "A witch," shouts the child.

The boys slow down. In passing, they eye Meijken from head to foot. Just as she thinks she's starting to escape their notice, one of them hollers something to the others, they turn their bikes, standing on the pedals they bounce up on the sidewalk and cut off her path, to circle around her screeching like gulls. Wheels sheer past her feet and handlebars knock her in her sides when she tries to break out of the whirling circle. She grabs a lamppost. She can hear metal whizzing by, rubber whooshing past her. Then her tormentors suddenly vanish.

In a doorway, a woman shouts something at the boys in a shrill voice. "Lily-livered hellions!" she yells. She quickly makes her way to her front gate, raising a balled fist. "Your parents are going to hear about this!" At the fence, she stands still. "Meijken?" she guesses. Disbelief is written all over her face. "It's you, isn't it, Meijken?"

All down the street windows suddenly glitter like eyes opening wide. There's Meijken! Where? Look, there, just look! See Meijken?

"Do you still remember me?" the woman asks. "From school?" she has moved closer, holding her collar shut at the throat. "Don't you want to come in for a minute?"

Meijken shakes her head. They won't see anything's wrong. They won't notice a thing.

"Are you all right? Should I call your husband?"

Again Meijken shakes her head. "I'm on my way home," she manages to say.

"With no coat on? And you're barefoot!"

"I'm on my way home," she repeats. She starts moving again.

"Meijken!" the woman calls. Meijken! the echo clatters down the row of houses. The windows beam. Did you see Meijken?

"Meijken!"

Blind and deaf, she propels herself around the corner.

She's almost there.

A strange name plate has been screwed on the door and Mother's curtains have disappeared—now there are blinds hanging in the windows. That isn't her style, something modern like that. Alarmed, Meijken looks at her childhood home. On the windowsill there's a strange cat. Her hand is already unsteadily reaching for the doorbell, when she suddenly remembers: that's right, Mother moved. She's living in Vesper Vitae now. The thought of almost having burst in on total strangers makes Meijken shudder. She turns around as fast as she can.

She's only a couple of streets away from the nursing home. It is encircled by a wide lawn with a pond in the middle surrounded by benches. Near the water's edge, leaning on his cane, sits an old man. "Merry Christmas," he unexpectedly calls as Meijken passes. She bows her head and ignores him. It's a little too late now to want to patch things up. She won't ever forgive him for not having stood up for her. She hopes—she hopes he'll fall into the pond and drown.

She pushes the glass door open and walks into the front hall. "Mother," she calls out, out of breath. She now feels the panic she was able to keep in check the whole way crashing over her in waves. She takes another faltering step. In the middle of the floor there's a gigantic Christmas tree and the strains of "Silent Night" filter through the empty space. Mother isn't there.

Radiant spots dance in front of Meijken's eyes as she moves farther into the hall. In the farthest corner there's a reception desk, behind which sits a young girl. She's flipping through a magazine while her head, sporting headphones, mechanically shakes back and forth. Her hair has three different colors. She is just blowing a bubblegum bubble when Meijken leans over and, in order to make herself heard above the canned sounds emanating from the headphones, asks in a loud voice, "Where's my mother?"

"Jesusaychchrist," says the girl, jerking her head up. She

pulls the headset off, caught red-handed. "Excuse me, ma'am. Good afternoon." There is gum sticking to her lips.

"Where is my mother?"

The girl briefly fixes her with a stare. Then she asks, "What is your mother's name?"

"Bentveld," says Meijken automatically. She can barely keep a grip on herself. She's going to fall apart right before this girl's eyes.

"Sorry, I'll have to look that up. You see, I'm only working here over the holidays." She checks the list. "Room 108. That's on the first floor, ma'am. And the elevator is over there."

Meijken clutches her stomach once again. She straightens her back. She moves first one leg, then the other. She's gaining speed again. She reaches the elevator. The door softly swishes shut behind her. She pushes a button. She waits, all her forces strained to the utmost. The door slides open. She finds herself in a hallway with numbered doors. The gray carpetting is soft and warm under her feet. She can smell vague food odors. It's Monday—that's when Mother always eats pigs in a blanket.

With an awkward move of her hand, Meijken wipes away the tears running down her cheeks. She is home. She is safe. With a sniffle of thankfulness, she pushes the door to Room 108 open. She stops on the threshold. She must have been mistaken about the room number.

In front of the window sits an old woman, dozing, a plaid throw around her shoulders that she holds closed over her chest with a bony hand. The toothless mouth is slightly ajar and there's a thread of saliva running from the corner of her mouth to her chin. The sunken upper lip is gray and wrinkled. The snow-white hair is so thin that her scalp is visible underneath. Suddenly the eyes under the heavy, violet lids open up. They are covered with a milky white film. A shudder travels through the brittle figure. "Are you there, child?" asks the woman in Mother's voice, turning her face towards the door.

Meijken can't speak. She steps into the room and feels how her chafed thighs burn.

"You know you're supposed to come straight to me," says Mother reproachfully. With a corner of the throw she wipes her chin. "To your own Mother!"

Her words send tears once again to Meijken's eyes. This is exactly what she has been craving. "I came here straight away, Mother," she manages to say.

"Not true! You were with…" Mother starts. She suddenly stiffens. She claws at the throw to wrap it tighter around herself. "Bonnie? It's you, isn't it, Bonnie?"

"No," says Meijken, momentarily confused.

Mother's face contorts, as if in fear. With an unsteady gesture she tosses the throw off. She tries to stand up, but falls back in her chair. "What did you come here for?" she stammers.

"To be comforted," Meijken whispers, "just to be comforted." She shuts the door behind herself. Now she's alone with Mother in the privacy of Room 108. Now everything will be made better. This time Mother won't hiss, "Did he have a knife? Did he have a weapon?" when she stands in front of her with bloody thighs. This time Mother won't snap, "A healthy girl like you certainly can't be forced to do that against her will," when she stands in front of her with the silt taste of that clump of flesh still in her mouth. This time Mother won't shout, "You asked for it, going into the woods all by yourself! You've shamed both yourself and us!" This time Mother will comfort her, Mother will rock her in her arms and hold her tight for just as long as it takes until she has forgotten everything and she's the old Meijken again, inviolate.

Meijken has the feeling that she's half-flying to cover the last few yards, as if her outstretched arms are wings that have lifted her heavy, heavy body. She smiles serenely as she nestles herself on Mother's lap.

Mother utters a cry. Her legs kick and flail. She tries to

say something, but after all there are no words for what has happened to her daughter, and she can only produce nonsensical sounds, as befits profound grief. On her lap, Meijken surrenders to her tears. But they are peaceful tears. This, she thinks, I should have done a lot sooner. A lot sooner. Every muscle in her body relaxes and a blissful feeling of warmth overwhelms her. She lays her head on Mother's shoulder. She throws her arms around her. Finally safe on her lap. Pressed closely against her she tenderly caresses the hands that once, above the steaming bath water, handed her a mixture of vinegar and brandy: so old and fragile they are now. "There, there," she whispers as Mother's voice dies away, "don't try to say anything." The time for accusations and reproaches is over for good.

Zwier has a lot to overcome before he puts a quarter in the public phone and punches in the number. He has no idea how he'll phrase his request. Merry Christmas to you, too, Gert, and seeing as we don't have anything to eat we'd really enjoy being your guests tonight. While he's listening to the signals from the receiver, he stares at his daughter who is standing beside the phone booth, near the bicycles, swinging a plastic tote bag with her bottle in it back and forth impatiently.

He hears the click establishing the connection. "Bonnie Bentveld speaking."

The palms of his hands get wet. On impulse, he slams the receiver back down. Mary Emma taps on the glass. "Why aren't you calling?" she cries.

He opens the door a crack. "Engaged," he manages to say. He pushes both thumbs into his eye sockets and presses until it seems his head will explode. "You just keep an eye on the bikes while I give it another try."

He finds more change, a handful of which he showers into

the device. With utmost concentration he punches in the number. Already after the second ring somebody answers. "Bonnie Bentveld speaking."

"The Balm residence, you should say," he grates. "Otherwise people will think they've got the wrong number."

"Oh, Zwier," says his wife. Now it's her turn to gasp audibly for breath. "Was that you just now, too?"

He shifts his weight to his other leg and leans one elbow on the glass.

"I was thinking, there can't be any breathers in Sibculo!" She continues, as if it hadn't been nine years since they had last spoken to each other. But her breeziness sounds forced.

Bitterly, Zwier confirms, "It doesn't seem to surprise you much that I'm in the country."

"Not at all," says Bonnie a little too hastily, "I had Mother on the phone a half-hour ago, so I've been filled in. Shouldn't go and stay with my family."

"True enough."

"But it's definitely a miracle that you're calling. They've been waiting for days to hear from you. After you smashed Gert's teeth in, I mean."

"Right," says Zwier, with that old tired feeling. Typical, he thinks, that she doesn't ask: but *why* are you here?

"Where are you staying for pity's sake?"

"At a campground in Beerze. Rose's Campground." He tries to picture her face, but in his recollection her features have been distorted and disintegrated for always, burning in the ashtray, her quartered body catching fire until there was no photograph of her left. He suddenly doesn't know what to say. This conversation has somehow started off wrong.

"Beerze," she exclaims. "Isn't that where that murder was committed last night?"

"What murder?"

"The hell I know. But they even thought it might have

been me."

"Oh, I was expecting you'd say they thought it'd been me."

"No, the body," says Bonnie, annoyed.

"Listen," says Zwier, "I won't deny that I've been possessed by murderous instincts for years. Possessed. But that's over. Don't ask me how, but I managed to overcome my wanting to kill you. And yesterday, by the way, I spent the whole evening singing Christmas carols."

"Zwier," says Bonnie. "It wasn't me, as it turns out, so you're off the hook." There is a silence. Then she says, "But I'm happy to hear you've forgiven me."

"Forgiven?" he bursts out. "Now don't take me wrong! That's putting it pretty generously. I've finally gotten to the point that I can tolerate the thought of your being alive at all."

"That ego of yours! It'll be your undoing some day. You really aren't the only one somebody ever walked out on."

"I ask," says Zwier, "that you not make light of the things I had to contend with." Countless, endless nights in his thoughts he has had discussions with her, millions of sleepless hours he has pleaded with her—there isn't a single word he wants to add. Questions that once seemed of the utmost importance don't need to be answered anymore: were you, before you left for your miserable mangrove swamp, already secretly planning not to come back anymore, my sweet, or did you come up with that idea once you were high and dry in Mexico? It's all the same to him. "Let's just forget it," he says listlessly.

"Agreed," says Bonnie. "It's certainly high time to finally take care of this like normal adults for once. The last time I was in The Netherlands already I was planning to get an attorney, except I didn't get around to it at the time. But this time, after the holidays, I'll get on it right away."

"Good," he says, nevertheless still unpleasantly taken aback at the thought that the person he has called his wife will from now on be entirely her own person. "Good. Fine."

Bonnie clears her throat. Her voice doesn't sound at all businesslike when she mumbles, "Still, it's too bad, isn't it, Zwier?"

He says nothing, unexpectedly caught by an all too lifelike image of a languid Bonnie in the steamy dimness of the tent, her stretched-out body down to its most intimate and remote places his and his alone.

She continues, huskily, "I can't tell you how often I wished that everything had happened very differently."

"Christ," says Zwier. "What did you think I was thinking?" He now leans both elbows on the glass. Hoarse, he utters, "After you, I never wanted anyone else."

"Well, how about me?" cries Bonnie. "How am I supposed to keep going, knowing that I only fall for bad men?"

"Oh, thank you."

"I always think I have to save you guys from yourselves."

"Us? Boy, you must be busy! How many of us have you already saved since you last honored me with your presence?"

"You know, dear," says Bonnie, "that primitive side of you, you really should at some point get that under control. Sometimes I think: a nice docile type, that would be the very thing for you. Somebody you don't have to compete with. You *think* you like strong women, but you can't handle them at all. At all!"

Zwier rips his glasses off his nose and, clamping the phone between neck and shoulder, takes the hem of his shirt and wipes the steamed up lenses clean. "Shall we change the subject?" he suggests.

"Yes," says Bonnie, "so tell me, for instance, what you're doing here in Sibculo."

"Aha," says Zwier. "Now we're getting down to business."

"Business?"

"Well, hasn't there been a small trifle you've been overlooking up till now?"

"What's that?"

"That we have a daughter," he roars. "Remember?"

He can hear the sharp intake of breath. Then, on the other end of the line, she lets out a long sigh, and he remembers other sighs. Will that woman, in spite of everything, always have the capacity to enchant him? He hates her.

Unsure of herself, she says, "Now it's my turn to ask you to kindly accept that I've had enough to contend with where that's concerned."

"Well, hon," snaps Zwier, "your torments are over."

"Zwier? What do you mean?"

He wipes the sweat from his forehead. "Do you have any idea how old your daughter is?"

"Eleven," says Bonnie formally.

"I can't believe it," says Zwier. "Good. Almost old enough to go to secondary school, right? So, what does her father do? Her father asks Leiden for a project in The Netherlands. In The Netherlands! I ask you! Interesting terrain for her father, wouldn't you agree? And what turns out to be the only thing available on short notice? Sibculo's monastery well. Ironic, right? On the other hand, fresh air is very healthy for a growing child. And you also have to realize that she isn't used to the civilized world. So, in fact, Sibculo is cut out for her. You see?"

"That tone of yours," Bonnie hisses. "That's what I basically don't understand."

"Let me put it this way," says Zwier restraining himself. "This is a sacrifice that's beyond me, after all the things I already had to give up because I had to raise a child by myself. I don't want to dig in The Netherlands, I don't want to be here a second longer than absolutely necessary, but what I really can't stomach is to have to do work that's miles below my level in a one-horse town out in the boondocks."

"But why did you leave Africa so soon? In any case you still had a half year…"

"Because, my beauty," Zwier erupts, "on the day of the unfortunate tidings, on the day they wrote me that I could go to *Sibculo* to look for a burial vault under a *monastery well*, I happened to read something in a Dutch paper that one of my students received in the mail. Namely, that a new book by the celebrated mother of little Mary Emma was going to come out! She just keeps on publishing! She just comes and goes as she pleases! She doesn't run into any obstacles in her career! She has been able to do exactly what she wanted to for the past eleven years!" He rakes his hair back. He could rip the phone out of the ground. "But those days are over, Bonnie. From here on in, Bonnie, our daughter is your business."

For a brief moment she is silent. Then she breathes, "Zwier!"

"You heard me. I did everything humanly possible to be able to be in the country at the same time you'd be here and make this clear to you. You don't write very often, as it happens."

"But this is—this is outrageous!"

"This is the only thing that has kept me going the past few months."

"But how can you…"

"You don't think in all seriousness that I came here for that well? I accepted that project only so that I'd be registered here for a house in which you, angel, are going to live with Mary Emma. And they also arranged a school for her. Very decent people here in Sibculo."

"You're just bullshitting!"

"I did everything in my power to clear the way for you. Your child has to go to school, and that's that. I'll give you a couple of months to arrange your affairs, but then you're coming here and taking over from me so that I can finally get on with my own life. Don't you think that after all these years I have a right to that?"

"But you can't do that to your daughter!"

In a monotone Zwier says, "That's a pretty strong statement."

"She doesn't even know me! She's forgotten all about me! I'm a complete stranger to her! We wouldn't even recognize each other!"

"We're coming to see you right now. Then you can see with your own eyes what a nice kid you've got."

"Forget it. I'm just about to leave. I have to go back to Amsterdam. This afternoon still. I'm late as it is."

"Then you can be there an hour later."

"I wouldn't dream of it. I've already got my coat on. And you can't just dump that child, Zwier!"

"That's not what I'm doing. I'm leaving her with her mother."

"Oh, no," says Bonnie. "Oh, no, not on your life, not on your life. If you're in that tight of a spot a boarding school..."

"Have you gone out of your mind? Have you gotten weak in the head? She isn't that kind of a child! It's impossible for her to hold her own with other children! They'll eat her alive! She has no inkling of the most normal..."

"Well, there you go! Only you know what's best for her. I'd make a mess of it, Zwier, you can figure that out, can't you?"

Enraged, he beats the glass siding with his fist. Simultaneously, he sees, as if through a haze, Mary Emma on the other side skipping up and he promptly turns around. Around the corner she pops up in front of him again almost at the same moment, shrieking with laughter. She puts her thumb to her nose and spreads her fingers when he turns away again. With both thumbs in her ears, wagging her fingers, she runs around and around the phone booth. Zwier feels the telephone cord tighten around his throat as he spins around trying to evade her. He half-covers the receiver with his hand. "You're taking over," he hisses. Then he untangles himself from the cord.

"Zwier," says Bonnie plaintively, "that won't work. How

am I supposed to earn a living in Holland? What am *I* supposed to do in Sibculo?"

He can hear the panic in her voice. "You egotistical piece of swill!" he shouts. "The issue here for once doesn't center on *you*."

"If I," Bonnie resumes, "thought for one second that I was a better parent than you, I'd have taken her with me right off. But you were able to combine her with your life and I couldn't! With me she wouldn't have had a life. Won't have a life."

Mary Emma is now pressing her face against the glass so that her nose and lips are flattened. Zwier stares at her with unseeing eyes. He feels around for where he presumes his heart is. He says flatly, hardly recognizing his own voice, "I beat her."

"No," says Bonnie after a moment, "that can't be true."

"I'm not responsible for my actions anymore. I'm at the end of my rope."

"You're lying. You'd never beat a child. Your own child."

"She's standing here next to me, with a black eye." With his free hand he holds the door shut that his daughter is trying to pull open from outside.

"Stop it!" shouts Bonnie. "You're going too far just so you can have it your way. You wouldn't ever touch a hair on somebody's head if they were defenseless. Your problem is that you only start slapping somebody around when they're stronger than you are."

"Oh yeah?" says Zwier. "And what about that lame duck of a brother-in-law of yours then? I managed to get a set of teeth out of him didn't I?"

"I don't believe you. I just can't believe that you'd lower yourself so much you'd..."

"Ask her yourself then!" He lets the door go. He sees his daughter tumble backwards and regain her balance in the nick of time. She slips into the phone booth, comes over to stand next to him and throws an arm around his thigh.

209

"Daddy," she bubbles exuberantly, ready to start in on a lengthy story. She raises her open, eager face toward him. Without looking directly at her, sweating, he presses the receiver into her hand.

Bewildered, Mary Emma says, "Hello?"

On the other side there's a strange sound, as if somebody were having trouble swallowing something down.

"Hi," an unfamiliar voice says softly.

Mary Emma looks up at her father for help, but he has covered his eyes with his hand. The other one is resting heavily on her shoulder.

"Hello?" she says again, bolder now. "Who is this?"

"This...this is Bonnie."

"Oh," says Mary Emma. She can hear her own voice float away, into the phone lines, to end up on the other side in somebody's ear.

"Well...this is quite a surprise, I...don't really know what I should say to you," this Bonnie says.

Mary Emma leans against her father's leg. She runs her thumb along the stitching on the seam of his jeans. She hooks her fingers over the edge of his pocket. His body heat is noticeable and she can smell his familiar scent.

"And you don't either," continues Bonnie. Now it's her voice that's rising up out of the long line and dribbling into Mary Emma's ear, causing a soft static in her head, as if Victor Hugo were still in the atmosphere wanting to signal her. For a moment Mary Emma forgets about the phone in her hand. She feels a longing mount up inside of her, so big, much bigger than she is herself, a longing that makes tears come to her eyes. But Victor Hugo's gone forever. And suddenly she remembers what it was that she still wanted to say to him: that she'll always be his ground control, no matter how far away in space he might find himself. How could she ever have forgotten to tell him that? A strange restlessness takes hold of her. She scratches her head and feels how the itch transplants itself to her shoulders, her back, her legs. All of a sudden she wants to scream.

"Cat's got your tongue, eh?" asks Bonnie, whose name she'd also completely forgotten.

Mary Emma can hardly make out her own voice when she whispers, "You're my mother, aren't you?"

"Yes...yes, I..."

"Are you calling all the way from Mexico?" she asks in awe.

"No, I'm here. In Holland, I mean..."

Mary Emma lowers the phone. "Daddy! You see? Those letters were a good idea! She found us! She finally found us!"

Sitting on the bottom of the stairs, Bonnie rocks herself while she listens to a long and enthusiastic story about an acrobat act. "And we've got the sack of coal, too," her daughter continues, "then Daddy throws me all over the place."

"Doesn't he hurt you when he does that?" she asks quickly, her temples pulsating. She can't forget that this conversation has but one purpose.

"He always catches me, right? It's just pretend!"

"So, Daddy," says Bonnie, recoiling from the word, from the image that it calls up, "is very good to you?"

"He gave me his cartridge pen!"

"And he takes good care of you?" Bonnie asks stubbornly.

"Sure, except when he educates me."

"Educates?"

"That I have to clean up my things and stuff."

"Yes, he's like that," says Bonnie, instantly bewildered over the fact that she shares this and other intimate knowledge with this girl. She gets hold of herself. "Is he sometimes mad at you, too?"

"Yes," says Mary Emma.

"And then?"

"Then I make it all better again. And you know what? We've got all these new clothes, Mamma."

Bonnie shrivels.

"And I bought Tummy Tone, too."

"Is that candy?"

Her daughter bursts out laughing. "That's for when you take a bath!"

"I'll bet you get really clean," says Bonnie foolishly. Does your father beat you? She has to get this over with as quickly as possible. Every word that the child says is one too many. She won't ever forgive Zwier for luring her into this trap. It isn't in anybody's best interest except his. "Mary Emma," she begins.

"When are you coming, Mom?"

Bonnie's throat constricts. "I'm not coming," she manages to say. "I'm...in the country for only a little while. I have to go on another trip very soon."

"Oh," says her daughter.

"Can you understand that?"

"No." She promptly starts to cry.

"Mary Emma," says Bonnie helplessly.

"But we have such a nice little house!"

"Pipe down. Now listen. I have to work. That's why...that's why I left then, too. To be able to do my work."

"Not so!"

"It is so," swears Bonnie.

"You left," sobs her daughter, "because I was a crybaby!"

"Oh my god," says Bonnie, "where did you get that idea? You were the sweetest baby in the world! Just as I'm sure you're the sweetest girl in the world now. Because I'm not with you doesn't mean I don't love you, Mary Emma!" She can't believe she's saying something so sentimental. Such cheap words—but still, they're true. Some of them are true. Some of them. Bonnie brushes aside the hair that's sticking to her forehead. Point a gun at my chest, she's thinking, and then will I repeat those words? I would if I could save my hide. But underneath lies something else, something older, something that has forced women since the dawn of human existence to be made into prisoners: how can I not love you, how else can I react but by helplessly reaching out when you cry, how can I ever leave you to fend for yourself? You come first.

"Mamma," sobs Mary Emma.

"Hush, now," Bonnie shushes automatically, "hush, hush." Later on you'll see the good side of it, you'll understand what we both escaped from: you were never a burden to me and so I've never had to curse you, or wanted to strangle you. You never ruined my life with the dictates of your needs, I didn't have to efface myself, sacrifice myself, so I didn't have to make you suffer that domineering manipulation mothers are so good at, either. You were never at the mercy of my love. And believe me, I know what I'm talking about. "Imagine," she says in a persuasive tone, "that you suddenly had *two* parents that wanted to educate you!"

Her daughter's sobbing calms down.

"Or does that sound like a good idea to you?" asks Bonnie.

"No," replies Mary Emma, audibly from the bottom of her heart.

"Well then," says Bonnie. "So, now you're just going to go on enjoying your Christmas. What are you going to do this afternoon?"

The child sighs. She sniffs. Then she says, "I put a letter in a bottle. We're going to throw it into the river."

"And what does it say?"

"Just about my life. That Victor Hugo's gone and stuff."

"What?" Bonnie stammers. Grateful, she thinks: you see? I don't understand a blooming thing about this! I know nothing about her! I'm the last person on earth who should raise her. She gropes around for her kleenex. The words slip out before she can stop herself, "Would you like to write me a letter sometime, too?"

It suddenly seems like the most normal thing in the world. She pictures herself on her motorcycle riding to a ramshackle post office, in the shade of which men are drinking, clucking their tongues when she gets off and runs to her box to take out a letter from her daughter.

"But we never have your address, though," Mary Emma complains.

"If I write you first, when I'm in Guatemala. Then you can write me back."

"And will you write again, then?"

"Only if you want me to."

Circumspectly her daughter says, "I think so."

"Is it a deal?"

"Yes. And you know what, Mamma?"

"No," says Bonnie. "I don't know a thing." She can't take any more. She simply can't take any more. She envisions plump knees with dimples in them, grubby hands and medium length uncombed hair—and then with a feeling of shame, she realizes that she's really just picturing one of the little girls in "The Family Circus," with an apron on. Or Alice. It's getting curiouser and curiouser, thought Alice, as she fell down the rabbit-hole.

"I fried eggs this morning."

"Big girl," says Bonnie. "Well then, shall we say goodbye now?"

"No, Mamma, no!" Panic.

"Yes, yes," says Bonnie softly. "And I'm very proud of having you for my daughter, don't ever forget that."

"You can't hang up!"

"No, no, if you still want to say something, I'll stay on the line."

"What should I say, then?" She's crying again.

"Whatever you like." Bonnie swallows her own tears.

"Do you know," her daughter hiccups at last, "how you're supposed to get a bikini line?"

Suddenly there's a fumbling at the front door. The sound makes Bonnie tense up. She wipes her cheeks. She sits up straight on the bottom of the stairs. On second thought she stands up. "I have to hang up," she says.

"Mamma! I want to have a bikini line!"

She partially covers the receiver with her hand. She says, "Can't you ask Daddy about that?"

"He doesn't know about things like that!"

"Sweetie," Bonnie exclaims, "I'll write you soon, honest, but I really have to hang up now." She doesn't want to get caught. She can't bear the thought that Gert and Meijken will gloat, chuckling to each other later, "The way she looked sitting there! Crying her eyes out!" Bonnie's fingers tighten around the receiver. She whispers, "And write me back right away." She hangs up.

For a moment she stands there as if in a daze. But, after all, she chose to live without memories—so this conversation, too, she will manage to forget, in the end.

Meijken gently closes the door to Room 108 filled with a serenity she has never known in her entire life. She has no idea how long she sat with Mother, her motionless hands in hers, or how often she pressed a kiss on the lips that once spat out such bitter and implacable words—it seems like a dream from which she only gradually awoke, refreshed, and with the feeling that she had been awarded her rightful place in the universe, as if the world at long last is turning around its epicentrum: around her. Without hurrying, she walks down the long corridor to the elevator and pushes the button. She has no further plans than to step into it and see where she ends up. The rest of her life stretches out before her like an exciting adventure. She can do whatever she pleases.

There's a pinging sound to indicate that the elevator has arrived. Meijken feels the happy smile on her face fade when the doors open. "So there you are!" her husband cries, reaching out to her.

He holds her by her upper arm as they cross the large entry hall, as if he were a police officer bringing her in, and showers her with a stream of words.

"For hours I was driving around, Meijken, for hours, but luckily people had seen you, and then I was able to deduce that you might have been on your way to Mother's." He stands still and pulls at her arm. "What possessed you all of a sudden?"

The coldness of the floor tiles bites into her feet. Surprised, she comes to the realization that she's lost her slippers.

"Meijken!" He shakes her. "I was crazy with worry!"

She looks at him. His lip is still a bit swollen. "What did you say?" she asks disinterestedly.

"What got into you so suddenly?"

"How do you mean?"

He raises his hands. "As if it's the most normal thing for you to take a stroll around the block! In your nightgown, at that! And why don't you have anything on your feet? Were you trying to harm yourself?"

Meijken looks at the Christmas tree, at the girl with the dyed hair behind the desk. She hears strains of "Away in a Manger." How did she get here? How had she managed to do that? To overcome her uncertainty she says brusquely, "It's Christmas, Gert. People visit with family."

"Yes, but you don't."

Again she looks at him. She can see the way he holds his head to the side, how one of his shoulders droops. That man. That pillow-stuffer. That's what she's given half her life to. Is that what she had in mind when she wandered freely through the woods and fields?

"Do you realize the kind of alarm you've caused?" he asks, anguished.

"No," says Meijken. "Sorry."

"Are your slippers upstairs at Mother's? Let's go get them first."

"No," says Meijken again. She doesn't have to go into that room again. There's nothing for her there any longer.

"Well dammit, Meijken!" he jerks her arm again. But there's no sense anymore in yelling at her or shaking her. A gruff tenderness wells up inside her when she realizes that their marriage is finished. Now that she's finally settled things with Mother, Gert Balm has no reason to exist in her life anymore. She takes his hand and squeezes it. He didn't deserve this from her.

"Sorry," she says.

"Then let's go home right now," he says harshly. "Bonnie'll probably be wondering where we are."

"Bonnie?" Meijken exclaims.

"Yes, she's alive and kicking. She's been sitting at our place since this morning already!"

"Really?" asks Meijken. She throws her head back. She starts laughing loudly. She sees the girl with the tricolor hair look at her disapprovingly. She sees the lack of comprehension in her husband's face. She sees herself: barefoot, in her nightdress. But no power on earth can hold her back. She laughs until she feels cramps in her sides. Bonnie! For the first time since her unfortunate birth, Bonnie's existence has completely slipped her mind.

"But what exactly did she say?" Zwier asks again. He is squatting beside the phone booth holding his daughter compulsively by the shoulders. Tears are streaming down her face. "That we're going to write letters," she hiccups, running the back of her hand along her nose.

"And what else?" He shakes her violently, no longer able to control himself.

"That she's going on a trip. And then she'll send her address."

"And then?"

"I don't know anymore," cries Mary Emma. She squirms free of his grasp and plaintively yammers in a high voice, "Sorry, Daddy, I can't help it, really I can't, but I don't know any more."

"Did you tell her," he grabs her roughly by the arm, "that I beat you?"

"No, Daddy, honest!"

He yanks her arm. "And why not, you backwards idiot?"

She gasps for air, her eyes are glassy with panic. "But I didn't say anything," she babbles.

"You stupid dolt," snarls Zwier, "you impossible...you... So, I don't beat you?"

"No, Daddy, no!"

"You're lying!"

In a reflex reaction she ducks her head down between her shoulders and holds up one arm for protection.

"So say it! Confess it! Admit it!"

"What?" she blubbers.

Zwier lets his arms drop limply at his sides, suddenly sober. Confess that you get beaten. Or else I'll knock the living daylights out of you again so you'll remember. He turns away. This is no longer the slippery slope, he thinks, this is hell itself. He throws his head back and inhales deeply a couple of times. The sky is amazingly blue. But the feeble winter sun offers no warmth at all. Beside him Mary Emma sobs quietly, his incomprehensibly loyal daughter. With the feeling that he is two thousand years old and lost forever, he asks, "Can I kiss it and make it better, Emmie? I didn't mean to scare you, honey."

Her shoulders twitching, she looks at him, unsure about his mood or his intentions.

"Hey, soldier. You're always still a top-notch ace." He manages to pull a strand of her hair teasingly. "Come on over here to your old father."

A glimpse of a smile appears on her face. Noisily she sniffs and then throws her arms around his neck, his millstone, his ball and chain, his lifelong companion, more inseparable than his own shadow.

The sunlight is bright on the water and the white gravel sparkles on the bicycle path along the bank. Squinting his eyes, Zwier bicycles behind his daughter through the overly bright landscape. He still isn't prepared to give up his dream altogether. He can still always pay Bonnie a visit in Amsterdam and try to convince her. The game isn't over yet.

Mary Emma's red jacket dances ahead of him like a moving spot. He finally realizes that up ahead she has already gotten off her bike and is now running down to the riverbank. "Careful," he shouts, "don't fall in!"

"Are you coming?" she's standing by the water's edge with his genever bottle. "I'm going to throw it in, you know!" She swings the bottle back and forth a few times and then flings it in a wide arc into the river. Relieved, she looks at him over her shoulder as he approaches, "Now it's going to the sea!"

Zwier sits down in the yellowed grass and pulls her down beside him.

"What would you like the most, Em? If you could choose?"

"Choose what?"

"Well, you've got two parents. If you'd rather live with your mother, then we'll have to arrange that," he says.

"Oh," says Mary Emma. She starts frenziedly scratching her head.

"Just think about it."

She says nothing. She chews her bottom lip. Her eyes get red.

"You don't have to say anything right away. Hey now,

Emma, no tears. What is it this time?"

"Aw, *man,*" she exclaims. She punches him in the thigh. She collects her skinny bones around herself and sits with her back towards him. Huskily, she says, "She doesn't even want to come visit us in our cabin. So you really shouldn't think that I can go live with her."

"But it doesn't always have to be the way she wants," says Zwier over his shoulder. "You've got a say in it too."

"What I want, you guys won't do anyway!"

"And that is?"

"You know. That both of you live in the same house. In the same country. With me."

"No, that won't happen."

"Well, so there."

"Don't get so uppity."

In a twinkling she is on her feet. Legs akimbo she stands in front of him, her hands on her hips. He is startled by her face. She's as white as a sheet. Her pupils are dark with desperation. "And what about you, then?" she exclaims. "Who's going to take care of you when I'm gone?"

"You don't have to worry your head about that, honey," says Zwier reassuringly, before it occurs to him what's gotten into his daughter: she's simply fighting for her life. Her father's trying to dump her and her mother doesn't want to have her. How could he think even for one second that she hasn't figured that out? Feeling guilty, he takes her hand, and sees himself all of a sudden as a little boy, holding his father's hand. Fathers were still reliable back then, they were there for keeps. They simply loved you. But the point here isn't whether he loves his daughter or not.

"There are all kinds of things you need me for, Daddy," Mary Emma resumes in a rush.

"Yes," he says, "too many to name. But..."

She interrupts him. "Maybe you don't know yourself even," she says persuasively. "But you really couldn't do without me, really you couldn't, Daddy. Because, for starters, without me you'd lose everything!"

Zwier shifts his position. He catches her by the knees and lets his head rest against her legs while the sounds of her words enter into him. Without me you'll lose everything. Without me the final remnants of your rationality will leave you. Without me your life will, always, be loveless. Because, who wants you? Only me! I'm the only one who won't ever leave you! And who's going to contradict Mary Emma Zwier?

"The problem," he says laboriously, "is really the other way around. Sometimes I'm afraid that I don't take very good care of you."

This time she doesn't try to deny reality. For a long time she is silent, while she picks at the remains of her nail polish. At last she timidly suggests, "But then you can just get some therapy, right?"

He flops on his back. Some counseling wouldn't do Professor Zwier any harm. "Emma?" he asks the sky.

"Yes?"

"We have to be realistic. I'm not a man to go in for therapy."

But for some reason or other he has a sneaking suspicion that he has less to say about that than he would like. It suddenly dawns on him that the roles have imperceptibly reversed and that he's the pleader now.

"What do you think?" inquires Mary Emma after a few moments of waiting in anticipation.

"Nothing," says Zwier.

"Why did you lie down?" She comes and sits beside him in the grass. He closes his eyes.

He says, "That way I can feel the earth turn better." What kind of world is this, he wonders, in which you can beat your kid senseless without a soul knowing or caring? In which anybody can have kids and do whatever they like with them? Who's ever going to explain this world to his daughter and make it understandable for her? He presses his fingers against his forehead. To pose the question is to answer it. The overwhelming desire to explain the world to his child himself leaves him momentarily speechless.

"Do you have a headache?" she asks, kindly laying an ice-cold hand on his forehead.

He presses a kiss on her palm and sits up. It's worth a try, he thinks. In any case, it's worth a try.

The sunlight is still playing on the river and in the distance a gull screeches. On the towpath along the river, someone is approaching them. There is something vaguely familiar about her. Zwier slaps the grass from his pants that are now noticeably soaked, while he looks into the sun in an effort to find out who, hands shoved deep into her jacket pockets, is headed their way, seemingly with a purpose.

Sunken down in her armchair as if nothing has happened, Meijken wiggles her toes nervously in the warm water of the footbath that her husband foisted on her: the neutral subjects of conversation have long-since been exhausted and the uneasy silences are getting longer and longer. Now and then, when Bonnie sneaks a peek at her watch, Meijken dares to look her over. For some reason or other she looks less self-assured and inaccessible than usual.

Gert Balm clears his throat. "And now way down to Guatemala," he says, making conversation. But Meijken can tell by his voice that even his thoughts are elsewhere. He'd like nothing better than to grill his wife more about what he calls "her outing."

"Yes," replies Bonnie, sitting on the edge of her chair. "I'm looking forward to that trip. But I'm afraid that it's getting to be time. I still have to go see Mother and otherwise I'll never get to…"

"First you're going to have something hot to drink," Meijken decides, waving impatiently at her husband. 'Tea, Gert."

But when he has left the room, the silence weighs heavier than ever. "Are you warming up a bit?" Bonnie politely asks, finally.

"I had a thick shawl on, I didn't feel the cold," says Meijken.

"Wasn't it odd after so long to…"

"No, no, not at all."

"But it's a, how should I say it, a turning point!"

"Maybe," says Meijken dully. From the moment that she was once again slapped in between her walls whose slightest irregularities she could draw with her eyes closed, she has felt the sensation of freedom slowly draining out of her. A single moment of significance means nothing. What follows is the thing that counts.

Facing her, Bonnie crosses her legs out of boredom and impatience. "You're starting to get a wrinkle between your eyebrows just like me," discovers Meijken in amazement. She touches the bridge of her own nose.

Bonnie says shortly, "We're all getting older. I'm not eighteen anymore, you know."

"When I was eighteen," Meijken says promptly, falling anxiously silent again. "When I was eighteen," she recommences. Suddenly she knows for certain that this is the only way to regain control over her own life. The right words will surely come of their own accord, the object isn't to think twice or hesitate; the opportunity has to be seized before this moment as well, wasted, will dangle isolated in time. Except it's impossible for her to tell her story as long as she's in this absurd tub of water. She raises one dripping foot. "Could you maybe…?"

"Oh," says Bonnie. She picks up the towel and, after hesitating briefly, kneels down.

Her honey-colored hair fans out near Meijken's knees.

With brisk hands, she dries her feet. Her bowed head is only centimeters, millimeters from Meijken's lap. To touch her now, to draw her close. With the feeling that she's plunging into deep, uncharted waters, Meijken says, "I have something to tell you, Bonnie."

At the same instant the doorbell rings. Bonnie cowers, as if the sound has frightened her. She exclaims, "Who can that be?"

"Minnie," says Meijken, bewildered. "It's just about Minnie's time, that's right."

"Minnie? The one with all the theories?"

"Stark raving mad that woman drives me sometimes," hisses Meijken, as tears of powerlessness well up in her eyes. After having waited her entire lifetime, she can't tolerate any delays anymore.

"Meijken Balm!" cries Minnie as she bursts into the room. "What's gotten into you all of a sudden? The whole village is talking about it! Oh, Bonnie! Dear! You're already in the country! We've all been terribly excited about your visit." Silvery pumps and a subdued black dress with silver stitching along the neckline.

Meijken has absorbed all the details by the time she says, "You're coming at a bad time, Minnie."

"What a Christmas," Minnie rattles on, ignoring her completely. "First that murder, and now Meijken's also gone berserk."

"Oh, yes, that murder," says Bonnie. "Why, for god's sake, did you think it was me, Meijken?" She looks outraged.

"I thought," Meijken stammers, not knowing anymore what she thought, "I mean, it could have been?"

"Oh, come on!" remarks Bonnie dismissively.

"No," Minnie interjects, "you shouldn't take it so lightly, dear. My theory is: today a stranger, tomorrow you. It's never been any different. I was telling Meijken just this week: from the moment they got up on their hind legs, they have equated brutish violence with life."

"They?" asks Bonnie.

"The very minute they start feeling a little yang and you don't stand a chance. That you got away this time doesn't mean a thing."

"I didn't get away from anything!"

"Does she understand me?" Minnie asks Meijken. "Does she understand what I'm talking about? It could just as easily have been her that was murdered! What difference does it make that we don't know this particular victim? We'll still always be dealing with the assailant! He's walking around scot-free, just like the rest of them! Although I'll also say that a woman who's taking a walk late at night out on the dunes is somehow asking for it."

"Asking for what?" Meijken blurts. "To be killed, you mean?" Her fierce intervention causes an amazed silence to fall, during which the ringing of the phone can be heard.

"Oh, no," Bonnie exclaims. "That'll be him again!"

"Who?" asks Minnie.

"Zwier! He called earlier, too."

"Zwier?" breathes Meijken. She feels dizzy.

"Yes, you don't know yet, but he's at a campground in Beerze."

"They come and go as often as they please," Minnie concludes. "Did Gert get that, you think? I don't hear anything."

"Oh, Bonnie," says Meijken, collecting her wits, "he probably wanted to speak to me. What did he say?"

Bonnie shrugs. She pulls the sleeves of her sweater over her hands and stares fixedly at her knees.

"I've told Meijken a hundred times already that she shouldn't have offered him a place to stay," explains Minnie. "One shouldn't choose sides in another's marital dramas, that's my theory."

"That bastard," mutters Bonnie. She starts biting her thumbnail. Then she says, "No, Meijken, it wasn't you he wanted to talk to. At least he didn't give me a message for you."

Meijken bows her head.

"But why did he call here?" Minnie wants to know.

"He said," Bonnie begins. She says no more.

"What?" inquires Minnie.

"Oh, a stupid story. That…from now on…I'm supposed to take care of Mary Emma."

"So," says Minnie. She purses her lips. "I'm not for men avoiding their responsibilities, but I can't deny that I think you should never have left your child with him."

"Oh, right," says Bonnie. She exposes her pointy teeth. "Did anybody ask you for your opinion? Do you think I could care less what you think? It just so happens I'm not planning to pay all my life for a single mistake."

"That conclusion," says Minnie, "seems to me to be on the simplistic side."

"For a fossil like you, maybe," says Bonnie crassly. "But nowadays we think differently about those things."

"I raised four," says Minnie with tight lips, "and I'll be the first to admit that it's sacrifice through and through, and nothing but. You have to throw in a hell of a lot of Tao to pull it off. But a child simply has to have a mother."

"From the day that I could think," spits Bonnie, "I've been busy avoiding mine. There are quite a few cases where a child would be better off without a self-sacrificing mother. All the things for which mine held me responsible, only because she'd had me so late in life! I was just about the death of her! All but dying she brought me into this world. I half tore her apart."

"Not true," Meijken declares loudly.

"And for that sacrifice I had to pay my whole childhood. Don't tell me about kids that need their mothers. It's precisely the other way around. What did you say, Meijken?"

"She said: not true," Minnie says coolly in her stead. "As if she knew anything about it, Meijken isn't a mother. Like she'd know. As far as she's concerned you could just as easily give your child away."

"Exactly," Bonnie confirms, her eyes spewing fire, "and because of that, my sister is the only person, to my knowledge, who has always respected my choice. She's the only one who never hassled me about it, whereas the rest of the world, without being asked, is always getting on my case. She's the only one who never called me to task."

"What did I just tell you?" asks Minnie. She gets up and smoothes her black dress. "It's easy for Meijken to talk. But let me go take a look see how Gert's getting on with the tea."

As soon as she has closed the door, Minnie de Kraaij allows herself to give in to the weakness in her knees. She is totally appalled, even though it's enriching to go with the flow as the young Transcendental Meditation people always say. But that Meijken never shut that unmannerly wench's trap, that she didn't even step in between, after all the things she's done for her! With love, of course. She just happens to like to make herself useful. Otherwise life makes so little sense for a single woman. But if people no longer appreciate her advice and insights, she'll keep them to herself. Apparently an epoch has somehow or other come to a close unnoticed, without anybody taking the time to tell her of the developments. With the feeling that she has been unforgivably wronged, she goes to the kitchen.

"Oh, Gert," she says.

He is standing at the counter with his back to her fixing sandwiches, and something in the way his shoulders are drooping tells her he feels as lost as she does. Meijken never appreciated that man enough. In her overweening desire to dominate everything, she has turned him into a clown, where another would have left him as he was.

He puts the knife down and rearranges a couple of slices of cucumber as he says in a monotone, "There was just a call."

"Yes," says Minnie, touching his shoulder. "We heard the

phone ring."

'It was somebody from the nursing home. They just found Mother dead in her chair." Then he starts slicing a tomato with mechanical motions.

Minnie opens the refrigerator and takes out the mayonnaise. From one of the drawers she takes a spoon. She spreads the tomato slices that appear from under his knife thickly with it. She says, "It must have been a shock for you."

"She must have passed away in her sleep. I mean, her heart must have failed, or something like that."

"And then, of course, she was very old."

He tears off a paper towel and dabs his eyes. "The only thing that allows me to put my mind at rest about it is that at least Meijken went to see her today. I just have to gather enough courage to tell her."

"I'm sure," says Minnie. "By the way, do you want any pepper or salt on these?"

"Maybe a little basil? I bought some fresh. I have no idea how I should tell her."

Minnie takes the potted basil from the windowsill. Without looking, she finds the scissors in the familiar drawer. She snips up a handful of leaves. Frowning, she says, "Let's not mention it for just a while, for just a little while. You know how hard I've tried half my life at getting Meijken to reconcile with her sister. For years I've worked for this moment. And you should see them sitting there together now. Don't say anything just yet."

"I meant it," says Bonnie. She has come over to sit on the armrest of Meijken's chair. She dangles her long legs back and forth. "You're the only one who doesn't get all excited about that motherhood stuff. You don't have the slightest idea how much that drives me crazy. Mothers are such grossly overrated figures. The whole notion of motherhood is overblown. Fundamentally exaggerated. I'm glad you feel that way too. Maybe I should have let you know earlier that I really appreciate your support."

Meijken has the feeling she's looking through a kaleidoscope: pieces of colored glass sparkle in front of her eyes, they veer away and never land in the places you expect them to, constantly forming new and surprising constellations. She can't manage to utter a word.

"Speaking of which," says Bonnie, standing up and stretching, "I'll really have to go and see Mother, like the obedient daughter that I happen to be."

"Wait," says Meijken.

"What for?"

I was going to tell you something, thinks Meijken, already well aware that she won't be strong enough to discard the only reason why Bonnie still has a little respect and affection for her. Will she always have to run into situations in which she simply can't win?

"What for?" Bonnie says again, sounding impatient. She sneezes into a kleenex.

Meijken folds her hands over her gigantic stomach. Her gaze shifts from Bonnie to the walls around her. Maybe what it's really about is her saving the rest of her own life, the life she's always allowed to be determined by others for far too long.

"Oh, that's right, too. You wanted to tell me something just now before that horrible woman barged in," says Bonnie with a sigh: what on earth can Meijken have to say that's interesting?

From habit, Meijken fingers the wart on her upper lip. It's gone. Her skin feels smooth under her fingers. She feels again. Her wart is gone. It isn't there anymore. During Christmas night one of those miracles had happened to her about which she'd heard as a child already, one of those miracles that were handed down from mother to daughter. And her mind is suddenly made up. "I just wanted to tell you I'm planning to go on a diet," she says.

It is so calm that Zwier, holding onto his daughter's hand, can see the approaching figure reflected in the river: corduroys, a leather jacket and around her neck a light blue shawl half-wrapped around her long red hair with the childish pins in it. In the barely rippling water, she waves. She calls out, "So, it seems you've managed to find those beautiful spots by yourself." She quickens her pace until she is standing right in front of him. "It's a gorgeous day, isn't it?" she says. Her voice sounds a little out of breath. She is a head shorter than he is and she has to tilt her head back to be able to look at him. Again she is smiling that special smile that makes her eyes light up. He has never seen a redhead with such dark blue eyes. "And Merry Christmas, too," she adds.

He feels Mary Emma's fingers tighten around his. "This is my daughter," he says, grateful for her presence. "Who already knows her *Donald Duck* backwards and forwards."

"Oh, hello. Your father was telling me Saturday that you were here on vacation together. Say, you took a nasty spill."

"Yes," says Mary Emma stoutly. She lifts her battered face toward Zwier. "Can we go now, Dad?"

"Where to?"

"To Uncle Gert's!"

'The plan's been called off. I can't reach them."

"But I was going to get some samples from him!"

"Maybe tomorrow," says Zwier.

"In those neat little boxes?" the girl from the bookstore asks his daughter. The sunlight shimmers in her long hair.

"Yes," says Mary Emma, warming up to her.

"If you come to the store after Christmas for your next *Donald Duck*, I'll make sure I've got some of those hotel soaps. And a shower cap, too, in a little pouch."

His daughter says very sociably, "Except our shower doesn't work." Then she spreads her fingers and explains, "Daddy did my

230

nails for Christmas."

"What a pretty color you two picked out."

"Azalea."

"See? Mine's aubergine." They hold their hands next to each other. Zwier can see the dirt under his daughter's nails. He knows her hair is full of lice. He's ashamed like he's never been ashamed before. Then his eyes catch her overjoyed face. "You left a little rim to let the air get to the quick," she exclaims, leaning over the glossy aubergine nails. "Just look, Dad! That's the way you should've done it. At least she knows what she's doing!" Full of awe, she eyes her new friend. After that she looks at Zwier, and all the joy disappears from her eyes. "But Daddy," she asks plaintively, "where are we going to eat if we can't go to Uncle Gert's?" Why, says her face, why do you always cause us so many problems?

"Well," says the girl from the bookstore, tossing the end of her shawl over her shoulder, "at my place the situation's just the other way around: the guests that were coming this evening had a mishap in the family. So, there I am with my turkey."

"Turkey?" asks Mary Emma, her voice laden with hope. "That's what we always used to get at Grampa's, too."

"With chocolate ice cream cake for dessert."

"That's my favorite kind of ice cream," says Mary Emma.

"Does your father like it, too?"

Zwier glances at the river calmly flowing by, as if the answer were hidden there. He becomes aware that the shoe that leaks has let water in again. He curls his bare toes. A foot has to be able to breath. A person's a nomad after all. Then he says, "I think it's time we introduced ourselves." Once again, beaten, he thinks: it's worth a try. In any case, it's worth a try.

About the Translator

After graduating as the first candidate of the Translation Program at the University of Iowa, Wanda Boeke received a Fulbright-Hays grant and continued to pursue literary translation in The Netherlands, France and Spain, working with a variety of novelists, poets and filmmakers there. Her translations of poetry, short stories and articles have appeared in The Netherlands, Great Britain, and the U.S. including contributions to the *Greenfield Review*, *Poetry International*, and *Dutch Crossing*.

She returned to Iowa in 1990 to join the staff of the International Writing Program for two years as the Program's translation coordinator.

Renate Dorrestein's *Unnatural Mothers* is the first novel the translator has published in the U.S. Also appearing this year will be her translation from the German of *The Natural Cat*, a book about the history, evolution and behavior of cats. At present Ms. Boeke is completing contributions to a women's anthology of Netherlandic poets from the Middle Ages to the present, a long-term project for which she was the permissions editor.

About the Author

One of Holland's leading feminist authors, Renate Dorrestein was born in Amsterdam in 1954. After a distinguished career in journalism as a correspondent for the magazine *Panorama*, editor of the feminist magazine *Ozij*, and columnist for the weekly opinion magazine *De Tijd*, she turned to her attention to fiction. In 1983 her first novel *Buitenstaanders* ("Outsiders") appeared. *Unnatural Mothers*, which was originally published in 1992, is her eighth novel, and the first to appear in an English translation. In 1993 Dorrestein was awarded the Annie Romein Prize for Dutch feminist fiction.

From 1986 to 1987 she was writer-in-residence at the University of Michigan, a position she has also held at the University of Iowa. She currently resides in Haarlem in The Netherlands.

Welcome to the World of International Women's Writing

Unmapped Territories: New Women's Fiction from Japan edited by Yukiko Tanaka. $10.95. ISBN: 1-879679-00-0. These stunning new stories by well-known and emerging writers chart a world of vanishing social and physical landmarks in a Japan both strange and familiar. With an insightful introduction by Tanaka on the literature and culture of the "era of women" in Japan.

Two Women in One by Nawal el-Saadawi. $9.95. ISBN: 1-879679-01-9. One of this Egyptian feminist's most important novels, *Two Women in One* tells the story of Bahiah Shaheen, a well-behaved Cairo medical student - and her other side: rebellious, political and artistic.

Under Observation by Amalie Skram. With an introduction by Elaine Showalter. $15.95. ISBN: 1-879679-03-5. This riveting story of a woman painter confined against her will in a Copenhagen asylum is a classic of nineteenth century Norwegian literature by the author of *Constance Ring* and *Betrayed*.

How Many Miles to Babylon by Doris Gercke. $8.95. ISBN: 1-879679-02-7. Hamburg police detective Bella Block needs a vacation. She thinks she'll find some rest in the countryside, but after only a few hours in the remote village of Roosbach, she realizes she has stumbled onto one of the most troubling cases of her career. The first of this provocative German author's thrillers to be translated into English.

Wild Card by Assumpta Margenat. $8.95. ISBN: 1-879679-04-3. Translated from the Catalan, this lively mystery is set in Andorra, a tiny country in the Pyrenees. Rocio is a supermarket clerk bored with her job and her sexist boss. One day she devises a scheme to get ahead in the world....

Originally established in 1984 as an imprint of Seal Press, Women in Translation is now a nonprofit publishing company, dedicated to making women's writing from around the world available in English translation. We specialize in anthologies, mysteries, and literary fiction. The books above may be ordered from us at 3131 Western Avenue, Suite 410, Seattle, WA 98121. (Please include $2.00 postage and handling for the first book and 50¢ for each additional book.) Write to us for a free catalog.